THE BEE WHISPERER

BARRINGTON BOOK THREE

SUSAN MACKIE

small town
publishing

For Emily and little Olive
This story was inspired by my daughter's passion for natural bee-tending. Through her, I've become more mindful of the natural environment.
Now I'm saving the bees too.

Susan Mackie

Books are the bees which carry the quickening pollen from one to another mind. **Jane Russell Lowell**

One can no more approach people without love than one can approach bees without care. Such is the quality of bees. **Leo Tolstoy**

FOREWORD

While the town of Barrington does exist, it is little more than a small village with a general store, hall and school.

I've imagined elements of nearby larger towns, such as Gloucester, to create the township of Barrington for this story.

Any similarities to people, living or deceased, are purely co-incidental and a product of my imagination.

The Barrington Tops, Bucketts Mountain, Barrington, Dilgry and Gloucester Rivers and Jems Creek do exist, and it is a stunning region to visit.

1

'Move away children! Quickly please! Into the library.' Alex McIntosh spoke quietly but firmly as he glanced behind him. The massive swarm hadn't moved, it was hanging from a large bottlebrush tree only metres from the classrooms. While he had no reason to believe any of the students were allergic to bee stings, he couldn't take any chances.

The last child safely inside the library, he stepped closer to the swarm. It was a large organism, thousands of bees clinging to each other, a queen bee somewhere in the middle protected by the heaving, moving bodies of the swarm. Fascinating. He would include some bee study in the curriculum this term. But first he needed a beekeeper to come and capture the bees and remove them from the school grounds.

Stepping back into the administration section, he spoke to Jenny. She'd been admin at the school for decades. Jenny would know the local beekeepers, he was certain.

'Well, the McGee's used to have hives, but I think they've gone out of it since old Hugh passed away.' She nodded emphatically. 'I really don't know of anyone else in the area.'

'Thank you Jenny.' Alex strode over to the library building, a few bees flew around his head, and it took all his willpower not to swat at them. He didn't want to stir them up. He stopped at the library door. Perhaps they would leave by themselves. He needed to google bee swarms.

Opening the door, he saw the children sitting in organised groups with their teachers. His own class was mingled with the grade ones and twos, reading quietly together. He cleared his throat, and the children paused their activity and looked expectantly at him.

'Do any of you have beehives at home? The swarm is likely to have come from somewhere quite close.' He watched as they all shook their heads or murmured 'No sir.'

'Thank you. Carry on.' Stepping outside, more bees flew around him and a few started to settle on the porch eave over the library entrance. Pulling his phone from his pocket he googled 'beekeepers Barrington.' Nothing. He tried again, using 'catch a bee swarm Barrington.' This time a few listings came up for Save the Bees Australia. They had information on bee swarms and people who would relocate them. Checking further, he realised Save the Bees was Victorian based. He swore under his breath. More bees settled on the library eve. The swarm was moving, to right above the only access to the library, with the whole school inside. He clicked on the call button, maybe these people could recommend someone, otherwise he would have to get Council to exterminate them. A last resort.

'Save the Bees Australia.'

'Hello. I see you're based in Victoria, but I'm hoping you may know someone local to remove a swarm. Barrington School, New South Wales.'

'Barrington? Really?' The male voice paused. 'There should be someone in your area at the moment. I'll send their contact details directly to your phone.'

Surprised, Alex grinned. 'Thank you very much.' Hanging up, his phone beeped. He saw the number for Ayla Forrest, Beekeeper, and pushed 'call'.

'Hello, this is Ayla.'

'Hello Ayla. Alex McIntosh here, Principal at Barrington School. The bloke from Save the Bees gave me your number. Are you nearby? We have a swarm here.'

The woman at the other end laughed. 'Do you? How fabulous! I'll be there in ten minutes.' She ended the call and Alex looked at the screen of his phone, slightly bemused.

2

Bees are at their most vulnerable and friendly when they swarm. The hive is a collective consciousness and when it has ample honey and favourable weather conditions the colony will split to reproduce. Swarming involves the old Queen and wisest bees leaving their established location to scout out a new location. @embodybee

Ayla grinned as she drove her old Kombi van around to the school. She knew exactly where Barrington School was, she'd been there two days ago, having a look at it as a possibility for Skye.

'Are we catching a swarm Mama?'

'We are. At the school.' Glancing across to her daughter for a moment, Ayla winked. 'Want to help?'

A small frown appeared on Skye's face as she gazed at her

mother, then she smiled and nodded. 'Of course. Don't I always?'

Parking at the front of the school, Ayla focussed on getting the gear out of the van. Beekeeper hats and veils for her and Skye, and an empty bee box. She had a spare top bar hive she could transfer them to later. She'd rubbed her Miracle Balm into the bee box only that morning; a mixture of beeswax, propolis, olive oil, lemongrass and coconut oil. The scent would attract the bees, help them feel at home. She hoped the teacher hadn't stirred the swarm up. They could move on just as quickly as they appeared.

As an afterthought she grabbed a third hat and veil. Perhaps the teacher would like to help. A long shot, but she'd offer it to him.

Movement in the schoolyard caught Ayla's attention. The tall man watched them for a moment, then proceeded through the school gate, reaching them in a few long strides.

'Hello Ayla, I'm Alex McIntosh. I'm pleased to meet you.' He held out his hand to shake hers, a warm smile on his face. 'I'm really, really pleased to meet you. The swarm has now settled on the eave over the library door. All the students are inside.'

His hand was warm and his grip strong. Tall and broad shouldered. Friendly eyes. Late thirties perhaps. His shirt sleeves were rolled up to his elbows, his skin tan. He had a real outdoorsy look about him. Not like any schoolteacher she'd met before.

'Serendipity. Happens to me all the time.' Ayla was amused as he blinked, considering her words, before lowering himself to look Skye in the eye.

'Are you a bee catcher too, young lady?' He smiled as he spoke, one knee on the ground, seemingly aware that the sheer size of him could scare a small child. The man had to be six four, at least.

Hands on hips, Skye answered in her usual feisty style. 'I'm a bee whisperer. Like Mama. And my name is Skye.' She held her small hand out. If he was surprised by her confidence and manner, he didn't show it. He shook her hand gently, smiled at her then stood.

'Seriously. Thank you. I hope you can catch them. Calling Council to exterminate would be a last resort.' He picked up the bee box and carried it toward the school. Ayla followed, Skye at her side.

Standing a few metres away from the swarm, Ayla could see it was massive, and a bit unsettled. She also noticed lots of small faces peering out of the library windows. Skye saw them too and waved. Some waved back and Ayla glanced briefly at her daughter, noting her excitement. Turning back to Alex, Ayla outlined her process to catch the bees. He hesitated. 'Aren't you going to smoke them? I hear that calms them down.'

'A swarm is a natural birth and very gentle, so there's no need for smoke to calm them.' She could see he still looked unsure.

'I have a spare hat and veil if you'd like to stay nearby and watch.' Ayla handed the gear to him. 'The children will be able to see most of the action from the windows.' She chuckled inwardly as he looked surprised, then fearful, although he quickly changed his expression to one of acceptance when he realised his students were watching.

'That's all you're going to put on?'

She frowned at the tone he used. Disbelief. He sounded like a teacher, even if he didn't look like one. 'Yes.' She had already placed the open box on the ground beneath the swarm. A few bees were buzzing in and around it, investigating. His expression grew more incredulous as Skye put her own hat and veil on.

'No gloves? No suit? Not even for your daughter?'

'No need.' Ayla looked again at the height of the swarm and the distance to the ground. 'Could I have two chairs please? I'd like to get the hive box a bit closer to them.'

'Of course.' He hurried off to another building, returning moments later with two wooden chairs. Perfect.

Ayla set the chairs up facing each other. She placed the bee box on one and stood for a moment on the other, rubbing her hands together.

3

Bright blue, with flowers painted on its side, the Kombi had arrived in exactly ten minutes. Alex was curious to see this bee catcher with the lovely voice. The door opened and she stepped out. Tall. Leggy. Long wavy honey brown hair. He chuckled inwardly. *Honey* brown hair. Wearing denim overalls, rolled up over the ankles, white tee shirt underneath and white tennis shoes. Her skin a golden hue, she looked like she'd stepped out of a country living magazine. And tall enough to be a model too.

Alex began to walk over. That's when he saw the child. A little girl in denim shorts and a floral tee shirt. A mass of very dark curly hair. About five. Cute as a button. They turned at the same time to watch him walk across. Then they smiled. He almost stopped. Beautiful smiles, white teeth. As he neared them he saw Ayla's eyes were a smoky blue, the childs were very dark brown, almost black.

Shaking her hand sent a small jolt through him. He saw her

mouth twitch, did she feel it too? Was she *laughing* at him? To hide his reaction he knelt down to meet her daughter.

He listened as Ayla explained her method but was surprised that she didn't put a full bee suit on herself or her child. Even when she said she thought it was a wild swarm of honeybees and probably not used to human intervention.

He took the hat and veil she offered, and in other circumstances would have watched from a distance. But the faces of his students were pressed against the library windows. The teachers too, he noted. Ayla gave off a calm confidence. Her little girl, Skye, was a bit bouncier. She giggled when her mother handed him the hat and veil.

He held his breath as he watched Ayla stand on one chair directly beneath the heaving mass of bees, rubbing her hands together with her eyes closed. He could see her breathing deeply. He wondered if she was meditating.

With her daughter standing only a metre away, he watched in open-mouthed amazement as Ayla, wearing only a hat and light veil, raised her hands to the bottom of the swarm and just held them there. A minute, then two, maybe three, and a quarter of the huge bee bundle nestled into her hands. She lowered them and gently shook them onto the bee box. She repeated this several times until all the bees were crawling around on top of the box, some moving further inside and a few flying around her head.

Alex stepped closer to her. 'Wow! I wouldn't have believed you could do that.'

'There's no real mystery. I have a gentle touch.' What she said was an understatement, but he sensed she had a certain reserve, a self-containment that prevented her from glorying in his praise. She seemed to sniff the air for a moment. 'Can you smell that? Lemongrass or maybe lemon myrtle in the air?' He nodded. 'Would it surprise you to know that it's a soothing smell? It will help us, and the bees to relax.'

He shook his head. 'Fascinating.' *She* was fascinating. He could listen to her all day. He glanced at the bees in and around the box and laughed. 'What are these ones doing?' He pointed at the bees at the entrance to the box. They seemed to have their bums in the air, flapping their wings.

'They're releasing a pheromone that lets their sisters know they have the Queen bee in here.' Ayla pointed to more bees, still flying overhead. 'They fly in a symmetrical pattern, a figure eight, their way of communicating to the rest of the colony. It's how I know I have the queen.'

'Amazing!' He nodded. 'Can we move them further away from the buildings and let the children out of the library?'

'No. If I move the box the foraging bees will die. I can't put the lid on until early evening, when the rest of the bees return. But we can let the children out now, they just need to walk past quietly.'

'Okay.' He glanced at Skye, standing right beside the bee box, oblivious to the bees flying around her, some darting in and out of their new home. 'How old is Skye?'

Ayla looked at her daughter, then at him and smiled. Really smiled. Her nose crinkled up a little bit and her blue eyes looked right into his. 'She's just turned five. We dropped by a couple of days ago to look at the school. We're going to be in the area for a while and I think she should start next year.'

'Brilliant. We'd love to have her here.' A look passed across Ayla's face, briefly, before she turned again to check on the bees. Was it relief he saw? Of course the school would welcome a new student.

Skye had pulled her hat and veil off and was sitting cross-legged on the grass, right beside the bees. While many of the bees had moved further inside, some were still flying around. He watched, fascinated, as Skye held her small hand toward the box and a few bees flew around it, then one landed on the top of her forefinger. She brought her finger, with the bee resting on top, toward her face and studied it, smiling happily. He drew in a breath. Such a beautiful, natural child. He wished he had a camera handy, the image would be worthy of National Geographic.

Ayla checked the bees, then slipped the lid halfway on. He watched as she nodded to Skye, then looked at him. 'You can let the children out now, but please ask them to come out quietly, and move toward the other buildings.'

4

The ancient ones believed that bees showing up at your place was a good omen. A sign of abundance to come. @embodybee

The teacher walked silently up the few steps to the library, opened the door, entered, then closed it behind him. Ayla noticed the faces at the windows of the building disappear immediately. A few minutes later the students walked quietly out in two neat lines. Some of the older students were holding the hands of smaller ones. Some as small as Skye. Ayla liked that. She could see Skye wriggling with excitement. She really liked being around other kids. Definitely ready for school next year.

The students moved to a paved area in front of the far classroom and the teacher, Alex, beckoned her toward him.

'Boys and girls, this is Ayla and her daughter Skye. Please say a quiet hello.'

In unison, the children chanted quietly, 'Hello Ayla and Skye.'

'Everyone at Barrington School thanks you very much for catching the swarm of honeybees.' He said this to Ayla, but then turned to the children. 'Did most of you see how Ayla caught them? With her bare hands?'

Some of the children called out 'yes!' and others nodded vigorously. The teacher continued, 'Of course, only an experienced beekeeper would do this, but I think we are very lucky to have Ayla show us how she works with bees.' The children nodded and she noticed Skye had sidled up to one of the bigger girls, who was now holding her hand. Skye grinned at her, her little face so happy and bright. Ayla's happiness level rose a few notches.

'Ayla, I'm going to send the children and teachers into their classrooms, but I'd like to speak with you for a few minutes, if that's okay?' He glanced over at Skye. 'Is it all right if Skye goes into class with Ruby while we chat? It seems she's made friends already.'

Ayla followed his gaze. Skye was standing with the older girl, still holding her hand. She waved at her mother happily.

'Um. Sure. She seems happy.' She watched as the teacher quietly sent the students into class. She noticed there were three buildings. The children followed their teachers into two of them. The older students, with Skye, were waiting with expectant looks.

'This is my class. Years five and six.' He said this quietly to Ayla, before turning to his class. 'Please follow Ruby, and Skye, into class and read quietly until I join you in a few minutes.'

The older girl, Ruby, with Skye skipping beside her, led the remaining children into the last building.

Ayla turned back to the teacher.

'Ayla, thank you again. So fascinating to see your relationship with the bees. I want to ask you two things.' She smiled inwardly as he held two fingers up and ticked the first thing off with his other hand as he spoke. Such a teacher. 'Firstly, I'd like to pay you for your services today. I understand you are a professional bee catcher. Are you able to give me an invoice?'

Laughing inwardly she studied him for a moment. He was being so serious and business-like. He had judged her already, and assumed she was too much of a hippie or free spirit to have an invoicing system.

'Sure. I can generate one on my phone now and send it to you. I just need your phone number.' She pulled her phone out of her back pocket, tapped into Xero, entered the details then looked at him with one eyebrow cocked. He stared at her.

'Your number?' She smiled.

'Oh, yes. Of course.' He reeled off his number. Ayla sent the invoice and his phone beeped. He tapped the phone sticking out of his shirt pocket. 'I'll have that fixed up today Ayla, thank you.'

They looked at each other for a moment.

'There were two things?' Ayla prompted him.

'Oh yes. Thank you.' He stumbled over his words a bit. 'Now that we've had the bees here today, and the kids have seen you catch them, I'd really like to do some bee studies this term. Age appropriate for the different classes. Is this something you can help with? Are you interested?'

Ayla nodded. She couldn't believe her luck. This was exactly what she needed to get to know the community. 'Yes, I'd love to.

I do a lot of bee talks at schools actually. And at libraries and farmers markets. The school ones have been supported by the Victorian government. The contract is with Save the Bees Australia, but they subcontract these out to local beekeepers as needed.' She paused. He seemed impressed. 'I have a lot of teaching materials, I'd be happy to meet with you to discuss what you need, and perhaps make recommendations.'

'Excellent. I'll make a time with you to do that. I have your number, I'll give you a call to discuss it further.' He paused. 'Would you like to come and see how Skye is getting on with my class?' He moved toward the classroom, and she fell into step beside him. 'Bring Skye when you come to do the talks too. If you're thinking of sending her here, she can get to know her way around and meet more of the children.' A little buzz of excitement filled her mind. The school would welcome them. They reached the door, there was a low buzz of chatter from inside. He paused for a moment and opened the door. The chatter stopped and all the children turned their faces toward him.

Skye jumped up, a book in her hand. 'Mama, I'm reading with Ruby!' The words tumbled out of her loudly, her excitement obvious. The older girl, Ruby, held her hand out to take the book from Skye, but she frowned and clutched it to her chest. 'My book!'

'That's all right Ruby. Skye can borrow the book and bring it back next week.' The teacher smiled at Ayla.

'Thank you. But no. Skye, please give the book to Ruby. And thank her for reading with you.' Ayla spoke quietly. Skye reluctantly handed the book back, then burst into tears, rushing to her mother, her arms around her legs, crying noisily. Ayla stroked Skye's hair, 'We're going to visit again and do a bee talk.

So I'm sure you can read another book then.' Skye stopped crying immediately, wiping her eyes with the back of her hands. 'Thank Ruby for reading with you, Skye.'

Ayla held her breath as her sweet girl ran back to Ruby, throwing herself into her arms and giving her a kiss on the cheek. Ruby looked shocked and glanced at the teacher, but she hugged the smaller girl quickly.

Ayla took Skye's hand and led her outside, after waving goodbye to the class. The teacher walked back to the bee box beside the library with them.

'Would you like me to carry it to your car?' He looked dubiously at the box, quite a few bees were flying in and out.

'Thank you, no, as I mentioned earlier, we need to wait until dusk. Skye and I will have our afternoon tea out here, while we wait.'

'Of course. Um, the toilets are over there, if you need them, and there's a kitchen in the front part of the library, if you want to boil the jug or use the microwave.' He pointed to the buildings as he spoke and Ayla chuckled to herself. He seemed a bit out of his depth. But she sat there and nodded, quietly thanking him. She waited until he returned to his classroom, before walking over to the van to retrieve the cooler bag of groceries. She had fruit, biscuits and cheese. They'd snack on the grass by the bees.

Less than an hour later the bell rang and the children began to head home, many of them calling 'goodbye' and 'thank you' to them as they left, some on pushbikes, others on buses or picked up by their parents. Ayla called out, 'You're welcome,' in return while Skye waved.

The teacher came out, standing awkwardly for a moment.

'Would you like me to wait with you, until you're ready to leave?'

'Thank you, but I've got this.'

He held his hand out. She stood up and placed hers in it and shook quickly. A little jolt of electricity got her again. She'd think about that later.

5

While Alex hadn't intended term to kick off with a bee swarm, it created a lot of interest from the students, and he decided to leverage this. The teachers in the younger classes read bee stories, painted and talked about how much bees like flowers. There was a lot of honey talk too.

In his own class, they talked about different bee types, including small native bees and honeybees, and about the relationship between bees, pollination and food production. The kids were keen and engaged, and he decided to contact Ayla soon to discuss this with her. Could they plant a small plot of vegetables and flowers on the school grounds to attract bees? Not close to the classrooms or play areas, behind the equipment shed, perhaps?

The day ended without further incident and he ran over the events in his mind as he and Ruby were driving home.

'How was your first day of your last term at Barrington

School, Rubes? He kept his voice light, she had started to transition from happy-talkative-child to stony-silent-teenager lately and he was never sure what he would get. And it could change from one moment to the next. When they'd arrived at Barrington School at the start of the year she'd been mostly happy and made friends with Lucy next door who was also new to the area, but Lucy was in her first year at high school and Ruby hadn't made any close friends at school. Lately she had been a bit snappy with him, and he was pleased, for both their sakes, that she was starting high school next year. She always seemed worse after spending time with her mother, but he kept his thoughts on that to himself.

'It was a good day, Dad.' She didn't elaborate but gave him a half smile as she spoke.

He pushed for more information. 'Best thing that happened today?'

'That's easy. The bee swarm. Watching Skye's mum catch them. With her hands! Have you ever seen that before Dad?' Ruby's face lit up, her eyes shining as she asked the question.

'No. I wouldn't have believed it either. It was amazing. Extraordinary.' He shook his head again at the vision of the quietly confident bee catcher, holding the swarm of bees in her bare hands. He grinned at Ruby. 'Don't try this at home.' She laughed out loud at his joke and his chest swelled. He didn't hear her laugh nearly enough.

'Skye said her mum is a Bee Whisperer. Skye said she's a Bee Whisperer too.' Ruby said this almost reverently.

'I've heard of horse whisperers, so I expect it's possible there are bee whisperers.' He nodded as he slowed to turn into their driveway. They were living in a timber home just past Copeland. He was renting the house from local farmer and builder, Robbie Stewart, who let them keep two horses at the property. Alex wondered whether Robbie might subdivide and sell the house and a couple of hectares to him. A conversation he needed to have at some point. He and Ruby were really settled here and when she started high school next year, the bus ran right past the front gate.

He'd barely pulled into the carport when Ruby was out, pulling her backpack from the back seat. 'I'll get changed and feed the horses. Then can I ride over to Lucy's please? I'll be back before dark.'

Not wanting to dampen her enthusiasm he nodded, but held up his hand as she was about to dash off. 'Call Lucy first and see if it's okay with her mum and Robbie. Then back by six. No later.' He used his teacher voice.

She cheekily poked her tongue out. 'I don't have any home-work tonight. You can ask my teacher if you don't believe me!'

Alex laughed. She had him there. He waved his hand, shooing her away. 'Quick. Before I change my mind.' He was out of the car now, pulling his own backpack out. Alex reached the kitchen, turning on power to the blender. He'd make her a banana smoothie while she got changed, she hadn't eaten since lunchtime.

As he threw frozen banana into the blender, Ruby rushed from her room, now in jeans and a long sleeved tee shirt. She settled on a stool at the kitchen bench, handing him the big jar of honey. He used a spoon to slide a good serving in with the banana, ice and milk, then held the jar up, reading the label.

'Come on Dad, turn it on, I'm starving, and Lucy will be waiting for me.' She nudged him and he turned the blender on.

'We have to stop buying this supermarket honey, Rubes.

Ayla said we should be able to source raw honey from local beekeepers, much healthier. Maybe at the markets.'

'Great. Markets. Come on Dad!' Ruby pushed two glasses toward him. He turned the blender off and poured the smoothie into one, which Ruby grabbed and drank while he was still filling his own glass.

And she was gone, shouting over her shoulder, 'I'll be back by six, Dad. Promise!'

Alex took his smoothie out to the side veranda and watched as she saddled her horse, a neat little bay gelding called Brute. He was anything but a brute, and Ruby adored him. She mounted and walked through the gate to the next paddock, running parallel with the road. She could ride the whole way across one large, long paddock. In the distance he could see the two story house Lucy lived in with her mum, Nicole and now Robbie Stewart. It had been the local courthouse during the gold rush years, but Nicole had renovated it into a home for themselves upstairs and short-term accommodation downstairs.

Once Alex finished his drink he changed into jeans and a tee shirt, then set about preparing dinner. Fettuccini meatballs with a bit of salad, Ruby would be hungry when she got back. He glanced at his phone laying on the bench as he cut up mushrooms and onions. He put the knife down, wiped his hands on a tea towel and picked it up. Finding Ayla's number, his finger hovered over the ring button. He hesitated. Did he want to speak to her about the school bee talks, or did he just want to speak to her? Hear her voice? Shaking his head, he set the phone down. Better he call her from school, during the day. An evening call might leave the wrong impression.

6

Every hive is a being with a unique personality. All of the bees in our backyard were originally wild swarms, all of them unique in their own way. The more you spend time with bees, the more the colony will get to know you and be comfortable in your presence. My daughter spends a lot of time in the backyard and will play close to the bees. It is beautiful to see her lack of fear, although she is aware that a sting can hurt. @embodybee

Ayla set the rescued swarm box in the garden by a large clump of lavender. The van doors were open, Skye was still asleep in her booster seat. It had been an exciting day for her. Ayla would use the time to get the bees settled, then check her vegetable garden and the chickens behind the old stables. Part of the roof had been damaged in the fires two years before, like most of the buildings on the property. The roof wasn't beyond repair, but she had other priorities.

The chickens were free range during the day, but Ayla had to lock them away at night. Being right on the edge of the State Forest there were dingos and foxes in the vicinity. She hummed to herself while she worked, glancing at her sleeping daughter every few minutes.

Taking a deep breath, Ayla stretched, then turned in a full circle. This place. This beautiful place. While the fire had left its mark on many of the buildings, the forest on the other side of the creek was already reclaiming the burnt trees. She could see a native lemon tree growing out of the fallen, burnt remains of another. Aranged around her garden were more than a dozen bee boxes, and the air was filled with the hum of their busyness. Ayla's heart seemed to resonate with the bees, and she felt at peace in this space. Safe.

'Mama!' Skye wailed and Ayla walked quickly to the van. Her daughter's face lit up when she saw her, holding her arms out, saying more quietly as Ayla scooped her up, 'Mama.' It was just a whisper near her ear, yet the sound spoke volumes.

'Dinner time baby. Let's have some of the bread we baked this morning.' Ayla carried her to the old house. The back of it had been devoured by the fire, but the kitchen, bathroom, two bedrooms and the front veranda remained. They had lived in the stables for weeks while Ayla partitioned off the burnt part of the house with recycled timber boards.

Skye scrambled out of her arms and ran ahead, up the three steps to the veranda. 'And cheese Mama. Cheese please.'

Ayla laughed. 'Of course cheese. And tomato and avocado. And tomorrow, a walk over to the river. It might be too cold to swim, but the walk will be lovely.'

* * *

THE DAY BEGAN TO WARM THEM DURING THE HOUR IT TOOK TO get to the river, walking along ancient logging tracks, gradually climbing to the top of the ridge, six hundred metres higher than the house and stables. Then a steep descent, this time following a worn cattle path, zig zagging down to reach the fast-flowing river. Clear water bubbled across rocks and fallen trees, creating small rapids on one side and a deeper pool closer to the riverbank where the water eddied into a lazy whirlpool.

Dropping her backpack, she glanced at Skye. It was a long walk for her small legs, but she was sturdy and a good walker. She was already stripping off her shorts and tee shirt, dumping them on the grassy bank.

'It might be too cold to swim.' Ayla chuckled as Skye ignored her, laying naked on her tummy on the edge of the bank, reaching her arm over to dip her fingertips in the water, her little bottom wriggling with excitement.

Grinning at her mother, Skye jumped up. 'Not too cold Mama. We can swim.' She nodded emphatically as she spoke and Ayla knew it was a statement, not a question, so she kicked off her walking boots before lazily undressing, until she too was naked.

'Let me step in first Skye. We need to stay in this pool by the edge, the current is too strong in the middle.' Dipping one leg into the water, up over her knee, she paused, breathing deeply while she became accustomed to the cold water. The other leg in, she threw herself backwards, completely immersing her body, before popping up again. Skye was already on the edge, poised to jump as Ayla surfaced. She landed in front of Ayla, going completely under, then breaking the surface before dog-paddling around her mother in a circle.

They frolicked in the water for a short while, Skye squealing happily as they paddled around but it really was cold, so they moved to sit on a smooth rock warmed by the sun, a good portion of it rising above the water line.

A flash of light caught Ayla's eye, and she looked over the river, her gaze following the cattle tracks up to the next ridge at the top. She squinted, there was another flash of sun glinting off metal. Then she saw them. Two horses with riders on the crest up high. Skye's squeals may have alerted the riders to their presence. Ayla turned her back. They were two far away to really see anything, but they may realise she and her daughter were naked. She was confident she wasn't trespassing, the survey plan she had studied clearly showed this portion of the river belonged to the fire-damaged and abandoned resort.

The riders disappeared from the ridge and mother and daughter lay in the sun until their bodies were warm and dry. The walk home would take longer, Skye would be tired, and Ayla would have to carry her some of the way. The thought didn't diminish her pleasure of the afternoon.

7

Alex stood near the front gate greeting the students as they arrived, some spilling out of two small buses, some dropped off by parents and many walking and riding their bikes. He liked to be visible and available in the mornings, sometimes parents preferred an informal 'word' about their child in passing, rather than making an appointment. He also enjoyed the way a number of the parents chatted by the front fence after their children had walked through the gates. They included him in their chat at times, and he was happy to be part of the broader school community in this way.

One parent, Melanie Evans, smiled as he neared. 'Morning Alex. No bee swarms in sight today?' Monday's bee swarm was still the hot topic of conversation.

'Morning Melanie. None in sight. I expect most households had 'bee' discussions over dinner the last couple of nights.' He raised an eyebrow as he smiled.

'Did she really hold the swarm in her bare hands? Melanie shook her head as she asked.

'She really did. No fear. Bees buzzing all around her. And her little girl. No stings. I'm pleased I filmed it. It's something I don't expect to witness again.' Alex knew he sounded impressed, but why wouldn't he?

They were joined by several other parents. Melanie turned to Nadia Fabianitz, who owned the general store. 'Nadia. We were just discussing the capture of the bee swarm on Monday. Was it the key topic of conversation at your table this week?'

'It would have been, but Joyce Wilson brought another snippet of information with the post, just before closing time.' Nadia raised her eyebrows and stepped away from the gate. Melanie stepped toward her, as did Alex, if only out of curiosity. What would trump the bee swarm?

'Well. You know Joyce. Likes a chat on the mail run.' Melanie and Alex nodded. 'Two of the Fraser boys say they saw nudists in the river yesterday afternoon.' Nadia paused for effect. Alex wished he'd not joined this conversation. It was gossip, not news.

Melanie looked a bit uncomfortable too. 'Quite a lot of folks skinny dip in the rivers and creeks on their own properties.'

'That's just it. She was in the Dilgry River where it runs through the old resort up in the Tops. We all know the owners abandoned it after the fires burnt them out. it's been up for sale by the bank for more than a year. Young Bill Fraser says he's seen smoke coming from the old homestead recently when he's been riding the ridge. It looks like someone is *squatting* up there. There may be more than one. Joyce said it might be a *commune of hippies*.' Nadia nodded emphatically on the last word, her hands on her hips.

'Ah, well. Perhaps something for the police to check. I must get to class.' Alex nodded to both women, turning to leave.

'Maybe Ben can check it out. He's the real estate agent with the listing.' Melanie turned to Alex. 'Go Alex, I'll mention this to Ben later.' She gave a weak smile and included Nadia in her next comment. 'Best we don't speculate. At the moment it's just second-hand news from Joyce.'

Alex shot Melanie a grateful glance. 'Thanks Melanie.' Then he walked back through the school gate, calling out to his daughter. 'Ring the bell Ruby, it's eight thirty.'

* * *

His mind returned to the conversation several times during the day. He wondered who would be squatting up there. It was a big property, he and Ruby had ridden up around it only a few weeks ago, curious to have a look at the ruins. He understood it was about eight hundred hectares, most of it forested high country. The resort was once the premier place to stay in the Barrington Tops, built about thirty years before, with the cabins and buildings on just a few hectares of flat ground before the heavily wooded country rose to over a thousand metres above sea level. He didn't know much more than that, although there was speculation that the last people to own it had not maintained their fire breaks.

There could be someone camping, passing through. There was a closed sign at the front gate where it met the road, perhaps travellers had gone in, curious like he and Ruby, and decided to stay for a few weeks. His thoughts segued from forest to bees.

Alex had put a proposal to the School Board to run the bee

keeping talks, which generated some interest. Nadia, Melanie and a couple of other parents suggested a small flower and vegetable garden as a project that all grades could get involved in, and perhaps even establish a hive of bees for the school as part of the project. He was waiting for final approval before contacting Ayla, although he had ensured her initial invoice was paid promptly.

* * *

BY FRIDAY, THE TALK AT THE SCHOOL GATE ABOUT *HIPPIE NUDISTS* had died down and Alex was looking forward to the weekend. Ruby was keen to ride up to the resort again, but when Lucy invited her to stay over on Saturday night, she changed her mind.

Early Saturday morning Ruby bolted down breakfast then rushed out to saddle Brute. The girls were going to practice some low jumps on a course in Nicole's paddock that Robbie had built, and Ruby couldn't wait to get started. She waved as she headed off, backpack and broad smile in place. Alex stood on the fence and watched her go. Fifteen minutes later he received a text.

> Here now. See you tomorrow. R 😊

> Be good. Call me if you need anything. Dad. x

A smiley-face emoji appeared, and he sighed. High School next year. He wondered if their relationship would change even more then. Probably. He should make the most of it now, some days she barely acknowledged him.

After putting a load of washing in the machine, Alex made a quick shopping list and drove into town. He stopped at the general store on the way home, to get a coffee. He'd called into the coffee shop in town, but it was packed with tourists, and he liked to spread his custom around. He sometimes worried how well Nadia and Frank did at the store. Although they had the last petrol before the high climb to the Barrington Tops, so he probably shouldn't.

'Hey Nadia. Good morning. I'll have a large cappuccino to go please.' Alex picked up the local paper and put it on the counter while he waited for his coffee. Nadia's husband Frank went out to serve someone at the petrol pump. Alex recognised Robbie Stewart, Lucy's step-dad.

'I doubt there are many places left in this country where someone will still pump fuel for you.' Alex grinned at Nadia as she set the coffee in front of him.

'People can do it themselves. Frank just likes to have a chat. And he cleans the windscreen while he's there. Everyone wins.' Nadia chuckled as she took his payment.

'Thanks Nadia.' Alex strolled back to his vehicle, coffee in one hand and paper tucked under his arm.

'Hi Frank. Robbie.' He loitered by the vehicle as Frank finished pumping the fuel and took Robbie's card inside for payment.

'Hey Alex. The girls are already going over those jumps easily. I've sent Harry out to raise them a little bit. He's doing some work on the front fence, so he's going to keep an eye on them.' Robbie's son Harry, about twenty years old, ran a building and fencing business with his father. Alex really liked the whole family and was happy they lived so close. Ruby adored Lucy, and Nicole. She didn't see her own mother much since she'd moved to Melbourne with her new husband. Ruby had chosen to stay with Alex when they divorced four years ago. But she had a week with her mum most school holidays. Although this year she had resisted, wanting to stay home to ride Brute. Alex had made her go for five days anyway, but if she put up a fight during the next holidays he'd have to speak to her mother about it. Maybe Sasha could come here for a few days. Not his favourite option, but he'd do what he could to keep communication open, for Ruby's sake.

'They're pretty handy on their horses, I've been wondering if it's time to upgrade Brute.' Alex and Robbie leaned their hips against Robbie's vehicle, facing each other.

'Not yet Alex. Another twelve months I think. I've got my eye on a couple of stockhorses Harry broke in. We've been working them ourselves. They might suit the girls next year.'

Alex nodded. He'd defer to Robbie's knowledge. While he had a horse of his own, mostly so he could ride with Ruby, he wasn't born and bred to it like the Stewart men.

'Been meaning to talk to you this week. I've spoken to Ben Evans today about the sighting of someone living up at the old resort. He's the listing agent, been working with the bank on the sale.' Robbie paused as Frank returned with his card and receipt. They chatted for a moment, then another car pulled in for fuel and Frank's attention was diverted. Robbie lowered his voice. 'Ben says the place went under contract a couple of months ago, it was mortgagee in possession. It's been purchased in a company name. Apparently they want it kept quiet while they decide whether they'll rebuild or do something else with the property.' Robbie scratched his head. 'I don't know what else you could do with it. It's all steep country, heavily forested and joins the state forest. You'd lose any cattle or horses you ran there. There's only a couple of fenced paddocks in the front section, on the flats.' Alex nodded, not sure where Robbie was going with this.

'Ben needs to find out who's up there, but he doesn't want a confrontation. He wondered if I might ride up, just check it out from a distance. He doesn't want to send the police up there in case it's someone just passing through, doing no harm. Thought you might fancy a ride yourself, this afternoon?'

Alex nodded, then squinted at Robbie and laughed. 'Mate. I think you're nervous to go up there by yourself. You've got nudist nerves!'

Robbie grinned. 'Good one Alex. You got me there. Harry was dead keen to investigate, but Ben suggested a more mature approach may be needed.' He chuckled.

Alex slapped him on the back, laughing loudly. 'Okay Robbie. Safety in numbers. I'll be your wing man to protect you from any rampant nudists we encounter.'

8

The beehive resonates and amplifies the universal tune that awakens, balances and guides life. This thought is not unique but collectively acknowledged from ancient to more modern times wherever the bee is native to the region. It is no wonder that honeybees are revered. They have served nature and humankind for over 200 million years. Their hum is part of our psychic fibre, subtly informing us that all is well. A direct extract from 'The Beehive Effect. Ancient Rites, Quantum Principles' by **Valerie Solheim.**

Saturday was bright and sunny, and considerably warmer than earlier in the week. Ayla and Skye baked bread and carrot cake early in the morning, then checked the bees. They had let the chickens out before baking, collecting ten eggs. Skye held one in each hand, Ayla had the rest, very carefully returning to the house and placing them in the egg basket on the kitchen bench.

Sitting on the front veranda, they dangled their legs over the edge while they ate home-made muesli for breakfast.

'What would you like to do today Skye? We need to make some jam out of the wild plums we picked last week, they're ripe enough now.' Ayla watched as her daughter considered the question.

'Swim in the river.' She nodded her head emphatically and her mass of curly dark hair bounced up and down. Ayla itched to tie it back, but this had become a battle lately.

'We can do that. It's warm enough. But it's a long walk and a hot day, and it's always harder coming back.' Ayla watched as Skye processed that.

'We can make a picnic Mama. We can swim and have lunch and a rest, then walk home.' She turned her large brown eyes on Ayla. 'We can take cheese for our picnic. I like cheese.' Skye nodded, her little face serious.

'Alright. A picnic it is. With cheese. And bread.' Ayla stood up. 'Come on, let's get ready and start before it gets any hotter.'

THEY WERE HOT AND SWEATY WHEN THEY ARRIVED AT THE RIVER. Ayla set her backpack with their picnic under a large gum tree that was almost strangled by a parasitic native fig tree, its branches entwined with the gum tree providing a canopy of shade. Skye set her smaller backpack down beside Ayla's and stripped off her clothes without hesitation.

'Swim now Mama.' She was ready to launch herself into the

water, and although she could swim to an extent, not enough for Ayla to let her enter the water alone.

'Wait Skye. We'll swim together, then have a snack.' Ayla drew off her singlet top and bra, then pulled her leggings off. She stretched, then stared up at the ridge where she had seen the horsemen on Tuesday. She squinted a little, then turned to Skye, excitement in her voice. 'Look Skye, up at the ridge. There's an eagle. No two eagles. They're wedge-tailed eagles.' She brought Skye in front of her and pointed to the eagles, circling slowly just below the ridge, dropping lower and lower.

'I can see them Mama. I can see the eagles too!' Skye picked up on Ayla's excitement. One of the eagles drew its wings into its side and plummeted toward the ground, while the other continued to circle above, the wind currents lifting it higher than the ridge. They couldn't see where the first one landed and Ayla almost held her breath as they waited for it to reappear. They were about to give up when it rose upwards, wings flapping furiously, a small animal held in its claws. Ayla couldn't make out what it carried, a rabbit or small wallaby most likely. They watched as it continued to rise, then landed on a large nest on a rocky outcrop on the side of the ridge. The other eagle landed beside it.

'The eagles have their lunch too Skye. They most likely have a baby eagle in their nest.' Ayla glanced once more at the eagles, then raised her eyes to the ridge. No other movement caught her eye. She stepped gracefully into the water, ducked under, then surfaced as Skye jumped in, swimming to her side. It was slightly warmer today, especially where the water had stilled in the pool at the edge. Ayla suspected the fast flowing water, coming down from the high country, in the middle of the river would be as cold as it was on Tuesday.

They splashed around, then Ayla gave Skye a swimming lesson, watching as she floated on her back, then turned to breaststroke to the riverbank. Skye scrambled out, turning to her mother. 'I'm hungry, let's eat now.'

Ayla's own stomach rumbled. She stepped up onto the bank, wrapping a sarong around her body, tied above her breasts. She wrapped a smaller one around Skye and laid their picnic out on the grass.

Skye curled up after they'd eaten, her head resting on Ayla's legs, and within moments she was asleep. Ayla lay back too, one arm behind her head, and allowed herself to clear her mind, the rhythm of her daughter's soft breathing lulling her into a meditative state. She slowly brought her thoughts back to the present, then gently placed a tee shirt under Skye's head, enabling her to withdraw her leg and get up.

Standing on the riverbank she gazed across to the ridge, her eyes searching for the eagles nest, camouflaged by vegetation unless you knew where to look. Spotting it, with at least one eagle settled on top, she stretched. Undoing her sarong, it dropped in a pool of silky fabric at her feet. Stepping from partial shade into the full sun, she stretched again, her arms over her head and turned around slowly, enjoying the warmth on her skin. Skye was still sleeping, so she walked to the edge of the river, preparing to step into the water.

Movement on the ridge caught her eye. She found the eagles nest again; nothing had changed there. Her eyes roved higher. Two horseman were poised at the very top of the ridge. She raised her chin, they were a long way away, but she was annoyed they had returned to watch her. The sun glinted off metal, or glass, like it had the other day. She squinted, staring up at the silhouettes. Movement caught her eye and she turned her back. The bastards were using binoculars! She straightened her shoulders, standing motionless. Let them look! Almost languidly, she bent to retrieve her sarong, wrapping it low on her hips. Turning back to face the ridge, she raised her hand in a wave, letting them know she could see them.

As she did an eagle drifted into view, wings extended, floating on an updraft. It was just below the spot where the horses stood, Ayla couldn't turn her eyes away. She was sure the riders hadn't seen the eagle yet, it was below them, drifting very close to the ridge. A gust of wind must have caught it, as it lifted several metres higher, almost to the same height as the horses. Ayla wasn't sure, but it looked like only a few metres of space separated horses and eagle. One horse pranced sideways, the eagle flapped its wings once and turned back to the north. The other horse half-reared, the rider appeared to cling to its neck for a moment, then both horses and riders disappeared from view. Ayla frowned, wondering if they were all right, but Skye woke in that moment and her attention was diverted.

9

Robbie and Alex set off within the hour, carrying water and sandwiches in their saddle bags. Alex added binoculars, he'd seen an eagle's nest up there with Ruby last time, although they hadn't spotted the adult eagles.

They rode steadily until they reached the foothills, stopping in the shade of a swiftly running creek to eat their lunch and water the horses. With only a short break they turned right, heading upwards through the Fraser property, toward the ridge. About halfway up they paused and dismounted, giving the horses well-earned respite from the steep ascent. Down in the valley to the east they could see the buildings of the resort, most of them fire damaged. Although much of the forest directly to the north was blackened in places, two years and steady rain had already regenerated some of it, they could see new green growth taking over.

'How many buildings were there, before the fire?' Alex

inclined his head toward the valley. Robbie stood alongside, pointing. 'That's the stables, yards and just to the north there, the original homestead. More of a cottage really.' He turned slightly. 'Here, to the west of the stables is the restaurant building and you can see where the holiday chalets were.'

Alex nodded, taking it in. He counted eight burnt patches, remnants of roofing iron and other debris laying in blackened heaps. Two small buildings seemed unharmed. Scorched perhaps, but still standing.

'I understand only two chalets survived and most of the main restaurant building. There was a tennis court there.' Alex looked where Robbie pointed. He could make out the high fence, but the surface was strewn with tree branches. Alex lifted the binoculars from his saddle bag and took a closer look. The large building and remaining chalets appeared abandoned, but when he trained his eyes on the homestead he could see signs of maintenance.

He lowered the glasses and handed them to Robbie. 'It's more than just squatting. There are chickens in the garden down there.'

'Chickens?' Robbie looked surprised, then trained the binoculars on the stables and house himself. 'You're right, there are several chickens, and just to one side some earth has been turned over. It looks like the start of a vegetable garden. I can't see any human activity.' He handed them back to Alex, who had another look around. On the other side of the house he could see some colour, a bit of blue.

'There's a vehicle parked on the other side of the house. I can just see the back of something blue.' He looked at Robbie. 'Should we ride down there?'

Robbie contemplated the question. 'No. We don't want a

confrontation. We'll advise Ben and he can get in touch with the new owners, and the police if need be.'

Alex nodded. 'Sure.' he looked at his watch. 'I saw an eagles nest up this way last time, although we came to the ridge from the other side, through the state forest. I don't think it was too much further, do you mind if we take a look?'

Robbie grinned, shaking his head. They continued on, the valley with the resort now hidden behind a low ridge, until the river far below came into view. They stopped again, Alex raised the binoculars, searching for the eagle's nest, until Robbie reached across, tapping him on the shoulder, pointing down to the river. Alex swung the binoculars down, as the woman stepped out from the shadow, standing in full view on the riverbank. He adjusted the focus, then looked again to see her stretch, then undo the thing she was wearing. Colourful thing. Sarong, that's what it is, women wear them to the beach over their swimsuits. He gulped, the material slid from her body, and she was naked, just standing there. Naked. Beautiful. Robbie made a noise, and Alex handed him the binoculars.

Robbie pushed them away. 'I've seen enough mate.' Alex nodded. He felt slightly ashamed, and put them back in his saddle bag, but he couldn't help looking again, without the glasses. She had turned, picked up the sarong and tied it around her waist. She turned back to them, bare chested, proud and absolutely stunning. She waved one hand.

'Shit, she saw us. Bloody hell, now I feel like a jerk.' Alex would have said more, but a massive eagle rose from nowhere, its wings stretched wide. Robbie's horse shied and he turned it, speaking quietly, settling it. Alex's horse reared, he crouched low on its neck, trying to calm it. The eagle flapped once and turned away on the wind, but not before Alex registered its wingspan was bigger than his horse. Robbie had trotted down the ridge a few metres, his horse still prancing sideways, when Alex's horse reared again, then shied sideways, cantering away. Alex fell heavily to the ground.

He was winded and felt blood oozing from scratches to the side of his face where he'd hit the rough undergrowth. Standing, he brushed himself off and watched Robbie canter after the horse, leading it back. He shook his head, reproaching himself, as Robbie handed him the reins. 'That's karma, for having a second look.'

Robbie laughed. 'Mate, the little I saw, I'd say she was worth a second look and a scratch or two.'

Alex wiped blood from his face with the bottom of his tee shirt. Just surface scratches, nothing deep. He turned to Robbie. 'I know who that is. And she has a blue kombi van.'

Robbie raised his eyebrows.

'It's Ayla. The bee whisperer.'

10

When I talk about bees, children hang on my every word, hungry to learn more about our pollinator friends, full of curiosity and love. These children give me hope for the future, as children are our future. Let's immerse children in the natural world around us, tell them about the big impact small creatures have. What is loved will be protected. @embodybee

The walk back was quicker than she expected, Skye had lots of energy after her sleep by the river, another swim, and then the last of the carrot cake. And cheese. Skye had finished off the camembert. Ayla shook her head, chuckling to herself. The kid loves cheese. Will eat a whole wheel of it if she finds it in the fridge.

A bit disappointed she hadn't heard from the teacher by the end of the week, she inwardly shrugged. He may have been challenged by the school board or parents group. Or the education department. She'd drop in next week, tell him the swarm had settled in their new home, a top bar hive, and see if he brought it up.

After Skye went to sleep, Ayla worked on her business. She had to hotspot from her phone for internet connection, which was a bit slow. She'd go into town on Monday, set up at the coffee shop. The owner, Debbie, had been really friendly last time. She'd take some activities for Skye, would get an hour or two in if she focussed.

Decision made, Ayla went outside to ensure the chickens were locked in properly and do a quick walk around the outside of the house. A dingo howled in the distance. She shivered. She'd seen paw prints around the outside of the chicken coop this morning. Probably a dingo.

Her thoughts segued from dingos to the riders on the ridge that morning. Twice this week they had seen her. Not that she cared, really. But she knew from experience that small towns could be hotbeds of gossip, particularly about newcomers and those perceived as *different*. While Ayla embraced people's differences herself, she was fiercely protective of Skye and did not want her to be subjected to small town prejudices. She sighed. Acceptance at the school would go a long way, she just needed an opportunity to demonstrate how much she could offer the school, and the community at large.

* * *

EARLY ON MONDAY MORNING AYLA DROVE DOWN THE MOUNTAIN. Skye was bubbly, bouncing a bit in her seat on the way, and talked a lot about going to the café, definitely a treat for her.

Parking behind town hall, Ayla gathered her phone, laptop and some pencils and paper for Skye into her satchel. Her daughter had dressed herself, looking cute in her favourite floral tee shirt with a pocket - she was crazy about pockets at the moment - and a pale pink ballerina skirt with spangles. She did a little twirl as Ayla locked the van, clapping her hands happily. Ayla glanced down at her own outfit. A slim white tank top, long wraparound batik skirt and handmade leather toe thongs, which matched the smaller ones Skye wore. Ayla had managed to get a wide cloth hairband on Skye, pink like her skirt, keeping her riotous mass of curly dark hair off her face. Ayla's own hair was tied back in a high ponytail with a strip of batik fabric.

Skye skipped and trotted in front of Ayla as they reached the main street, turning to follow the footpath to the café. An extremely tall man standing outside a real estate shop grinned at Skye, then looked Ayla in the eye, smiling as he said hello.

Returning his smile, she said 'good morning' as she walked by. Her spirit lifted a little as several more people, locals she thought, smiled or nodded at them as they passed by. Okay, most were smiling at Skye, her unbridled happiness as she skipped along hard to resist. But after they saw Skye, and smiled, they looked at Ayla, still smiling, and nodded or mouthed 'hello.' An older lady said, 'your daughter is gorgeous' as she passed by.

At the counter of the café, Ayla said hello to the owner, Debbie. They'd been in twice before and she was pleased when Debbie remembered their names.

'What can I get you today, Ayla?' Debbie smiled down at Skye, 'and for you, Miss Skye? A milkshake perhaps?'

Glancing down at Skye, Ayla waited for her to answer. Skye

seemed to think about it for a moment. 'Yes please, a banana milkshake, with honey.'

Debbie laughed. 'That's the only way we do them here. Raw honey too.' She turned to Ayla, 'Dirty chai latte for you Ayla, like last time?'

'Yes please. Large.' Ayla grinned, really chuffed that Debbie remembered. 'And two of the chocolate brownies please.' Taking a quick survey of the café, she spotted a table down the back, out of the way. 'I'd like to access your Wi-Fi today, I have some work to do. May we sit down the back there, away from the crowd?'

'Of course. Here's the password. Take all the time you need.' Debbie processed the payment for their morning tea.

With Skye set up, kneeling on a chair, paper and pencils in front of her, Ayla punched the password into her laptop and loaded her graphics app and Instagram. Debbie brought the drinks and brownies to the table herself, setting the milkshake in front of Skye.

'Here you go Skye, banana milkshake, with honey, and a chai for Mum.'

'Thank you.' Skye put the straw in her mouth, taking a sip. She looked at Debbie with a serious expression. 'It's very lovely.'

Debbie laughed and smiled at them. 'Thank you Skye. I have chocolate brownies for you too.' She placed two plates on the table, and Ayla saw that Skye's brownie was neatly cut into four smaller squares. She glanced at Debbie.

'Little hands,' was all she said, before turning back to Skye. 'Tell me what you're going to draw today Skye.'

'A big sunflower with a bee on it.' Skye was emphatic and Debbie seemed both surprised and pleased. 'How lovely, I can't wait to see it.' She turned to Ayla. 'Sing out if you need anything else.'

'Thank you very much Debbie, this is perfect.' Ayla meant it. No pressure, the use of the cafe Wi-Fi and a table out of the way was absolutely perfect. She'd give the café and Debbie a shout out on Instagram, the least she could do.

An hour passed, and Skye was getting restless. Debbie came over to clear their table.

'May I see your picture Skye?' She cleared their empty dishes onto a tray, wiping up a few crumbs in front of Skye with a cloth.

Skye turned her page around, it was her third attempt and Ayla knew her daughter was pleased with it. 'Wow!' Debbie sat down on a chair at the end of the table, next to Skye. 'May I?' She reached for the picture, which Skye, suddenly shy, handed to her. Debbie studied it, for what seemed like minutes. She lay it down on the table and turned it so Ayla could have a look too. She'd been so busy at her laptop that she hadn't given it more than a cursory glance.

'This is very, very good.' Debbie nodded, quite seriously. Ayla leaned closer to the picture. It was good. The page was filled with a large sunflower, with a bee poised in the very centre and another flying to one side. It was all in proportion and brightly coloured. Ayla had sharpened two different yellows, a green and a blue several times during the morning. She knew Skye was creative, but this was stunning.

'How old are you Skye? I really love your picture, it's absolutely beautiful,' Debbie asked Skye directly. Ayla liked that.

'I'm five. I'm going to school soon.' She picked the picture up, studying it for a moment, before reaching for the red pencil. The tip of her tongue poked out between her teeth as she drew a small heart shape to one side of the sunflower, then coloured it in vigorously. When finished she nodded at the picture, seemingly satisfied with her handiwork, then handed it to Debbie, who had watched, fascinated. 'This is a present for you Debbie.' She pointed to the little red heart. 'Love from me.'

Ayla watched as Debbie took the picture, looking at Skye. Were there tears in her eyes? Debbie placed the picture on the table, then leaned over, putting both arms around Skye, giving her a hug. 'This is the nicest present ever, Skye, thank you. I just love it.' She stood, carefully picking up the picture with one hand and the tray of dishes with the other, before walking away.

'I need to pee, Mama.' Skye was standing. Ayla glanced around, not sure if there was a bathroom at the café or if they'd have to go to the public restrooms in the park nearby. She started to pack her gear away hurriedly, Skye often didn't give much warning when she needed to go. Debbie materialised beside her.

'Where's the nearest toilet please Debbie?' Ayla glanced at Skye, who was jiggling from one foot to another.

'We have one out the back, through the kitchen.' Looking at Ayla trying to put her gear away, she added, 'Leave your stuff if you're not ready to go, I'll keep an eye on it.' She pointed toward the kitchen, 'Just go through there, Cathy will open the door for you.'

Nodding her thanks, Ayla took Skye's hand and walked quickly through to the kitchen. Returning a few minutes later, she found Debbie, coffee in hand, sitting at their table. 'I've got a short break, thought I'd sit here until you returned.' She started to stand up.

'Please stay, I'll order another coffee too.' Ayla walked to the counter, a younger woman was serving now. She ordered a small chai and a wholemeal cheese sandwich for Skye.

Ayla asked Debbie about the town and her business, learning she had grown up here, but had studied and worked overseas before returning to marry and set up the café. An older woman approached the table, rather large and lumpy, dressed in black pants and a red polo shirt sporting the Australia Post logo.

'Debbie, have you heard the news?' Her voice was rough, and she barely nodded at Ayla, ignored Skye altogether and pulled a chair over from the next table. Ayla saw annoyance flit momentarily across Debbie's face.

'Hello Joyce. This is Ayla, and Skye.' The woman nodded, glanced at them, then turned to Debbie, speaking quickly.

'There's squatters up at the old resort, the Fraser lads saw them. Nudists, they are.' The woman, Joyce, nodded her head enthusiastically. 'Ben Evans and the police will have to go up there, move them on. It's owned by the bank now, see?'

Debbie had started to stand. Ayla was sitting very still, shocked to hear the woman's words. She glanced at Skye. She was drawing another picture, in a world of her own.

'Joyce, I don't know anything about it and neither do you. The Fraser boys may have seen campers.' Debbie spoke firmly, her hand under Joyce's elbow brought the woman to her feet.

Joyce looked mutinous. 'Definitely nudists they said. We don't need their likes around here. they'll be moved on, you mark my words.'

'I understand the boys were on horseback on the ridge. A long way from the river and even further from the resort. Glimpsing someone having a swim in a secluded spot hardly constitutes a nudist colony.' Debbie's lips had narrowed, she spoke firmly. 'Cathy has your lunch order ready, Joyce, if you'd like to go up to the front counter.'

Debbie turned back to Ayla as the woman ambled to the counter. She was joined by two middle-aged ladies in tennis gear who had been sitting at a table at the front. Debbie shook her head as Joyce repeated her story loudly to the women, who were tut-tutting and looking shocked, while several other people at nearby tables listened with obvious interest. 'Small towns Ayla. The good, the bad and the ugly.' She jerked her chin toward the women, still speaking together at the front. 'Gossip is definitely the ugly.' She walked determinedly toward the group.

11

Alex chuckled as he touched the side of his face, the small cuts and scratches from his fall on Saturday quite visible. A couple of his grade six boys had asked just before lunch, wide eyed and feigning innocence. 'What does the other bloke look like, Sir?' He'd given them a stern look, but they had grinned at him regardless. Ruby had already told them he fell off his horse. He and Robbie hadn't shared the details with anyone, except Nicole. Alex had said he would like to speak to Ayla first, let her know questions were being asked about her presence at the resort property. He wanted to give her the opportunity to leave, without getting into any trouble.

He picked up his phone, the students were at lunch and the teachers were either in the lunchroom or on playground duty.

Ayla answered after a couple of rings. Her voice was lovely, warm and soothing. He could listen to her all day.

'Hello?'

'Ayla, hello. It's Alex McIntosh from Barrington School.'

'I know. How are you?'

Of course she knew, his name was in her phone. He mentally slapped himself. 'Fine, thank you. I'd like to catch up for a chat if you have time this week. About the bee education program, and er, other matters.' He pictured her eyebrows raising as she responded.

'I'd love to. I have time this afternoon if that suits. I'm currently in town, could drop by when school finishes.' She paused. 'Other matters?'

'This afternoon is perfect, thank you. Um, we'll talk then. Say half past three?' He didn't want to pre-empt the discussion about seeing her at the river.

'See you then.' She ended the call. He looked at his phone for a long moment. Why had he said he'd speak to her? Robbie could have called Ben Evans, told him she was there, possibly living in the damaged homestead. Had been there long enough to have chickens and start a vegetable garden. He needn't have involved himself. He was just happy Robbie agreed they wouldn't mention her skinny dipping, he certainly didn't want her to know he had seen her, clearly, through the binoculars.

* * *

THE BLUE KOMBI VAN ARRIVED AS THE CHILDREN WERE LEAVING. Some of them waved to Ayla and Skye. He watched from his office as she knelt to speak to Nadia and Franks' son Oscar, at the gate. She certainly had a way with children, although why should he be surprised, she was a mother herself and her own child, a delight.

With the children gone, even Ruby had taken the bus, he walked outside to greet her.

'Hello again Ayla. Hello Skye.'

They smiled in unison, catching him unawares. Both so gorgeous. He wondered momentarily about Skye's father. She was olive skinned, with dark hair and eyes, yet her features were fine, like her mother's.

He led them to an outdoor table by the playground; there was a lovely breeze. Skye ran toward the swings, but her mother called out. 'Wait Skye.' The child stopped but did not return. 'Is it all right if she plays over there? We can see her from here.'

'Of course.' He nodded as Ayla waved to Skye, who continued onto the play equipment. Alex turned slightly, so they could both see her.

'Thank you.' Ayla spoke quietly, looking directly into his eyes. He saw her eyes flick to the left, taking in his recently acquired scratches, but he wasn't keen to discuss those.

'I've got approval from the school board to run a bee-oriented program this term. I have some ideas, but I'd like to hear your thoughts first, given you've done this before.'

'That's great news Alex, I'm really excited to share bee education with your students.' She reached into her backpack, retrieving two neatly bound folders. 'This one is for you. I've marked the modules that might be most appropriate for your school, covering the entire cohort, but with more advanced studies for the senior students.'

He knew she'd done this before, but he was super impressed by the presentation. So much of the work was already done, it just needed an expert to take them through the modules. He flicked through, taking particular note of the sections she'd marked. It was perfect. He looked up, nodding. 'This is very good, Ayla, exactly what I was hoping for.'

'The base information has been produced by Save the Bees Australia, but they like individual educators to put their own spin on it. Everything I do is very bee-centric, rather than beekeeper centric. If you want to develop the program further we can have the kids start a vegetable garden that includes native flowering plants, and I can bring a hive here too. We can eventually harvest honey and use beeswax to make sustainable products.' She sat back, her eyes shining. He could see how passionate she was, and he was enthralled by her long term vision. He couldn't wait to learn more.

He outlined his budget, and some further ideas and Ayla nodded, tapping notes into her phone. He saw she had priced the modules, but a small percentage went back to the Save the Bees people. He liked that too.

Skye called out, she had been playing on the monkey bars but was now sitting on a swing, her legs not quite long enough to push off from the ground. 'Can you push me Mama? Please!' Ayla looked at him, and he stood when she did, walking across to the little girl together. Ayla pushed her a couple of times, and once she had started she was able to continue swinging without further help. They moved to one side, standing together, their shoulders almost touching.

Ayla turned. 'You said there is something else you'd like to discuss?'

He nodded, cleared his throat, then looked at the ground for a moment. She didn't speak, he raised his gaze, looking straight into her eyes. 'Um, you're, er currently living at the abandoned resort up near The Tops.' It was a statement, not a question, but she answered anyway.

'I am. We are.' She looked at Skye. 'Why do you mention it?' Her voice had changed, a defiant note had slipped in.

Darn. She was going to make this hard. 'As we've met, you helped with the swarm last week, and I realised it was you, I said, er, I offered, to speak to you.' He was stumbling over his words.

She looked at him, her eyes slightly narrowed. 'Why?'

'Why what?'

'Why does anyone need to speak to me?'

'Um, it seems, that you're, um, living there.' He didn't know whether he should say *squatting* or *trespassing* or perhaps soften it and use *camping*.

'Yes. We've established that.' Now she just sounded annoyed.

'Look, there is talk in town, apparently, and, uh, the real estate agent, Ben Evans, has the listing. He wanted to check.' He hesitated. 'There is talk of sending the police up there to move you on. I really just wanted to warn you, give you a chance to move, you know, without any trouble.' He took a breath. 'If you need somewhere to move to, um, my mate Robbie Stewart and his partner Nicole have accommodation available.' Her eyes were steely now and he trailed off. He knew he'd handled it badly and was regretting getting involved. He hoped she'd stay around long enough to run the bee program.

'Oh. The real estate agent and the police are coming to, what did you say? Move me on?' She still looked miffed, but he could also see laughter in her eyes. Damn, she should be taking this seriously.

'Yes. Ayla, I just want to warn you.' He stopped. She was laughing.

'Thank you Alex. Thank you for the warning. I am forewarned and will be ready for the, uh real estate people and the police to arrive.' She stepped over and gave Skye another push. 'I'm pretty sure this can be resolved amicably. There won't be a shoot-out.' Now she was really laughing. 'Although my bees may sting them if they get rowdy.' She doubled over, giggling uncontrollably. He was flummoxed. Skye jumped from the swing and ran to her mother, giggling too. 'What's funny Mama?' Ayla shook her head. Taking her daughter by the hand she picked up her backpack and turned to Alex, stifling her laughter.

'Will we start the bee program next Monday, in the afternoon? And perhaps Friday afternoons we can spend the last lesson working on the bee garden. Get them to bring an old shirt to wear over their uniforms.' She wiped her eyes with the back of her hand, she'd laughed so hard she had tears. He nodded, still trying to process her reaction. As Ayla started toward the school gate. He fell in beside her.

'Next Monday is fine.' He knew his eyes held doubt, but she smiled. Then, quite unexpectedly, she turned to face him. Raising her hand she gently touched the scratches on his face, her own so close he could taste her sweet breath on his mouth. 'Big eagle. Spectacular really.' She winked, turned and strolled to her van. A gust of wind caught the edge of her wraparound skirt as she lifted Skye into the vehicle, showing her long tanned legs. She smiled at him over her shoulder and sang out, 'Nothing you haven't already seen.' He blushed, but raised his hand in farewell, not sure if he was grinning or grimacing. In that moment Ayla smiled. Really smiled. She was radiant and beautiful and just a little bit wild.

Alex held his breath, processing his strong reaction to her. To Ayla. He turned toward his own car, then frowned and glanced back. The van was moving away. Why was she not concerned about being asked to leave the old resort? He wished he knew more about her, it was obvious she was something of a free spirit, yet she had demonstrated business acumen and professionalism with her online invoicing and quick response to his initial call out. She was certainly an enigma. Shaking his head, he silently admonished himself. Why was it important to him, anyway?

12

The sting and the thorn. The duality of life. Working with bees is a sweet, sticky, sensory experience. It is an intense frequency to navigate, and the stings must be breathed into and accepted as medicine, or your love will turn into fear. There is something romantic about the bee and the rose. I want BIG LOVE. The beauty of the rose comes with the potential to get hurt. I am not afraid. Kiss my lips with honey and sting my ego when appropriate. @embodybee

Driving back up the mountain Ayla pondered the day's events. While she was annoyed she'd been discovered at the property, she knew she'd be found there sooner or later. Later would have been better. Her mind turned to the teacher. She wasn't sure if she should be angry that he'd been the one snooping around, although the woman at the café, Joyce, had only mentioned the Fraser boys.

Home again, she ran a bath for Skye, and prepared a vege-
tarian risotto for dinner. Dinner and three story books and Skye
fell asleep on her lap. Once she'd moved Skye to her bed, Ayla
worked on the bee program for Barrington School, making
some adjustments to ensure all ages were included.

It was time to manage her socials. She spent a couple of
hours each evening on it, and again in the mornings before
Skye woke up. Her phone service was slow, but enough to get a
bit done. There were a huge number of comments on this
morning's posts and a lot of shares and saves. Good. Searching
in Instagram, she found the account for the café – she'd give
Debbie a shout out for running an awesome business, it was the
heartbeat of the town. Scrolling through the café feed, Ayla
liked some of the photos, especially the homemade baked
goods. She commented on the chocolate brownies, smiling as
she did, they were so delicious. Moments later, while still
designing the post about the café, she received a message from
the café account.

> Found you! Hi Ayla, it's Debbie.

> Hi Debbie, I'm just about to post a
> shout-out for the café, thanks again for
> today.

Ayla finished her post and tagged *@coffeeismycalling*. She
knew it would pinpoint her location, but the cat was out of the
bag anyway on that score. She walked to the kitchen to put the
kettle on, hearing lots of pings from her phone. Her followers
were loyal, and they'd want more details about what she was
doing. While she wasn't quite ready, she could trickle out a bit

of information. Small amounts, so she could manage the fallout.

Back at her phone, Debbie had tagged her in a post. Ayla opened it up. Skye's sunflower picture came into view. Ayla blinked as she read the words, a small sob catching in her throat. The kindness of strangers really moved her.

Welcome to Barrington Ayla and Skye. So lucky our little town attracts lovely people. Skye, age 5, made the picture. #suchatalent #straighttothepoolroom #welcometobarrington #thebeewhisperer

Then Debbie sent another message.

> Holy crap! You're famous! 57.3k followers. Really? You're insta royalty! And my insta is going nuts now with your peeps liking and following everything. THANK YOU! 🙌

Ayla grinned. Being an influencer has its benefits.

> Watch out, they'll be lining up for those brownies! 😜🙌

Debbie sent a thumbs up.

A mug of herb tea in her hand, Ayla peeked at Skye, sound asleep, arms and legs akimbo on top of the covers. She set the tea on the side table and pulled the doona up - the nights were cool at this altitude - then stood for a minute just looking at her. Such a gorgeous girl, she wondered where her life would take her. She'd travelled around the world with Ayla since she was twelve months old, but the move to Barrington was deliberate. They need to put down roots, get Skye started at school, make a real home for themselves. And perhaps others.

* * *

AT THE END OF THE WEEK AYLA DROVE DOWN THE MOUNTAIN FOR supplies. She parked behind the town hall and walked through to the main street, coming out near Ben Evans Real Estate. Ayla paused as she neared the shop. Should she go in and speak to the man? But the image of the riders on the ridge, spying on her through binoculars, gave her pause. While she knew the teacher was one of them and had thought one of the Fraser lads might be the other, what was to say it wasn't Ben Evans himself? She'd never met him. Ayla took Skye's hand and walked on.

Entering the café, Skye skipped to the table down the back they had sat at previously.

'Morning Debbie.' Ayla glanced around, all the tables outside were full and most inside too. Maybe Saturday was normally a busy day, with lots of tourists in town for the weekend.

'Hello Ayla.' Debbie's smile was bright. 'A lot of people around the last two days. I'm wondering if your shout out this week is bringing some focus to town. Wendy in the tourism office said most accommodation is fully booked for the weekend.'

'Oh, I expect it's just the time of year Debbie.' Ayla wanted to divert attention from herself, but she noticed a group of young people at a nearby table were staring at her.

Debbie nodded and glanced around. 'Of course, You're right. Would you like your usual? I'll bring it to you.' Ayla reached for her wallet and Debbie shook her head emphatically. 'Not today Ayla. Go. Sit with Skye.'

A few minutes later Debbie brought coffee, milkshake and

cake on a tray. 'Hello Skye, I have banana milkshake for you, and I hope you like carrot cake.' She passed a coffee to Ayla, smiling. 'Our brownies sold out yesterday and Cathy hasn't had time to bake another batch.'

'Hello Debbie. Is that my picture?' Ayla looked where Skye was pointing. Hanging on the wall just inside the entry was Skye's drawing, beautifully framed in what looked like cedar or rosewood. Ayla looked at Debbie, eyebrows raised.

'It's really, really lovely Skye. I put a picture of it on my social media on Monday night and a lot of people asked me about it on Tuesday. My husband Jamie framed it for me, it's quite famous.'

'I'll draw another one for you.' Skye set to work.

Ayla wanted to ask more questions, but Debbie pre-empted her, speaking quietly. 'I took it home on Monday and asked Jamie to frame it. It truly is lovely.' She glanced around the café, still busy, 'I had no idea then, the interest my post would generate. I didn't hang it until Wednesday, but a lot of people asked about it.' She grinned at Ayla, 'Honestly girlfriend, who *are* you?' She laughed again.

Ayla smiled, perhaps she had an ally, if not a friend yet, in Debbie. It felt good. Down to earth and a business owner and mum too, she'd told Ayla she had a one year old son the first time she went to the café with Skye.

Debbie looked directly at Ayla. 'You're living up at The Tops aren't you? It's you they were speaking about the other day.' Ayla nodded, wondering where Debbie was going with this. Debbie leant over the table, closer to Ayla. 'I'd say a few people around here are in for a shock. And I think they've totally underestimated you.' She straightened, glancing toward the front counter, where a small queue had begun. 'Gotta go, hope you enjoy the carrot cake.'

Ayla watched Debbie walk briskly back to the front of the shop, smiling and greeting her customers by name. Skye was engrossed in another drawing, this one looked like lavender. And bees of course. Ayla took a breath, smiled inwardly, then opened her laptop, she needed to send some emails.

13

Gritting his teeth, Alex spoke sharply. 'I thought you *wanted* Lucy to come over today?'

Ruby glowered, her face mutinous, arms folded across her chest. 'I don't.'

'Why Ruby? Earlier in the week, it was all you could talk about. We were going kayaking and swimming in the Barrington River. I've hired the kayaks.' Alex moved toward his daughter. She was hovering in the kitchen doorway, but as he took a step toward her, she backed away. He tried again. 'What will I tell Lucy?'

'Nothing. Don't care. I'm not going.' And she turned and ran to her room, slamming the door. He could hear her crying and wasn't sure if he should go in or not. He hesitated outside her door. Not. He'd let her cool down a bit.

Picking up his phone, he called Robbie. 'Mate, Ruby's feeling a bit off. I'm really sorry but I need to cancel plans with

Lucy coming over today. I'll cancel the kayaks too unless you want to take Lucy yourself?'

'Don't cancel them. I'll talk to Nik. We'll take Lucy down the river. It's running pretty high at the moment, it's a pity Ruby isn't up to it.'

Alex sighed, shaking his head. Ruby had been so excited on Wednesday and Thursday, then yesterday she'd been moody and didn't want to go to school. He'd made her go, but perhaps he should have let her stay home. He didn't think she was sick, but she hadn't eaten much dinner last night. He walked to her door, she wasn't crying now. He knocked lightly. 'Go away. Just leave me alone, Dad!'

He decided he'd leave her to sulk if that's what she was doing. He'd get the washing out and drive into town for groceries. Maybe she'd be in a better mood when he got back.

Standing in the laundry, sorting the whites from the colours, he chuckled. He was quite good at the domestic stuff. Ruby helped around the house a lot too, although he hadn't got her started on laundry duties just yet. He lifted the lid of their top loader, then frowned. A few damp items were clinging to the inside of the drum. He reached in. Ruby's undies, pyjama bottoms and school sports shorts. Then he realised. Poor Ruby, starting her period and her mum not here to talk to. And it explains the moodiness. No wonder she's upset and didn't want to go kayaking and swimming.

He threw the damp items back in and added the whites he had sorted. After turning the machine on he walked back to Ruby's room. He knocked. 'Go away Dad.' She was sobbing quietly. He opened the door and walked in. Ruby glared at him. She was sitting on the bed, her back against the bedhead, knees drawn up.

'Ruby, I've just put some washing on.' He paused, then sat on the edge of the bed. 'I see you did some already. Ruby, it's okay, you can talk to me, I understand.'

She put her head down on her arms refusing to look at him. He tried again. 'Would you like to call Mum, have a chat with her about this?'

'Already called Mum. But she's not here.' Ruby lifted her head and looked at him sadly. He opened his arms, and she fell into them, crying on his shoulder. 'My tummy hurts, and I woke up feeling really sad.'

Alex held her gently and patted her back. 'Um, there's something we can get from the chemist, for the tummy pains. We can go into town when you're ready.'

Ruby flung herself backwards. 'I'm not going anywhere. Not like this. I don't want to see anyone!' She watched him stand. Her voice softened. 'Can you get the stuff please Dad? Tampons. And pads.'

Inwardly groaning, Alex nodded. 'Of course. No problem. Girl stuff. I can do that. Used to get that stuff for Mum.'

'Eeuww, Dad!' Ruby put her hands over her ears. Alex walked out, closing the door quietly. He had bought these items before. But he hadn't enjoyed it. He went back to the laundry, hanging out the first load of washing and putting another in the machine. Then he drove into town.

WALKING AROUND THE CHEMIST, HE SEARCHED FOR THE SECTION he needed. Napro something for period pain. He couldn't find it, maybe it was near the Panadol. He found the *feminine hygiene* section and stood there, staring at the array of items. Does a young girl, only eleven-almost-twelve, use the same items as a woman in her thirties who's had children? He picked up a packet of pads. A big packet. He didn't want to do this too often. He turned the packet over, frowning.

'You look confused. For a teacher.' Ayla was standing at the end of the aisle.

Momentarily startled, he stared at her. 'Hello again. Er, yes. Ruby. My daughter. You met her last week. She, er, needs...' he waved his arm, indicating the whole section of shelving. 'This. She needs this but I'm not sure exactly which.' He breathed out loudly, then smiled at Skye, standing beside her mum, staring at him. 'Hello Skye.'

'Hello.' She wandered to the other side of the aisle and picked up a packet of brightly coloured hair clips.

Ayla moved closer to him. 'Ruby's mum?' she arched an eyebrow.

'Remarried. Lives in Melbourne.' He reached for another big pack of pads. 'This. This will do.'

Ayla reached over, took the packets from him and returned them to the shelf. 'They won't do. They're for heavy periods, and after childbirth.' She ran her hand along the shelf and gathered two smaller packets, brightly coloured. 'These are for young girls, just starting.' She handed him a similarly branded packet of pads. 'And these, for night-time.'

'Thank you.' He looked at the packets. 'And she has tummy pain. There's an over the counter medication, do you know what it's called?'

'Pfft. Ginger and cinnamon tea. Homemade if you can, but the supermarket will have a version. Put a teaspoon of raw honey in it.' She took Skye by the hand, putting all but one packet of hair-clips back on the shelf. 'Do you have a hot water bottle?' He nodded. 'Hot water bottle on her stomach when she has pain, better than pills.'

'Thank you Ayla.' He followed her to the checkout, waited while she paid for the hair-clips, then placed his items on the counter. 'Do you want a bag for these?' The young cashier spoke loudly.

'Yes please.' He paid and stepped out, looking around for Ayla and Skye. They weren't in sight, so he walked to the car. He'd go home, see how Ruby was feeling.

14

A swarm is a sign of abundance. When bees swarm the old colony gets a brand-new queen full of natural genetic diversity.
@embodybee

Ayla shook her head, holding Skye's hand tightly as they walked back to the car. She was thinking about the teacher and was shocked by a wail from Skye as she tugged her hand free. 'Oww! Mama you hurt my hand!' Skye frowned at her, rubbing her hand.

Kneeling by the car, Ayla put her arms around her daughter, whispering, 'I'm sorry Skye-baby, I didn't mean to squeeze your hand so hard.'

"My hand hurts.' Skye held her hand so close to Ayla's face, she couldn't focus on it, so she kissed it instead. 'Does it feel better now?'

'Yes.' Skye leaned forward and kissed Ayla on the nose, giggling. 'Can we get ice cream from the store? That will make it feel more better.' She nodded vigorously, her dark curls tumbling around her face.

'Hmmm. Let me think. Ice cream.' Ayla lifted Skye into the car, helping her do up her seatbelt. 'I need to stop at the General Store for fuel, let's get ice cream there.'

'Goody!' Skye clapped her hands and Ayla grinned. She could remember wheedling ice cream out of her own mum when she was young.

A few minutes later they were at the store. Ayla pulled up at the bowser, waving to Frank as he walked out to pump the fuel for her. His son Oscar, one of the older boys at Barrington school, began to clean her windscreen. Frank was usually very chatty, but Ayla sensed a reserve in him today. He didn't meet her eyes when she asked him how his day was going, although he murmured something about the weather and a storm coming. She lifted Skye from the car and told her to run in and look at the ice creams, knowing it would take her ages to choose one. Another car pulled in, so Frank turned his attention to it while Oscar finished the windscreens, he'd done the back one too. Ayla moved the kombi away from the fuel pump and walked inside to choose an ice cream with Skye and pay.

A little bell over the door tinkled as she entered. 'Hello Ayla, Skye is over by the ice cream.' Nadia's tone was friendly, her smile broad.

Relieved, Ayla smiled back. 'Hi Nadia, thank you, this might take a few minutes.' Ayla walked past the newspapers and magazines to the ice cream freezer against the far wall, where Skye was peering through the glass at a colourful array of products.

"Mama, I like this one.' She pointed to a bright packet. 'Or this one, or maybe the one with the lion on the front.' She was excited but whispering her words, as if speaking too loudly might make the ice creams disappear.

Chuckling, Ayla leaned over the display. The bell over the door tinkled again, it was Frank. Ayla had her back to them but could hear the conversation. Normally she wouldn't tune in, but something about the tone of Frank's voice caught her attention. 'Did you speak to her?'

'No Frank. It's none of our business.' Nadia spoke more quietly than her husband.

'People around here have been asking. It's a small community. She's right over there, probably listening anyway. Speak to her or I will.' Ayla stiffened. There was no one in the shop besides her and Skye. She pulled out the brightly coloured ice cream Skye selected and turned toward the counter, Skye beside her. Nadia smiled but Frank gave her a funny look and left through a door marked 'private' behind the counter.

'I'm just going to pop Skye at the picnic table outside with her ice-cream and I'll be right back in to pay.' Ayla looked straight at Nadia as she spoke, keeping her tone even. Nadia nodded, murmuring 'of course.'

Once Skye was settled outside, Ayla walked back in, wallet in hand. 'The fuel too, Nadia.' She took a breath. 'What is it Frank wants you to speak to me about?'

Nadia looked uncomfortable. 'I'm sorry Ayla. There's talk. It started with Joyce, the mail contractor, but a few people, locals mostly, have been coming in asking me if it's true. They've seen you getting fuel and supplies here, thought I might know.' She let out a breath, shaking her head. 'I've told them all, including Frank, that it's none of our business, so I'm going to ask you a question, well, two questions really, but you don't have to answer them.'

Ayla nodded. 'I understand Nadia. Ask.'

'One. Are you and Skye living at the abandoned resort and two, are you, um, walking around naked up there?' Nadia rolled her eyes as she spoke, making Ayla giggle.

'Yes definitely.' Ayla nodded. 'We are living up there. You can confirm that to whomever asks.' She paused. 'As to the nudity thing. No. Not walking around naked at all.' She saw Nadia smile, then raise her eyebrows. 'Except when I go for a swim in the river. The swimming spot is on the resort property, so unless, um *watchers*,' she emphasised watchers, 'are trespassing or using binoculars from the neighbouring ridge, they really wouldn't, um, *see* anything.' The door marked 'private' had clicked open an inch or so and Ayla knew Frank was listening. With a wink to Nadia, she added, 'I manage to control my desire to remove my clothes when I'm out in public, you know, doing the shopping, driving around, getting fuel.'

Nadia snort-laughed. 'Thank you Ayla. I don't see why anyone would have a problem with that.'

Ayla laughed, reached across the counter and touched Nadia's hand. 'Thank you Nadia. For being direct and asking me, rather than whispering behind my back. Perhaps you can advise ... Joyce is it?' Nadia nodded. 'Advise Joyce of the facts.'

Nadia looked like she wanted to ask further questions, but she didn't. Ayla was grateful. She sensed Nadia was an ally. And perhaps Frank would be too if there was no longer any mystery about her presence in the area. She glanced outside, Skye was almost finished her ice-cream, her face and hands were covered in chocolate. Nadia passed a small packet of wet wipes across the counter, then nodded toward the door. 'You might need a couple of these.'

Laughing, Ayla took two, and walked to the door. Before opening it, she turned back. 'Thank you Nadia. Really. Thank you.' Nadia lifted her hand in a wave and Ayla stepped outside.

15

Ruby was lying on the sofa reading when he returned. She looked up as he walked in, smiling wanly. He leant over the couch, kissing the top of her head. 'How're you feeling Rubes?'

'Yeah. Okay. Better than I was this morning.' She stood up. 'Want a smoothie Dad? I have it ready to go.'

'Yes, thank you.' He followed her through to the kitchen, two bags of groceries in his hands. He began to unpack them while she turned the blender on. He handed her the paper bag from the chemist, not sure if he should say anything.

She opened the top, peeked inside, then looked at him, a wry smile on her face. 'Good work Dad. Betcha hated asking for help to get this stuff.'

He laughed, happy she could tease him. 'Actually, I had two packets of the *wrong* stuff in my hands and was about to go to the counter when Ayla and Skye walked in. Ayla set me straight, so it's really no thanks to me at all.'

'Oh. Really? Ayla and Skye?' Ruby looked surprised, then blushed. 'So she, um, *knows.*'

'It was either her or Mr Whitlock, the Chemist. I'm certainly glad it was Ayla.' He watched as Ruby chuckled, then nodded. 'Yeah. Me too, I guess.' She slid off her seat, picked up the package and left the room. Returning a few minutes later she gave him a slight nod.

'Oh, and that's not all. Ayla said we should make some ginger and cinnamon tea if you have pain and put a hot water bottle on your tummy. Better than the medicine from the chemist. You know, more natural.' Alex wasn't sure how much of this conversation Ruby would be comfortable with and he expected her to storm off and slam the bedroom door any minute, but instead she looked thoughtful and nodded.

'Ginger and cinnamon? We've got ginger growing and there's cinnamon in the pantry. It seems to be worse at night, so maybe we should make some tea later.' She poured the smoothie mixture into two glasses and handed one to him.

'Yeah, we'll give it a go. I'll pull a bit of ginger this afternoon. I'm not sure how much we use.' He reached for his phone on the counter and slid it toward Ruby. 'Maybe you should google how we make the tea?'

'Good idea.' Ruby perched up on a kitchen stool at the counter, sipping her smoothie and scrolling through his phone. 'Oh, here's a recipe. We don't need much, but we should grate a bit of ginger, then put it in a strainer or something.' She jumped off her seat and stepped into the kitchen. 'We've got that little ceramic teapot in here somewhere, Gran used to use it.' She rummaged around in a bottom cupboard then leapt to her feet, waving the teapot in the air. 'And it's got its own little strainer in it. Dad, we'll use this.'

'Excellent. Oh, and Ayla said to put a spoon of honey in it. I guess we do that once you've poured it into a cup.' He pulled a jar out of the grocery bag. 'I picked this up from the coffee shop, Debbie said it's local honey, the raw stuff.'

'Awesome.' Ruby handed his phone back. 'Is Ayla coming to school next week?'

'Yes. Monday afternoon. She's going to start with your class, then she'll do some interactive stuff with the younger grades.' He was watching her expression, he could see that Ayla had made quite an impression on Ruby. 'Are you keen to learn more about the bees?'

'Well, yes! Like, without bees there's no food. That's what Ayla says. I'd like to do what she does, you know, hold the bees in my hands without getting stung. Skye did it too, you know, sat by the bees and didn't care and didn't get stung.' Ruby was animated, waving her hands about as she spoke. He knew she had a way with animals and generally preferred to be outdoors, no matter the weather. That's why her refusal to go kayaking had taken him by surprise.

'Alright then, what would you like to do this weekend Ruby? I know you don't have much homework.' He grinned at her, and his chest swelled when she grinned back. 'You know, Robbie, Nik and Lucy picked up the kayaks anyway, they were going to put them in the Barrington River this morning like we planned. Do you want to make a picnic and meet up with them this afternoon? You won't have to swim, we can just share a picnic on the riverbank.' He waited while she considered this.

She gazed at him thoughtfully for a moment, then spoke quietly. 'Yes, we could do that.' Then her voice rose as the possibilities played across her mind. 'I can bake scones and we can take a picnic basket down there and I can hang out with Lucy for a bit.' She wriggled off her seat again. 'I'm just going to see if we have everything for the scones.' She pulled some items from the pantry, then opened the fridge door, looking at him. 'Cream. We don't have any cream. For the scones. We need cream.' Her face fell.

'I'll drive back to the general store, they'll have cream.' He stood, waiting for her to respond.

'Yes! Thanks Dad. I'll start the scones while you get the cream.' She hugged him briefly, then took a large mixing bowl from the cupboard. He walked out to the car, whistling softly.

Five minutes later he drove into the grounds of the general store and saw Ayla's kombi van parked to one side. He caught his breath when he saw it there and flushed with pleasure. He shook his head. What is wrong with him? Acting like a schoolboy with a crush. But he knew, although he didn't want to put it into words yet, that something about Ayla, and her little girl, affected him. An odd feeling of protectiveness came over him, something he usually only felt for Ruby. Yet it was obvious that Ayla was quite capable of protecting herself and Skye. He suspected she secretly laughed at his slightly old-fashioned ways.

He parked beside her van and stepped out. Skye was perched on a bench at a picnic table just outside the store facing him. Ayla had her back to him, bent at the waist wiping Skye's hands with something. A washcloth perhaps. He walked toward them, and Skye waved, calling out, 'Hello teacher.' Ayla straightened, then turned.

'Hello again Skye, hello Ayla.' He was right in front of her now. He could see a smudge of chocolate on Skye's cheek.

'Alex. Twice in one day.' Ayla was cool, raising an eyebrow. She wore no makeup, yet her skin was smooth, her eyes clear, her lashes dark and long. With her hair flowing around her shoulders she looked beautiful. Natural and beautiful. Stunning. He found her stunning. His heart seemed to beat a little faster when he was near her. He hoped she couldn't tell.

'Yes. Small world. Well, small town anyway.' He smiled, willing his heart to slow down. Looking into her eyes he felt, rather than saw, her relax slightly. 'I've come for cream. Ruby's making scones and needs cream.' Without knowing why, he kept talking. 'We're going to take a picnic to the river.'

Jumping off the bench with a little bounce, Skye took his hand, shaking it until he looked down at her. 'I like scones. We can come to your picnic.' He was surprised but looked at Ayla. He could see her mouth beginning to form a 'no' but before she could utter the words he continued. 'Of course you can come. Ruby would love that, she has so many questions about bees.' Ayla looked doubtful and still on the verge of declining when he played his trump card. 'And she wants to ask you about the recipe for the tea you mentioned earlier today.'

Ayla smiled, her eyes crinkling at the edges. Glancing down at Skye, who was still holding Alex's hand, she nodded. 'Okay, a picnic. If you're sure. I have honey in my van, but not much else to contribute.' Glancing at the door to the shop, where he could see Frank hovering, she asked, 'Where is the picnic spot and what time?'

'There's no time to go home first. Follow me back to our place and we'll help Ruby prepare the scones, then we can go to the picnic together.' She reached for Skye's hand, then took half a step back. He thought she seemed ready to flee. 'I'll just get the cream, then we can go.'

Skye must have sensed her mother's hesitation. 'Please Mama. A picnic.' Ayla nodded. 'Okay, we'll wait in the van.'

He rushed inside, chose two tubs of dollop cream from the dairy cabinet, then placed them on the counter. Frank and Nadia had been watching the interaction between him and Ayla. Frank jerked his head toward the door. 'You know *her*, do you Alex?'

Alex didn't like the way Frank said *her*. 'Yes I do. Ayla is a talented beekeeper and educator. She's starting a program at school on Monday afternoon.'

'Excellent. That sounds really interesting. We were amazed by the way she caught that wild swarm the other week, wish we'd seen her do it ourselves.' Nadia nudged Frank, who just nodded and muttered a 'hmm.'

SEEING AYLA READY IN HER VAN, ALEX BACKED OUT AND DROVE out to the road, checking in his mirror that she was following him. He was excited in a bringing-a-friend-home-from-school way and the concept made him laugh out loud. While he knew Ruby would be surprised to see Ayla and Skye, he also hoped she'd be pleased.

Ruby came out to the porch when she heard him drive in and waved madly at Ayla and Skye as the van parked beside him. Ayla waved back then stepped out, reaching in to help Skye out of her seat.

'Hello Ruby. I hope you don't mind us dropping in. Your Dad mentioned scones and Skye invited herself.' Ayla laughed, setting Skye on the ground. Ruby walked toward them, bending down to speak to Skye first. Alex couldn't hear what she said, but when she stood up Skye was holding her hand. 'It's great Ayla. I've made a huge batch of scones.' She turned to him. 'I hope you bought two cartons of cream Dad.' He held them aloft and she grinned.

They trooped inside, Ayla carrying a large glass jar of raw honey. Ruby was right, she'd made a lot of scones. Skye sat up on a high stool at the kitchen counter, as Ruby and Ayla cut the scones in half. 'Is it best to put the jam and cream on now or do it at the river?' Ruby asked Ayla but Alex was about to answer, when Ayla said, 'By the river I think Ruby. We can take the jam and cream and maybe a small amount of honey. If we wrap the scones in a tea towel they'll stay warm.'

Skye suddenly stood up on the stool, crying out, 'Horses! Look Mama, horses!' Alex lunged, one hand on her small back, ensuring she didn't fall. He steadied her and pointed to Ruby's horse. 'That's Brute. Ruby rides him. The other one is Cal. He's the one I ride.' Skye wriggled to get down, so he lifted her to the floor. She grabbed him by the hand, tugging him toward the door. 'I want to see the horses please.'

Charmed by her enthusiasm, he hesitated, looking at Ayla. 'I need to check they have water in their trough, and we can give them some hay.'

Laughing, she said, 'I couldn't stop her if I tried. She's horse mad.' She shoo-ed them off with a wave of her hand and Skye almost ran for the door, still holding his hand.

'Wait Skye, let me get my boots on.' He hopped on one leg,

putting one boot on, then the other, while she waited, almost jogging on the spot with excitement.

He glanced back at Ayla and Ruby, now sitting side by side at the kitchen bench. He hoped Ruby would ask Ayla about the tea recipe, provide an opportunity to connect. He knew, intuitively, that Ayla would answer any questions Ruby had and was relieved she'd agreed to come.

Out by the horses, he showed Skye how to pat Brute and Cal when they came to the fence for the hay. She was gentle, murmuring to Brute as she ran her hand down the side of his face. Alex turned the tap on to add water to their drinking trough, and she knelt, watching through the fence as the horses drank noisily. He wondered what she was thinking, as she studied them quietly.

Ruby appeared on the porch. 'Dad! We should go now.' Skye saw Ruby and waved, then said a soft goodbye to each horse. Brute nuzzled her hand when she held it out. She showed no fear. She turned to Alex, raising her arms. 'You can carry me.' It was a statement, not a question, so he picked her up and settled her on his hip as he walked back to the house. Ayla appeared on the porch with Ruby, holding their picnic basket. A warmth washed over him as he walked toward them. He reached the porch, about to set Skye down. She put her small hand up to his face, turning him towards her. 'Thank you teacher.' She kissed him on the side of the face and something inside him melted. He set her down on the porch, but he could still feel her gentle touch on his face. He looked at Ayla, but she had turned to her daughter. 'Want to go to the bathroom first?' Skye nodded, and Ayla handed the picnic basket to him, then took Skye inside the house.

Ruby stepped closer to him, putting her arms around his waist, her head against his chest. 'I thought today was the worst day. Ever. But it's turned out all right.' He stroked her hair and murmured, 'the day's not over yet Rubes. I think it will get even better.'

16

Honey has the potency to make you fall in love with the landscape on a deep cellular level. @embodybee

Choosing to take her van and follow, Ayla wondered if she'd done the right thing. She hadn't met Robbie Stewart or his partner Nicole. She now knew Robbie had been with the teacher on the ridge, but had refused to use the binoculars, which impressed her. She had tried not to laugh when Alex confessed the binoculars were his, and he'd taken them that day hoping to see the eagles. He'd been embarrassed, apologetic and sincere at the same time, while ensuring his friend remained blameless. She believed him. He was a bit old-fashioned, perhaps his career as a teacher made him hyper-sensitive to protocol. Working with children, negotiating with parents, she didn't envy him his work. And Skye liked him. She was sometimes reserved with adults. But still, despite his warmth, he wasn't at all her type. Way too conservative.

Slowing down, she pulled off the road behind them. There was a Landcruiser, and kayak trailer already parked in a gravel section by the riverbank. Movement caught her eye. Two kayaks paddled into view, moving quickly toward the edge of the river. She watched as Alex and Ruby ran toward them, stepping into the shallows to steady the front of the kayaks as the paddlers got out, pulling the empty vessels up on to the grassy bank. Skye squirmed to get out of her arms, so she set her down. She ran straight to Ruby, who laughed and took her hand. The other girl, Lucy, knelt down to speak to her. Skye was beaming from ear to ear as the girls walked toward her, Skye between them holding their hands.

'Ayla, this is Lucy.' Ruby introduced her friend, who smiled and said a shy 'hello.' 'We're going to get the picnic stuff.'

'I'm helping the big girls.' Skye nodded her head vigorously. Ruby and Lucy looked delighted. 'Come on then Skye.' They led her over to the teacher's car and Ayla strolled across the grass to Alex and his friends.

The woman, Nicole, walked toward her, hands outstretched. Quite a bit shorter than Ayla and maybe a few years older, she took both her hands. Her greeting was warm, genuine. Ayla relaxed slightly. 'It's wonderful to meet you Ayla, I have so many questions about the work that you do. I'm Nicole, but everyone calls me Nik.'

Smiling, Ayla said hello. 'It was a spontaneous decision to come and find you. Alex mentioned scones and Skye decided for us both, in that instant.'

'Scones will get you every time.' Nicole laughed, then turned to Robbie, who had stepped closer, holding his hat in his hands. 'This is Robbie, and you already know he was on the ridge with Alex the other day.'

Ayla could see Robbie's embarrassment at Nik's words. He looked at her, while not as tall as the teacher, he was slightly older, but still a good looking man. 'My apologies Ayla. We did ride up your way to see if there was activity at the old resort, but when we saw you at the river we were searching for the eagles Alex had seen a few weeks ago.' The teacher came and stood shoulder to shoulder with his friend, as if in solidarity.

She pictured them, for a moment, accidentally viewing her at the river. And instinctively she also knew that catching a glimpse of a nudist was not why they were there. She giggled, taking his hand firmly in hers. 'Well, it occurs to me I could ask you both to strip off and have a swim, you know, to make amends.' She was laughing and Nicole joined in, while the men looked slightly confused.

'Oh, you should Ayla, it's only fair.' Still laughing Nicole nudged Ayla and pointed at Robbie's horrified face. He jammed his hat back on his head and looked to his friend for support. But Alex was laughing now too. Robbie took his hat off again and slapped it against his leg.

'You got us good there Ayla. You had me for a moment.' If there had been a hint of tension between them, it dissolved as he spoke, and smiled at her, his eyes crinkling. Ayla nodded in acknowledgement and felt her own shoulders relax.

Looking across at the three girls, setting up the picnic on a rug near the kayaks, Ayla winked at Robbie then turned to the teacher. *'You're* not completely off the hook, I'm keeping that particular request in reserve.' She didn't know why she said it, she knew it was flirty and suggestive and indicated interest in him even though he was not at all her type. But right in that moment she meant it. Nicole caught on straight away and chuckled, grabbing Robbie by the hand, she pulled him toward the girls and the picnic.

The teacher stepped closer. He was right in front of her, looking into her eyes. She looked back at him. At his height, his strength. His arms, chest and shoulders filled out the polo shirt he wore. Raising her chin, she silently challenged him, still internally wondering why she did. He leant closer. 'There are children here right now, but Ayla, I accept your challenge. Right time, right place and I won't hesitate.' Something sizzled between them and she sensed he was totally out of his comfort zone in his response to her. They both were. She hadn't felt this sort of chemistry for a long time, but she remained cool and broke their eye contact. Stepping toward the picnic she glanced at him over her shoulder. He was watching her with an intensity that sent warmth rushing through her. 'Until then.' She said it quietly. He nodded and followed her to join the others.

THEY SHARED THE PICNIC. NICOLE HAD PACKED SANDWICHES AND fruit and they finished with Ruby's scones. Ayla loved the way Ruby and Lucy included Skye, playing games with her while the adults sat on the grass chatting. She felt comfortable with these people, and when she added it up, she had more than a few friends and allies in the area. The teacher, Robbie and Nicole, Nadia at the general store and Debbie at the café in town. She'd lived a nomadic life for years, travelling the world, even after Skye was born, and had spent a lot of time in other parts of Australia too.

There'd been other places, other small towns, where her *off grid* lifestyle raised eyebrows. Many people weren't kind and the last place she had tried to settle with Skye had turned sour. It was a smaller community than Barrington and she'd left when she heard children teasing Skye, calling her names. While she understood there may always be a portion of a community that disliked their differences, she wanted to know that she would have friends and allies too. Supporters. And that Skye could make friends with other children, grow up in a community feeling accepted and loved. Sitting on the grass by the river with the teacher, Robbie and Nicole and seeing Skye happily playing with Ruby and Lucy, she drew a breath. Maybe this was the place. Maybe they didn't have to be so isolated. Maybe they could become *part* of this community.

'A penny for your thoughts Ayla.' Nicole spoke quietly. Robbie and Alex had moved closer to the kayaks, discussing the river and its currents.

'It's nice here Nik. Really nice.' Ayla pulled a piece of clover out of the ground and studied it for a moment.

'It is Ayla. It's great to have the river flowing so well, we've had a few years of drought and you couldn't kayak this far without having to carry them across the dry riverbed in a few places.' She gazed at the river, then back at Ayla. 'But that's not what you meant, is it?'

'Not exactly. Meeting you, Robbie and Lucy today, and Alex and Ruby, has helped me feel we may be in the right place. That we should stay here.' She turned to Nik. 'We've been a bit nomadic. For years really. Since Skye was only a few months old. But she needs to start school. And find friends her own age. And maybe not be on our own all the time.'

'I understand. Lucy and I were on our own before we came here. We met Robbie, and his son Harry. And then other locals.

Not everyone will be on your team Ayla, but if you have enough, good ones, then you'll be okay.' Nicole watched Lucy play a clapping game with Skye. Ruby was sitting behind the little girl, braiding her hair. Ayla followed her gaze. Skye was sitting happily, as she had her hair done. She hated Ayla touching it, the best she could do lately was put a hairband in it.

'And Skye's dad? Not in the picture?' Ayla turned when Nik spoke. She generally didn't discuss Skye's father, but she sensed Nik was asking, not to be nosy, but to understand Ayla and Skye.

'He was a beautiful holiday romance in Spain. It was already over when I left to come home, only discovering I was pregnant a few weeks afterwards. He's a lovely man, but we're never going to be together as a family. I've taken Skye to visit twice, it's important she knows her father and his culture, and we stay in contact. He has an extended family that love Skye too.' She paused, glancing again at Skye, happily chatting with Ruby and Lucy. 'He married a couple of years ago, has a baby boy with his wife. I'm happy he acknowledges Skye as his daughter and welcomes us when we visit. His wife was a bit touchy when we met her at first, but it's better now and they have said they will have Skye stay when she is older, if she wants to spend time there.' Ayla watched Nik as she digested this.

'Then you've done a great job, Ayla. I can already see that Skye is a happy and confident child. I know from experience that it's not always easy, but that's a story for another day.' Nik stood, brushing the grass from her legs. Ayla saw a shadow of sadness in Nik's eyes and internally promised herself she would make time to get to know this warm, generous woman.

They strolled over to the men. 'We'll load the kayaks onto

the trailer Nik, maybe put in again tomorrow, depending on the weather.' Robbie pointed to the west, dark clouds were rolling in.

Nicole nodded and turned to the girls. 'Lucy, help Ruby pack up the picnic stuff and put it in the cars, looks like rain heading this way.'

'I'll do this Nik, with the girls.' Ayla stepped across, picking up the picnic blankets and folding them while the girls packed everything back into the basket. She saw Nicole and the men had the kayaks on and were tying them down, as large rain-drops started to fall.

'Quick girls, to the van.' Ayla ran ahead, opening the back of her van for the three girls to jump in. They were laughing and giggling and it warmed Ayla's heart to see how happy Skye was in their company. She ran back to the trailer to see if she could help, but they'd finished. Nicole beckoned Lucy from the van, opening the back door of the Landcruiser for her, then she turned and threw her arms around Ayla. 'So nice to meet you Ayla, I look forward to many more picnics and get togethers. You know where we live, I work from home, so drop by anytime.'

Squeezing the smaller woman back, Ayla felt tears in her eyes. 'Thank you Nik. I will. I'll drop in next week.' She waved at Lucy through the car window, 'Bye Lucy, see you soon.'

Running back to the van, Ruby had already secured Skye in her booster seat and was sitting beside her. 'Thank you Ruby. It's been such a nice day. You make the best scones.' Ruby nodded happily, jumping out of the van to run to her father's car, the rain now pelting down. Robbie moved their car and trailer onto the road, waving as they left.

Walking to the back of the van, Ayla checked the door was

closed properly. The teacher materialised beside her. They stood looking at each other, rain coming down heavily, soaking their hair and clothes. She leaned toward him. It was instinctive, spontaneous. He lifted his hands and held her face gently, looked at her for a moment, then leaned in and kissed her softly on the lips while the rain streamed down their faces. It was fleeting, but full of promise.

'Come back to our place, dry off.' What he was really asking went unsaid. She cocked her head on one side, then shook it. 'Not today, Teacher.'

'Teacher?' One side of his mouth moved up in a half smile. She hadn't noticed that before.

'It's your name in my head. And what Skye calls you.' If he asked her again to follow him home, she would.

'Drive safely, Bee Whisperer.' He spoke quietly into her ear, the rain drumming loudly on the roof of her van. 'That's your name in *my* head.' He held her door open and waited while she started the van, then he walked to his car in the rain, waving to her before he got in. She raised her hand in a wave as she turned the van onto the road.

Skye was asleep before they reached the main road. Despite water pooling on her seat and the floor of the van, Ayla sang quietly to herself all the way home.

17

'You're soaked Dad! What took you so long?' Ruby reached into the back seat, dragging a tea towel from their picnic basket, shoving it at him as he started the car.

Alex wiped his face and rubbed some of the moisture from his hair, before handing the tea towel, now wet and limp, back to his daughter. 'Oh, I just helped Ayla get the back of the van closed.' He glanced at Ruby from the corner of his eye as he drove slowly onto the road. The taillights of Ayla's van were barely visible ahead of them, the rain becoming heavier as they followed her out to the main road.

Ruby was silent for a moment, leaning forward to peer through the windscreen, the wiper blades beating in quick time across it. She said something quietly that he couldn't catch, the rain was drumming loudly on the roof.

'What?' He almost shouted. He was right behind the van now, Ayla was driving slowly, carefully. Rainwater was washing across the road. The conditions were dangerous, and he wished she had agreed to come home with them and wait it out.

'You like her don't you? Ayla?' Now he heard Ruby clearly, but he wasn't sure how to respond. While he'd always been honest with his daughter, he had never discussed his romantic interests with her, not that there had been many. About eighteen months after the divorce he'd dated a woman, Michelle, for a few months, but it became a disaster. Ruby had disliked her and behaved badly, and Michelle, who had little experience with children, couldn't understand why he had to organise their dates around Ruby. The romance faded as Michelle only agreed to see him if Ruby was with her mother or staying with friends. There was no future for them and if he was totally honest with himself, while the sex had been good, they had little else in common.

He slowed for their driveway, Ayla's van now out of sight. 'I do Ruby. I like her very much.' He almost held his breath as he waited for Ruby to respond. He parked close to the house and switched the engine off, then turned to look at his daughter.

Ruby nodded, looked across at the horses standing in the paddock, their backs to the driving rain, then reached out, touching his shoulder. 'I like her too Dad. And Skye. I like them both.' She hesitated. 'Why have you never had a girlfriend Dad? Mum remarried. Is it because of me?'

He shook his head, smiling at her. 'Oh, I dated a few times. You might not remember.' He reached out, touched her cheek, sweeping a thick hank of damp hair behind her ear. 'But it's not your fault. There is no fault. I haven't met anyone I really like, in that way.'

'I think you like Ayla. In that way.' Ruby made an oh-yuck face at him.

He laughed. 'Would it bother you? If I saw more of Ayla?' He made the oh-yuck face back to her and she giggled.

'No. It wouldn't bother me. She's nice. Skye is cute. She could be my little sister.' Ruby grinned and his heart flipped over.

'Oh you're getting way ahead of me Rubes. Don't go there, you might scare them off.' They shared a smile and his heart swelled. He sighed and looked through the windscreen where little rivers of water rushed across the path to the front door.

'Come on, let's make a run for it!' Alex scooped the picnic basket from the back seat and ran inside behind Ruby.

They stood on the porch, kicking off their shoes. 'Go have a shower Dad, I'm not really that wet. I'll make hot chocolate.' He leaned over and kissed the top of her head. 'You're the best.'

SITTING TOGETHER IN THE KITCHEN, HOT CHOCOLATES STEAMING between them, showered and dry, Alex looked out at the horses. 'Wish we had a stable to put them in, or even a lean-to for shelter. But it's not really cold, just wet.'

'They're horses, Dad. Robbie says they're used to rain. See how they stand with their backs to it? Robbie says they huddle together if they're cold, but Brute and Cal aren't doing that, so they'll be fine.' Ruby spoke confidently and Alex made a mental note to thank Robbie for the horse-lore he was teaching her. She suddenly seemed more grown up, and he realised that in another six years she'd be done with school and ready to head off to university, or travels. When did he get this old?

Ruby went to her room to read, and he began to go through the notes on the bee program Ayla had given him, to be ready for Monday's lesson. The rain eased during the afternoon, although the washing on the line was wet and he decided to leave it out, tomorrow was predicted to fine up. His phone vibrated, where it sat on the charger in the kitchen. He picked it up, a text from Ayla.

> Home safely, thanks for a great day. 🙂

> We had a great day too, thanks for joining us.

He was tempted to add a kiss, but as she hadn't he just hit Send.

> See you Monday.

> Can't wait, just reading through your materials now. Kids will love this. 😎

She sent a thumbs up to his text and he set the phone down. He was excited to see her on Monday afternoon, but he needed to keep it professional in front of the students.

18

Pollination is an intimate dance, the foraging bees are all female,
but only the queen will mate with a male bee. @embodybee

The rain stopped during the night and Sunday was fine. Ayla stepped outside just after dawn on Monday and gazed around the valley. The air smelled fresh and earthy, and she stopped by her hives, watching as the bees began their days' work. Stretching, she turned around once, then stood beneath the silky oak tree, itself dripping with nectar.

Closing her eyes, Ayla listened to the gentle hum of the bees. The unique vibration of each hive was to her, the sexual expression of the bees. They fly into the sexual organs of flowers, but are so artful they never harm them, and in turn transform the sweet nectar into honey. Her thoughts conjured an image of the teacher, and while he appeared to have considerable physical strength, she also sensed a gentleness. She shivered, before opening her eyes and drawing in a large breath of sweet air.

The beauty of the valley always amazed her, the deep greens of the forest and high, steep rocky ridges. An eagle glided high above, wings outstretched against the blue sky, and her steps were light as she walked from the yard toward the old stables, where the chicken coop crouched along the back wall.

Mud around the door to the coop revealed animal prints. The dingo had been around again. Ayla drew a breath and looked across the creek, almost expecting to see the movement of a stealthy shape in the undergrowth. Water dripped off tree branches, and the creek, usually small enough to cross in a few steps, was racing high and fast, reaching the top of its banks. Water was still coming down from the high country and the creek might continue to rise. She opened the door and let the chickens out, counting them as she did. Eleven. Good, they all looked well. She'd leave the eggs for now, Skye would want to help collect them when she woke.

Back in the yard she looked again at the creek and moved each hive about half a metre closer to the cottage, moving them more would risk the foraging bees returning to the wrong place. Satisfied, she went inside to check on Skye.

WITH ERRANDS TO RUN IN TOWN, AND THE BEE PROGRAM AT THE school early in the afternoon, Ayla and Skye set off in the van late morning. A few kilometres along the way, at the Jems Creek crossing Ayla slowed. The water was almost over the low cement bridge and running wide and swift. It wasn't raining down here, but when she looked toward the west she could see it was raining in the Barrington Tops. The range was fifteen hundred metres above sea level at its highest, while she knew the resort went from around three hundred to one thousand metres. She drove across the bridge, hoping the downpour would ease. She knew this crossing became impassable at infrequent intervals. 'Not today,' she murmured to herself.

In town, she drove around to the council offices. With her satchel over her shoulder, she took Skye's hand and walked through the double glass doors. The day was warm. Ayla had chosen to wear a dusky pink sundress with leather sandals, with a colourful cotton scarf tied loosely around her shoulders. Her hair was in a long braid down her back. Skye was in pale pink shorts and her favourite floral top. While she hadn't let Ayla braid her hair, she had managed to get it into two high pigtails which curled down past her shoulders. She was meeting with Council about living at the resort and wanted to make certain she had her facts straight. She knew what she had to do to get what she wanted. And what she wanted was to stay at the resort.

An hour later she left the building, feeling lighter. One step closer to her goals. 'You've been such a good girl Skye, while I was talking to the people. Would you like to go to the café for lunch?' Ayla lifted Skye into the van, ensured her seatbelt was fastened, then walked around to the driver's side, sliding in and closing the door.

'Yes please Mama. To Debbie's café?' Skye nodded emphatically and her curls bounced up and down on her shoulders.

'Yes, we'll go to see Debbie.' Ayla started the van and moved off.

'Can I have a milkshake? And a chocolate brownie?' Ayla was about to speak but Skye quickly added, 'please?'

'*May* I have a milkshake, not *can*. And yes, you may. I'm hungry too, so perhaps a sandwich or frittata for lunch.' Ayla parked in her usual spot, and they walked through to the main street. Not as busy as Saturday but again they received some 'hellos' from passers-by and lots of smiles for Skye.

Walking into the café, Debbie waved from a table to the side where she was serving a young family. Ayla waved back, hovering at the front counter while Skye skipped down the back to 'their' table.

'Ayla, hello. You and Skye look fresh and chirpy today.' Debbie smiled as she moved behind the counter. 'Lunch? Or just a drink and snacks?'

'Hi Debbie. Yes, we feel fresh and chirpy today.' Ayla felt she was speaking to a friend. It felt good. 'Lunch today. Milkshake for Skye, my usual chai latte and I'll have frittata and salad please and a cheese sandwich for Skye.' Ayla glanced around. 'I see you're busy again today.'

'Flat out. I'm hiring a part time cook to help Cathy in the kitchen and training a couple of school leavers for afternoons and weekends, just as extra support.' Debbie grinned. 'I think it's you, Ayla. We're getting a lot more tourists the last couple of weeks, even on weekdays, and quite a few ask about you and do I know where you live. And I've had lots of offers for Skye's picture.' She leaned a bit closer, grinning. 'Which I'm not selling at any price, by the way.'

Ayla glanced around. She recognised a few locals, regulars she'd seen before. But there were many tables of tourists too, she could tell by the clothes they wore. 'I'll stay in the back then.' She began to move away when she heard a woman say quite loudly, 'There she is. That's Ayla. The Bee Whisperer.'

Debbie gave her a cheeky grin and nodded toward the table nearby where a young couple were now standing. 'Your fans, I think.'

Ayla turned. The young woman waved, still standing at her table. Ayla glanced at Skye, she was already drawing at the back table, oblivious to the conversation at the counter.

She smiled at the young couple and walked across. 'Hello, nice to see you.'

'Hello Ayla, I'm Courtney and this is Brad.' The young woman was genuinely excited to see her, and Ayla responded with a big smile. Where would she be without her fans and followers?

'Hi Courtney, Brad. What brings you to Barrington?' As Ayla asked the question, Debbie arrived with drinks and snacks for the couple.

'*You* do Ayla. You've been sharing so much of the area, of this café, that we had a few days off and thought we'd come up. It's beautiful here. We're staying at The Lofts and we're going to kayak down Barrington River tomorrow.' She paused. 'Can we get a selfie with you?'

Ayla laughed. 'Of course! Thank you for visiting the area. It is stunning. There's a lot to see and do here.' They huddled together for a selfie, which Brad took. 'Enjoy your lunch, and your time in the area. Tag me if you post the selfie, I'll share it.'

'Oh gosh! Thank you Ayla. Will do. Maybe we'll see you around this week?' Nodding and smiling, Ayla moved away, walking back to the table where Skye was still busy.

Debbie appeared with their drinks, giving Ayla a cheeky grin. 'Told you! Girlfriend, you've got fans!' She laughed as she said it and Ayla chuckled. But Debbie referring to her as *girlfriend* really touched her. She'd like nothing more than to be friends with this woman.

They were still eating their lunch when the young couple, Courtney and Brad, dropped by their table to say goodbye. Courtney smiled at Skye. 'And this is Skye. She's even cuter in the flesh.'

'Say hello, Skye.' Ayla spoke quietly. Skye frowned, her concentration broken, and looked up. Courtney was smiling and Skye's face changed to a dazzling grin. 'Hello.'

Courtney had her phone in her hand and looked at Ayla, her question unspoken but obvious. Ayla shook her head. 'No. No pics of Skye but thank you so much for saying hello and coming out here to Barrington.'

'Of course. Bye Ayla, bye Skye.' Courtney and Brad turned and left.

Debbie arrived with their lunch. She stage-whispered to Ayla, 'Do you think Brad can speak?' Ayla snort-laughed, almost choking on her last mouthful of coffee. Debbie patted her on the back a couple of times, laughing too.

'Um, I don't think Brad needs to speak. Conserving his vocals, I'm sure.' She made eye contact with Debbie, both still chuckling.

'Ha, ha, you're right.' Debbie nodded and returned to the counter. Ayla checked her phone, nearly time to head to the school. She felt lighter, happier than she had in ages. Yes, she knew there would be detractors, there always were. But she was building relationships here. Friendships even.

19

Alex saw Ayla pull up in the van. It was lightly raining again, which was a pity. He'd hoped she could do her first talk outdoors. He instructed the other teachers to move their classes into the library. It was big enough for the whole school, all sixty-five students, if a little cramped. He wanted Ayla to give a broad overview for about twenty minutes, then he'd send the children back to their respective classrooms, where she would spend around fifteen minutes in each one, with the teachers taking over from there. She would start with the youngest and come to his class last.

The students were excited, they liked anything that deviated from their normal lesson plan, and after seeing Ayla catch the swarm bare handed at the start of term, some of them had attributed almost magical powers to her. He frowned slightly as he left the library, planning to help Ayla carry in any props she may use. He'd just heard two of the older boys whispering, referring to Ayla as the *nudie lady*. He didn't have time to address their comments, Ayla was walking toward him, but he would watch for any disrespect and speak to the main offenders when she left.

'Hello Ayla.' He reached across to take the box from her arms and their hands touched. It wasn't accidental and her eyes widened when he held his breath for the shortest of moments. She felt it too, he knew. But she greeted him with a friendly, 'Hello again.'

Skye had a miniature wooden beehive in her hands, he could see that it came apart. 'That looks like a very small beehive, Skye.' Best concentrate on the little one while he pulled himself together.

'Hello teacher.' This was from Skye. Ayla looked quickly at Alex, then turned to Skye.

'Mister McIntosh, Skye.' Ayla nudged her daughter.

Skye frowned, then said, 'Okay.' Looking up at Alex she giggled. 'Hello Mister Mac.'

'Good enough, Skye. Most of my class call me Mister Mac!' He was delighted, she had a great sense of fun.

Turning to Ayla he asked if there was anything more to get from the van.

'Oh, yes please, I have an easel and a pack of posters.' He trotted over to the van, found the items and returned.

With his hand on the library door, he asked, 'Are you ready?'

'Absolutely.' He was amazed at her quiet confidence. A lot of people were nervous speaking to groups.

Alex introduced Ayla and Skye, although the kids all knew who they were, then stepped to one side. Within minutes she had set up the large colourful posters on the easel, taking them off one at a time as she explained the life cycle of bees and their relationship with pollination and food and honey production. The kids were entranced. Ayla was animated and fun and told them they could interrupt to ask questions. Hands shot up and she pointed at them in turn to ask their questions, some of which she answered and some she asked if any of the students knew the answers. He was amazed. She was a born teacher, creating a very natural two way interaction with the kids without seeming to try. Skye stayed close to her mother, placing the posters in a neat pile as Ayla removed them in turn from the easel, but he could see her sneaking looks at some of the kids her own size. She had waved at Ruby when she first arrived, and Ruby waved back.

The initial talk over, it was time for the kids to return to their classes, where Ayla would start them off with age appropriate activities. He stood beside her as the teachers took the children out.

'Do you need all of this in the first class?' He had one hand on the easel.

'No, thank you. I'll take the easel home, but I thought you might like the posters for now, you can put a few up in each classroom, if that suits you. I can order a full set from Save the Bees if you'd like the school to have its own.' She started for the door, holding Skye by the hand.

'Yes, do that. Order a full set for us. I'll see you in my classroom in about thirty minutes or so.' He watched her walk across to the junior class, Skye skipping beside her. Kelly Rogers, Miss Rogers, was a fabulous teacher and he was sure she'd integrate Skye with her students while she was in the classroom.

At the door to his own class he heard Ruby shout at one of the boys. He hurried inside. Ruby was standing, red in the face, glaring at Sam Fraser, younger brother to the ones who'd seen Ayla at the river. 'She's not! She's lovely! Don't say that!'

'Settle down.' He clapped his hands sharply. 'Ruby, take your seat.' He looked around at the faces turned toward him. He'd expected some talk. He needed to address it right now.

'Ayla is a guest and a friend of the school, and you will treat her with the respect we give to all visitors.' He turned to Sam Fraser. 'I heard part of what you said. That she is a hippie. Do you know what a hippie really is?' Still looking at Sam, he continued, 'Did Ayla teach you anything today Sam?' The kid hung his head and mumbled something.

'I beg your pardon Sam; can you repeat that for the class?' Alex wasn't taking any prisoners today. He could see Ruby watching him, from the corner of his eye.

'I said yes, she knows a lot about bees and growing food and stuff.' Sam was blushing and Alex didn't want to labour the point.

'And do you know what a hippie is, Sam?' The kid squirmed in his seat.

'I thought not. It's really a lifestyle choice and it's a term that was coined in the nineteen seventies.' He moved his gaze steadily around the class. 'Sam here, says it like it's a bad thing, but it isn't at all. And while I don't believe Ayla actually is a hippie, let me explain what it is.' A few minutes and a brief explanation later, with all the kids still looking at him, he asked, 'Do any of you have any more questions about Ayla that don't concern her bee keeping work?'

The kids shook their heads with a series of 'no Sirs.' He had seen Ruby settle down as he addressed Sam, and hoped she had control of her emotions. 'Alright, I want you to form groups of four, and each choose a crop that is grown locally. Write down all you know about how it's grown and what food is made from it. Many of you are on farms, so you'll know lots of good stuff. Then when Ayla comes in I'd like you to ask her about your chosen crop's relationship with bees.'

He watched as they formed groups and was surprised when Ruby chose to sit with Sam Fraser and two other boys. He walked across. Ruby's cheeks were still slightly flushed, but she was calm as she spoke to Sam. 'You know the most about farming and crops, Sam. So what crop should we choose?' Sam blushed so hard his ears turned pink. Alex took another look at his daughter. She was pretty and feisty, and he suddenly realised that some of the boys probably 'like' her. By sitting with Sam she effectively put an end to anything further he might say about Ayla, and he seemed embarrassed, yet pleased, by her attention. He stepped over to another group, helping them with their ideas. His daughter was a smart girl. Where do women learn this, how to manipulate men with a word or gesture? So subtle. He shook his head in quiet wonder.

They worked on their projects for a further twenty minutes and Alex was pleased at the level of discussion around local crops and farming. The bee program was good for the school in many ways.

Ayla arrived at the door, Skye beside her. He welcomed them into the classroom and explained what the groups were doing. She nodded and moved to the first group, asking questions about their project, creating a discussion that many of the students joined in. Some kids, like Sam, didn't always participate in class discussion, but he did today. His group had chosen him as their spokesperson, and he was confident in his farming knowledge. Ayla nodded and took it all in her stride, even when an argument about the necessity of pesticides in farming came up, when she explained its danger to bees and challenged them to ask more about the pesticides used in local farming. She touched on the long-term sustainability of food production and Alex could see some of the boys in particular, who already worked on their family farms, were keen to understand.

Skye had sidled over to Ruby when they arrived, and she had pulled a chair over for her to sit at the table with the group. Alex was touched by his daughters' thoughtfulness for the younger child.

It was almost time to ring the bell for the day and Ayla finished off with an explanation of what they'd do on Friday, setting up a vegetable and flower bed to attract bees. She reminded them to bring an old shirt to wear over their uniform. Sam raised his hand.

Ayla nodded to him. Sam spoke clearly and Alex raised his eyebrows, this from a boy who was hard to engage at school. 'Would it be better to set the garden bed above ground? That's how we do ours at home. And bring some good soil in for it.'

'It would. Good question Sam. But to do that we'd need help from some parents to provide a load of soil and some logs or other material to raise the garden bed. I'm not sure that could be organised for Friday.'

'My Dad will do it.' This was Sam again. Alex was surprised. The boy spoke with confidence.

Alex nodded at Sam. 'Ask at home Sam, and maybe some of you can check if any parents are available to help put it together on Thursday after school. I'll provide logs to make the sides. I'll send a note home with everyone tomorrow.'

Alex turned to Ayla. 'Sam's right. If we want a good crop we need good soil, and the raised garden bed makes sense.'

Ayla nodded, smiling at the children as she said goodbye. Skye seemed reluctant to move from her place beside Ruby.

'Ruby, can you ring the bell please, it's home time.' He watched as Ruby stood, taking Skye by the hand and went outside the classroom to ring the old fashioned bell to end the school day.

As the students were noisily packing up and getting their backpacks he called out, 'If any parents want to speak with me about the working bee on Thursday, just get them to call me here at school tomorrow or speak to me at the gate if they drop you off.'

Ayla was quietly packing her resource materials away as the children left the class. Ruby and Skye returned.

'It's raining really heavily again Dad, I'll come home with you rather than catch the bus.' Ruby was still holding Skye's hand.

'Alright. I'm going to leave now too, as soon as the kids have been picked up.' He looked at Ayla. 'Wait a moment Ayla and we can leave together, I'll help carry your things to the car.'

'If it's alright with you, I'll leave everything here. I'll have different stuff on Friday, but next Monday we'll use some of this again.' Ayla pointed to the neat stack of posters and the small box of items by his desk.

'Okay. That works.' It had been ten minutes since bell time and most of the kids would have left the grounds, but he glanced over at the shelter shed as he locked up. No one about. Good, they could go.

Ayla picked Skye up, holding a coat over her head she ran across to the van. Ruby raced ahead of Alex and got into their car; he'd given her the keys to unlock it. He ensured Ayla had started her vehicle before he started his own, then waved to her as she drove off.

'A few surprises today, hey Rubes?' He grinned at his daughter.

She grinned back. 'Yup.' But didn't elaborate. That was enough. Her happy smile warmed him as they drove carefully home. The rain was heavier than it had been on Saturday. He suddenly wondered if Ayla would be able to get back to her place. He would text her when he got home, for peace of mind.

20

My daughter has been surrounded by bees since birth. She loves them and intuitively knows to be slow and gentle in their presence. They are her friends, and she whispers her secrets and joys to them. She has been stung. She knows they can hurt. But her curiosity and love for bees is stronger than the pain. @embodybee

Ayla looked doubtfully at the rain. Visibility was poor, and she drove slowly. About ten kilometres past the teacher's place, two cars coming toward her flashed their lights. She knew this meant danger of some sort. In the city it would mean radar or police ahead, but out here it was more likely to mean a tree was across the road, or a bridge was flooded. She pulled to the side of the road and stopped, leaving her hazard lights on. She wouldn't risk the bridge crossing. She pulled out her phone, googling local accommodation to see if anything was available in town. Nothing. She wondered if Nicole and Robbie might have something. Nik had talked about their accommodation business only two days ago.

She didn't have Nik's number but knew she called her place The Courthouse. It came up straight away on facebook and Ayla clicked call.

'The Courthouse, this is Nik.'

'Hi Nik, it's Ayla.'

'Oh hello, nice to hear from you. Are you nearby, would you like to drop in?'

Ayla gave a small laugh. 'Yes please. But more than that. Do you have any accommodation available tonight? I think the bridge at Jems Creek is flooded.'

'Of course! We'll sort you out. Are you far away?'

'I can be there in about fifteen minutes if that's not too soon. But I can nip back into town and pick up supplies if you need anything. Something for dinner perhaps?'

'You don't need anything at all, just come straight here.' Ayla could hear genuine welcome in Nicole's voice and sighed.

'Thank you Nik. Thank you very much. We'll be right there.'

Careful not to get too close to the edge of the road, Ayla slowly turned the van around. Her phone beeped as she drove. She'd check the message when she stopped. Pulling up to one side of Nicole's house, Ayla leant forward, peering at it through the rain before she turned the van off. A magnificent old building, two stories high, built out of sandstone with wide verandas on both levels. She hoped Nicole would give her a tour; the place was glorious.

Picking up her phone she quickly scanned the message. It was from the teacher.

> Don't go home. Jems Creek over bridge. Come here, we have a spare room.

Smiling, she messaged back.

> Thank you, but I've turned back. I have a room at Nik's. ☺

> That's great. You're welcome here too, anytime.

Ayla sent a thumbs up emoji and waved at Nicole, who was standing at her front door beckoning them in. She undid Skye's seatbelt, pulling her onto her lap, wrapped her coat around her, then stepped out of the van, Skye and her satchel in her arms, and ran to Nicole sheltering beneath the veranda.

They laughed when they reached cover and Ayla set Skye down as Lucy stepped out, smiling shyly.

'Hello again Lucy.' Ayla's greeting was interrupted by an excited squeal from Skye. A black and white dog had appeared from behind Lucy and within seconds Skye was on her knees, arms around the animal, while it licked the side of her face.

Not wanting to show she was somewhat afraid of dogs herself, Ayla spoke quietly, but firmly, to Skye. 'Stand up Skye, don't let it lick your face.' She watched as Skye reluctantly stood up, but her right hand was still petting the dog's head.

As Ayla spoke Lucy stepped forward. 'Sit Minnie.' The girl said it quietly but the dog immediately sat on its haunches, although it's tongue was lolling out as it gazed lovingly from Skye to Lucy and back.

Nicole, perhaps sensing Ayla's discomfort, turned to her daughter. 'Take Skye through to the kitchen Lucy and put the kettle on please. Minnie can stay out here now.' Without hesitation Lucy held her hand out to Skye, taking her into the house.

'Thank you Nik. I'm a bit nervous around strange dogs.' She let out a breath as Nicole gave the dog a hand signal and it trotted along the veranda and turned the corner out of sight. 'I really appreciate you having us.' Ayla hoped her words conveyed just how grateful she was.

'We're really happy to have you here.' Ayla saw Nicole glance along the veranda after the dog. 'And you needn't worry about Minnie. Lucy has had her since the day she was born and she's very well trained.' She smiled reassuringly and Ayla nodded, hoping she looked more relaxed than she felt. 'She's quiet and gentle and has a real thing for small people. She won't hurt Skye.' Grinning, she looked up at Ayla, then touched her arm gently. 'Or you.'

Her words reassured Ayla and she let the tension go from her shoulders and smiled. 'Truly. Thank you, Nik.'

With a grin and a shrug of her shoulders, Nicole glanced again at Ayla. 'You're very welcome. What made you realise the bridge might be closed?' She took Ayla's coat, hanging it in the hallway as they moved inside the house, closing the front door.

'We were about ten kays up the road, when two cars coming the other way flashed their lights. I thought it was either the bridge or a tree over the road. How did you find out?'

'Nadia from the store called. She was trying to catch Alex at school to let you know and thought he may have stopped in here.' She shook her head. 'Small towns hey? They have their good points. Nadia knew you would be at school this afternoon, but she didn't have your number.'

Despite the situation, Ayla did a happy dance in her mind. She wasn't used to having people care for her in such a practical, immediate manner. Thousands of followers on her socials gave her plenty of support, and she was grateful, but this in-person un-selfish help was next level.

Following Nicole inside she gazed around at the room they entered. She saw an office to the right and a wide staircase leading up to the next level. The stair treads were worn slightly in the centre and had a dull reddish sheen.

'Rosewood?' Ayla looked at Nik, seeking confirmation.

'You know your timber. Yes, the stairs and the window casings and architraves are all local rosewood. It was built in the eighteen eighties. The exterior is hand hewn sandstone blocks, or bricks. The floors are all hardwood, even the walls. Some of the outbuildings were built later, and we've renovated of course, but we've been careful to keep the integrity of the original design.' Nik's eyes shone as she spoke, and Ayla could see her love for the building.

'It's amazing Nik. Did you and Robbie take this project on together?' Ayla tried to recall Nik's words at the weekend. Had she said she'd arrived with Lucy and then met Robbie? Suddenly nervous, she wondered if she'd spoken out of turn and opened her mouth to apologise, but Nik, already starting up the stairs, touched her arm lightly.

'I bought it for us. Lucy and me. We had plans to renovate but weren't entirely sure where to start. But we met Robbie on our very first day here. It's a bit of a story. He's our neighbour, he owns the house that Alex and Ruby are in, and that's where he and Harry lived at the time.' Nik continued upstairs, Ayla beside her.

'Robbie is a builder, Harry too. So I hired them to help renovate. We did the stables first.' Nik paused. 'I'll show you what we've done there tomorrow if you're interested.' Ayla nodded, keen to hear more but they had reached the top of the stairs, which opened to a hallway, and she could see a large kitchen off to the right. Skye was perched on a high stool at the kitchen counter and Lucy was lifting something out of the oven.

'I'm really interested, and I have questions.' Ayla grinned at Nik. 'So many questions.' Nik chuckled and nodded, her eyes twinkling. She walked towards the girls.

'How do your muffins look Lucy? My mouth is watering.' Ayla watched Lucy's face light up. She seemed a sweet girl, in her first year of High School. Ayla had noticed at the river that she had a quiet confidence, although not as talkative as Ruby. Both girls had been lovely with Skye. Lucy turned the steaming muffins onto a cooling rack.

'Chocolate chip muffins Mama.' Skye, wriggling with excitement, touched a hot muffin with the tip of her finger.

'Hold on Skye, they're still a bit hot.' Lucy lifted Skye down and turned to Ayla. 'Can I show Skye my room? I have some books we can read.'

'Of course.' Ayla felt a little bubble of contentment rise up in her chest and exchanged a happy look with Nik as the girls left the room, Skye skipping beside Lucy.

'Lucy has a lovely nature Nik, you must be really proud.' Ayla leaned closer to the muffins. 'And she cooks like a professional!'

Laughing loudly, Nik nodded. 'I am. And she does. Thank you.' She paused. 'But only two years ago she was timid, wouldn't speak to anyone accept me and I was home schooling her. Bee Bee of course.'

'Bee Bee?' Ayla frowned, wondering what it meant.

'Before Barrington.' Nik turned around slowly, gesturing around the room, and beyond. 'We'd been through something.' She drew in a breath and Ayla wanted to tell her she didn't have to explain. But Nik, smiled, sadly, and continued. 'Domestic violence, a bad situation. And while Lucy wasn't hurt directly, she saw me ...' Nik stopped and brushed a tear from her eye. 'Saw me hurt. Badly. Was powerless to help me. For a while I thought she'd never recover. But we moved here. Met Robbie and Harry on our very first day, and Scout the next day. It took a while, but Lucy regained her confidence. We both did.' She reached across to the kettle, turning it on, then set four cups out while she continued. 'Best decision I ever made. Moving here, buying this place.' She reached for a cannister, opened the lid and held it under Ayla's nose. 'Tea? It's chai. Or I can offer coffee. And I'll make a hot chocolate for the girls.'

Ayla inhaled, the chai smelt fresh. How wonderful. 'Chai tea is perfect, thank you. But keep talking, I have questions. Who is Scout?'

'Aaah, Scout. Robbie's border collie. She was heavily pregnant when we moved in and Robbie would bring her here while he was working. Scout lured Lucy out of the shadows, really. And Minnie was the runt of that litter. She almost didn't make it. Robbie gave her to Luce.'

'That's a lovely story. I need to be better with dogs.' Ayla took the steaming cup Nik handed to her. 'I was bitten by a large dog when Skye was very small. After it happened the dog's owner just walked away from me, leaving me sitting on the edge of the footpath, both legs bleeding and my baby crying. It was awful. When it knocked me over I really thought it was going to grab Skye.' Ayla shuddered.

'Oh, no wonder you're nervous around dogs. I can vouch for Minnie however, and Scout too. She's out with Robbie and Harry, they're building some new yards on a property out on the Barrington West Road, but they'll be back soon.' Nik pushed the muffin tray closer to Ayla. 'Want to try one?'

'Yes please! Shall we call the girls?' As she spoke Skye skipped back into the room, carrying two picture books and wearing a broad smile, Lucy right behind her.

'Mama, I've picked out two books to read with Lucy tonight. Our room is right next to hers and we've got a really big bed!'

Ayla laughed and lifted Skye onto her lap, admiring the books and cutting a muffin into quarters for her. Lucy sat beside Nik and they all chatted together as they sipped their drinks and devoured the muffins.

'Halloo! We're home!' The arrival of Robbie, and son Harry, seemed to fill up the large room and Ayla watched, entranced, as Robbie kissed Lucy on top of her head and then placed his arms around Nik, kissing her loudly on the lips, to squeals of delight from Skye and laughter from Lucy and Harry. Harry shook her hand, smiling in welcome. He was a younger version of his father and while he was only in his early twenties, at most, he was tall and broad shouldered and very masculine. Ayla smiled to herself as she saw admiration in the young man's face as he gazed at hers, but he was well-mannered, like his father and turned his focus to Skye. He asked her about the books she held and next moment she had slid from Ayla's lap to Harry's and was laughing while he read There's a Hippopotamus on our Roof Eating Cake, using funny voices.

Sitting back, Ayla observed the dynamic in the room for a

moment. There was an atmosphere of happiness and family that she'd rarely experienced and for a moment she wondered if her nomadic lifestyle had been a mistake. But she saw how easily Skye responded to everyone, her little face laughing and happy, and nodded to herself. Skye was confident and delighted to be part of the fun. She was raising a well-balanced, happy child and Ayla let out the breath she was holding.

21

The rain seemed to be letting up and Alex pulled a wad of exercise books out of his satchel as Ruby washed up after dinner. Their afternoon had seemed a bit flat. The possibility of having Ayla and Skye stay then not needing to, had sapped the brief flame of excitement he had harboured and he could see Ruby felt the same. Finishing the dishes Ruby murmured something about having a shower and Alex turned his attention to the compositions he was marking.

His phone buzzed and he grabbed it quickly, hoping it might be Ayla. But the number was unfamiliar.

'Alex McIntosh.'

'Alex. Hello. It's Melanie Evans. Tiffany came home excited about the plans for the Bee Garden. Ben is happy to arrange the working bee for Thursday afternoon, if you haven't already made any calls.'

'Melanie, thank you, that's brilliant.' Alex could hear the enthusiasm in his own tone, and mentally tried to dial it down a bit. 'Sam Fraser said his dad can provide the soil. Does Ben want to call him or should I?'

'Oh that's good news.' Alex noted a slight hesitation with Melanie's next words. 'You know it was Sam's brothers who, er, saw Ayla, um, at the river?'

Alex spoke more firmly. 'I do. Sam's confidence in his dad's support surprised me. But pleased me at the same time.' He stopped for a moment. 'Do you think he may have dobbed his father in without thinking it through, and that he might not be keen to help?'

'Maybe. We've probably all done that when we were kids.' She chuckled. 'But let Ben handle it. He knows Jim Fraser very well. And we can get the soil from Drum Murray if Jim doesn't want to be involved. Leave it with me.'

'I've promised the timber to frame the garden bed up. I know Robbie Stewart has plenty and I'm sure he'll deliver it, if asked.' Alex nodded as he spoke. He'd give Robbie a call in the morning.

'Good. It's sorted then.' Alex liked the way Melanie stepped forward to help. She worked full time at the Vet Clinic but was one of the most active parents at the school. She was practical and organised and he really appreciated it.

'Thank you for calling Melanie and for organising this with Ben. It's a huge help and on behalf of the school, greatly appreciated.' He hoped she could hear the sincerity in his voice.

'No problem Alex. Always happy to help. I'll catch up with you at school on Wednesday morning and let you know the numbers and who is doing what.'

Alex set the phone down, as Ruby returned, hair damp, wearing leggings and one of his old jumpers which almost came to her knees.

'Hot chocolate Dad?' She filled the kettle before he answered.

'Love one, thanks.' He grinned. 'I don't suppose we have any scones left? We could microwave them for a minute, there's left-over cream in the fridge and a new jar of strawberry jam.'

'Yes! Good idea. I'll sort it.' He watched his daughter for a moment, as she busied herself in the kitchen. While lately she had wavered between sullen pre-teen and the happy child he'd always known, he knew there were challenges ahead. But he was proud of her. Proud of the way he was raising her, mostly on his own. He doubted himself at times, but watching her competence in the kitchen just now, and knowing how bright and intuitive she was, well, he felt that whatever they may go through together in the next few years, she'd be okay. They'd be okay. A lump of emotion seemed to rise in his chest for a moment, just as Ruby looked up at him, the jar of strawberry jam in her hands.

She cocked an eyebrow. 'What?'

He closed the exercise book he'd been marking and reached for another. 'Nothing.'

'Nooo. There was something. You were looking at me funny.'

He tried to make light of it, his smile lop-sided. 'Funny ha ha?'

Ruby set the jar down and stepped toward him, hands on her hips, but frowning. 'Don't do that Dad. I'm not a baby. What is it? What's going on with you?'

He sighed. Too bloody intuitive. But he'd always been honest with her. 'It's you Rubes. I was mentally congratulating myself for the way you're growing up. For the person you are.' He shook his head, glanced away, then looked back. 'But really, it's you I should be thanking. You're a great kid, and I'm feeling particularly lucky right now.'

He watched her face flush with pleasure at his words. She stepped over to him, nudged him with her elbow. 'You're okay too Dad. We get on fine. Most of the time.' She hurried back into the kitchen, returning with the scones, already cut in half and lathered in jam and cream. Perching on her chair she took a big bite out of her scone, then nodded toward the exercise books.

'Have you read mine yet?

'No.' He shuffled through the books, drawing one out of the pile with Ruby's name on the cover. He opened it, scanning her research on bees and food production. He wasn't surprised to read her stance on farming without pesticides and other chemicals but was fascinated by an additional piece on the practice of mono-cropping in relation to almond farming. He read it carefully.

'This is very good Ruby, but wherever did you find the information? Or even know what to look for?'

'Ayla gave us all a Save the Bees sticker. They have a website. I checked into it and there's a lot of information about mono-cropping and how bad it is for the bees.' Her voice grew strident, passionate. 'It's killing the bees Dad. All those city folk wanting almond milk in their coffee is killing the bees!'

'I didn't know that Ruby. We must ask Ayla for more information on this.' He took a bite from his own scone, chewing thoughtfully for a moment. 'No-one in this region grows almonds, so that's something at least.' He sat back, watching her relax a bit. Ayla and the bees had really triggered something in Ruby. In a lot of the kids at school. Even traditional farm kids like Sam Fraser.

'And the question I really want answered is?' He paused, pulling a Dad-joke face.

Ruby giggled. 'What question?'

He held up his hands, making tiny milking movements with his thumbs and forefingers. 'How do they milk the almonds?'

She laughed out loud, then punched his upper arm. 'That's a stupid joke, Dad!' But for Alex, the joke was silly but the moment was very, very nice.

Hours later the rain had become little more than a light drizzle, Alex lay in bed thinking over the conversation with Ruby. Ayla's arrival in their community had really struck a chord with Ruby. Not just with Ruby, with him, the school, the parents. Even the detractors, like Joyce Wilson had been touched by Ayla's arrival. There was something really special about her. He couldn't quite put his finger on what it was. As he finally drifted off to sleep he saw her again, standing on the riverbank, naked and beautiful.

22

The bee collects honey from flowers in such a way as to do the least damage or destruction to them, and she leaves them whole, undamaged and fresh, just as she found them. **Saint Francis De Sales.**

Ayla woke early, although she had sat up late chatting with Nik in the lounge. They'd shared stories while drinking herb tea, long after the others had gone to bed. Skye had been happy to let Lucy read several bedtime stories and had fallen asleep quite quickly. Lucy had then gone to bed to read herself, after wishing Ayla a shy goodnight, with Robbie following suit soon after. Harry had a room at the back of the house downstairs, in what would have been the cook's room when the house was young, with a small ensuite. He wandered off when his father did, but not before Ayla caught him looking at her, his eyes dark with passion. She'd held his gaze for a few seconds, he was bold for one so young, but he had looked away first.

Leaving Skye asleep, Ayla dressed quietly and walked downstairs carrying her canvas runners. Finding her way outside via the laundry, she could see where the dogs had slept on the covered veranda. The rain had stopped overnight and the dogs weren't there now. She sat on the step and pulled her shoes on, thinking she would find a quiet spot to do some stretching, although the ground was too wet for yoga. She stepped on to the path, following it toward the rear of the house. She could see the converted stables beyond the back garden gate. Still looking toward the stables, she turned the corner and walked straight into Harry, leaning against the wall, pulling his boots on. He was taller than her, broad shouldered yet lean through the waist and hips. He wobbled against the wall, only one boot on, and she reached out to steady him.

He took her hand, and now with both feet firmly planted on the ground, drew her towards him.

'Ayla.' His voice was husky and her body responded in an immediate, visceral way. One strong arm around her, he pulled her against him. Ayla relaxed into him for a moment, he was young, sexy as hell, emanating the masculine virility of youth. She could feel his body stirring against hers and thought how easy it would be to give in, enjoy the moment. His eyes held a question and she considered it for less than a second. He was her new friend's stepson, not yet twenty-one. She kissed him lightly on the lips and pulled back. Harry released her immediately, pulling himself to his full height, his cheeks blazing.

'Ayla. I'm sorry.' He bent his head, touched his belt buckle for a moment. Her gaze followed the movement and she saw his arousal had been swift.

'No. I'm sorry. I'm a guest in your home. And old enough to know better.' She smiled on the last words and he let out a breath, his relief obvious.

'You're just so...' He gave her a crooked grin. 'Beautiful. You're really beautiful Ayla. And I am sorry, I shouldn't have man-handled you.' He lifted his chin, glancing up at the house. 'I know better. I've been raised to respect women, not grab at them.'

Stepping closer to him again, Ayla raised her hand to his cheek. 'I know that Harry. But don't apologise. I reacted to you too. But I have a couple of years on you Harry and I'm a mother, life is not simple these days. I can't act on this. And Nik is my friend. At least, I hope she is.' She stepped back and he nodded. Ayla grinned, then whispered, 'But if I had met you before. Before Skye. We'd be horizontal right now. You're hot, Harry Stewart!'

He threw back his head and laughed. 'You're not just gorgeous, you're fabulous.' A door closed nearby, and she heard footsteps on the side veranda. 'The girls my age are nothing like you Ayla.' He gave her a wistful glance, before bending to pat Minnie who had appeared at that moment, Lucy right behind her.

'Morning Harry. Ayla.' She stopped, looking from one to the other. 'I'm just going to feed the horses, but I think Skye might be awake now.'

'Morning Lucy.' Ayla placed her hand gingerly on Minnie's head, giving her a light pat. 'I'll go in, check on Skye and I'm happy to start breakfast, if everyone is up.'

'Mum is in the shower and Robbie's making coffee.' Lucy looked at Harry. 'Can you help me with the hay for the horses?'

Harry wrapped an arm around Lucy's shoulder. 'Come on Luce, we'll do it together and maybe you'll have time to whip up some pancakes before we have to go to work?' Lucy nodded happily and Ayla watched them walk toward a large shed to the right of the stables, the dog trotting beside Lucy.

At the top of the stairs Ayla met Nik coming out of the bathroom. They spoke for a moment before Aya heard Skye call out 'Mama!' She hurried to their room and found Skye sitting up in bed, one of the books from last night on her lap.

'Hungry Mama. And I need to wee.' Ayla scooped her up, hugged her tightly, then led her to the bathroom.

By the time she had Skye dressed and the bed made, everyone was in the kitchen and Ayla could smell coffee and pancakes and bacon.

A chorus or 'morning Ayla, morning Skye' met them as they walked in. Ayla grinned and 'morning'd' everyone happily. Skye ran straight to Lucy, who scooped her up for a hug.

They sat around the massive dining table, helping themselves from an array of food on platters in the middle of the table. Ayla chatted to Robbie and Harry about their work for the coming days and Nik mentioned she had guests checking in to the stables at the weekend.

'Even though the rain has stopped, you won't be able to get over Jems Creek until at least midday Ayla, as the water is still coming down from the Tops.' Robbie looked at Nik, who nodded. 'Why don't you stay here with Nik this morning. Have a look at the conversion of the stables and the renovations downstairs too.'

'I'd really love to see what you've done, Nik. Yes, thank you.

But will we be interrupting your own work? You run an accounting business from here too, don't you?' Ayla was pleased to be asked, she was keen to see the work they had done.

'I fit my work in around other chores, and since we've been open for guests, I'm not taking new accounting clients on, so it's part-time really.' Lucy was already clearing the table and Nik glanced at the old fashioned clock on the wall. 'Twenty minutes Luce, before the bus comes.' Turning to Ayla, she added. 'Quite a few of the design ideas were Lucy's, she's really got an eye for it.'

'Have you Lucy?' Ayla was impressed. 'Is it something you want to do later on when you've finished school?'

'It is. Maybe architectural design. I like interior design too, colours and such. I haven't quite made my mind up.' Lucy's pretty face was animated, and her demeanour less reserved than Ayla had noted previously.

'It's great to have a passion Lucy, I really admire that. And if you can make a living from it when you're older, even better'. Ayla spoke directly to Lucy, who grinned at her, then at her mother.

After she left the room to get ready for school, Robbie and Harry departed, friendly goodbyes to Ayla and Skye and Robbie's kiss on the lips for Nik.

Skye had wandered off to the loungeroom with her book and Ayla started washing up, Nik clearing away the table as she did.

* * *

THE CONVERTED STABLES WERE GORGEOUS. AYLA GAZED AROUND as Nik explained the changes they had made and where they had sourced recycled materials. She was impressed with the the the beautiful work Robbie and Harry had done. Skye skipped around the room, poking into cupboards and opening doors. It was effectively a two-bedroom cottage with a large living area and kitchenette and a luxurious bathroom between the two rooms with the bedrooms opening to the side veranda.

'No wonder you have bookings coming in Nik, this is really beautiful.' Ayla was in awe. 'Robbie and Harry really did all the building work?'

'They're really good. We needed a plumber and electrician, but the boys did the rest. And it didn't cost as much as I'd thought, as a lot of the materials are recycled.'

'I can see that. It's really impressive.' Ayla walked into the first bedroom again, then the bathroom. 'Stunning. Absolutely-bloody-stunning.'

Nik beamed, then after a moment frowned. 'But I made a mistake with this. I should have done more research.'

Ayla was surprised. 'Really? What mistake? It's perfect.'

'Even though it's two bedrooms, the bathroom and living space is shared. So, I'm often full with one couple. To maximise the two bedrooms I should have had two bathrooms, ensuites, and maybe separate living areas.' Nik walked back into the living area as she spoke.

'Oh, I see. Of course. Unless two couples are travelling together and don't mind sharing.' Ayla grinned at Nik, 'but I hope you charge more when it's just one couple having the whole place. People from the city would be happy to pay a premium to have this to themselves!'

'Ha ha, I do now. I didn't in the beginning but spoke to Wendy at the local Visitor Centre and she helped me change the structure of my rates.' She paused. 'Weekends are booked out months in advance and now I only take two night minimum stays. The mid-week trade is building too, but more slowly.'

'Well done though. You haven't even been open a year.'

Skye ran ahead and was playing on the veranda with Minnie as they strolled back to the house chatting comfortably. Although Nik was at least a decade older, Ayla felt a strong connection to her. She'd been through a lot, personally, and protected her daughter, then had the courage to start over. Nik was a strong woman, in a subtle kind of way.

Back in the house, Nik stopped. 'I had an idea for downstairs, from the start. But I haven't really made it happen. I have overflow accommodation here that's family friendly. I could have offered it to you and Skye last night, but I didn't want you to feel like guests, I wanted you upstairs as part of our family.'

Her words resonated with Ayla, who took a deep shuddering breath, then stepped closer to Nik, enveloping her on a tight hug, saying quietly, 'Thank you. That's the kindest thing.' She couldn't say any more for fear of releasing a torrent of happy tears.

Nik hugged her back fiercely. 'Robbie and Harry have made us a family. It's been such a shift for me and Lucy. Such a happy shift. I wanted to share that with you and Skye.' Ayla nodded, unable to speak for a moment.

Nik opened a door, leading Ayla inside. There were two bedrooms, one fitted with a double bed and bunks and the smaller room with a double on the bottom and single bunk on top. There was a kitchenette and living and dining area with an eight seat table, comfortable lounge chairs and a sofa. Against one wall was a bookshelf and open chest filled with children's toys. A family style bathroom with bath and shower and a separate toilet was on one side of the house. Ayla glanced up, probably in the same position as the upstairs bathroom, easier for plumbing. The accommodation was family friendly, without the luxurious appointments in the converted stables.

'I was going to put a laundry in, but there's already a large laundry we use, that anyone staying here can access.' She stopped, looked up at Ayla. 'I wanted to make this a place of safety for women and their children escaping from domestic violence. A place to come and stay while they heal. Even for older women leaving marriages or on their own through the death of a spouse, and vulnerable for any reason.' Ayla nodded, listening intently as Nik continued. 'You'd be surprised the number of older women who end up homeless after losing a spouse, or upon retirement.'

'This is beautiful and generous, but tell me why it hasn't really happened?' Ayla followed Nik out to the hallway, where she quickly showed her the office. An area where guests could check in or ask questions, but also where Nik ran her accounting business.

Closing the door to the office, they were about to return upstairs. 'I'll just get Skye from outside.' Ayla stepped out through the open front door, calling for Skye, who came running, Minnie at her side. Her little face was flushed and happy. Taking Skye's hand she followed Nik upstairs and sat at the kitchen counter while Nik boiled the jug. Skye perched on the sofa brushing the hair of a doll, one Lucy must have found for her.

Looking wistfully out the window for a moment, Nik poured the tea before speaking. 'I just don't know how to connect with these women, the ones that might need a place to stay. Advertising would bring all sorts, maybe scammers too. I've spoken to a couple of government departments and they weren't really helpful. I need to develop a sort of private network, where people can come to me by referral. I just don't really know how to do that.'

Ayla nodded, her mind racing. She had some ideas straight away but wanted to work through them before sharing with Nicole, wanted to iron out any potential problems. 'I have some thoughts on this Nik. But leave it with me, I'd like to work through them before sharing.'

'Really?' Nicole's face lit up. 'Okay. Let me know when you want to chat some more about this.' She paused. 'And can I ask what it is you're doing up there at the old resort? I'm sure you're not trespassing, or camping. Is it a secret?'

Ayla grinned at Nik, then shook her head. 'Not a secret at all. But you're the first person to ask.' She reached for her tea, while Nicole chuckled as she settled on a seat by Ayla's side.

'It's like this.' And Ayla began her story.

23

A small knot of parents were huddled under umbrellas by the school gate when Alex and Ruby pulled in. Rudy had forgotten her sports shoes and they had turned back to get them, making them slightly late. But the parents were early, and they usually didn't hang around when the weather was bad. It was just a light drizzle, but enough to take cover.

Ruby rushed into the school yard, saying hello to a couple of adults before disappearing around the corner of their class-room. Alex hesitated by the gate. Melanie Evans turned, giving him a discreet nod. He stepped closer.

'I was just telling Nadia that Ben was able to speak to a few parents last night and we've got several committed for the working bee. Drum Murray is supplying the soil.'

Alex raised his eyebrows, wondering if Jim Fraser was against the plan, but before he could ask Melanie rushed on. 'Jim Fraser is on board, but Drum's farm is closer, so he's bringing soil. Jim will supply some gardening tools and we have several parents providing suitable plants.'

'That's great Melanie, an excellent response, please thank Ben for me.' Alex hoped he sounded pleased and not surprised. But Ben Evans was well known, and respected, he'd grown up here, and probably knew the families of the student body well.

'Have you spoken to Robbie Stewart about the timber for the framing?' Melanie waved to Nadia, who said goodbye and moved toward her car, chatting with two parents as she went.

'I called him this morning. He has timber he pulled out of an old barn, that's not suitable for building. He'll drop it here on Thursday some time. And he and Harry will stay and help.' Alex nodded, almost to himself, mentally ticking off the list of items he thought they'd need.

'That's great Alex.' She paused, glancing around. He followed her gaze. Some older students were playing handball in the shelter shed and the younger ones would be in the library or their classrooms, waiting for the bell to ring. He looked at Melanie, she obviously wanted to add something to the conversation.

Melanie met his eyes, smiled sheepishly, then leaned in a bit. Alex leaned toward her, not knowing what she would say but feeling sure it would be light-hearted.

'Are you wondering why there is a larger-than-usual working bee commitment?' He nodded. He was wondering. Exactly that.

'It's Ayla. Ben told them Ayla would be here on Thursday to meet the parents who help out.' Alex straightened, frowning. But Melanie was grinning now. 'So many parents want to meet her, apparently. I'm sure it's all about the bee program and nothing to do with rumours circulating about her, um, lifestyle.'

'That's good, I think. But I hope none of them are planning to, um, grill her about those rumours?' Alex was suddenly uncertain. He felt protective of Ayla, although he had no reasonable explanation for his feelings.

'Nah. Don't worry Alex. It's curiosity mostly. Dad's and mum's will come and I'm sure once they meet Ayla they'll be at ease.' She patted his shoulder. 'It's a good thing. De-mystifies her.' Melanie turned then, opening the gate and walking through. Alex was still watching her, unsure. 'Perhaps you should see if you have any other projects that a parent working bee might undertake, get them signed up while they're here.' She laughed and walked to her car. Alex grinned to himself. Ayla. No one could be ambivalent about her, that's for sure.

24

When the flower blossoms, the bee will come. **Srikumar Rao.**

The bridge across Jems Creek was only centimetres above the rushing water. There was debris to one side of the crossing and a large tree branch wedged on the up-stream side. She'd call council and let them know when she reached the house. Although it was likely it had already been reported by locals.

The four kilometre road into the resort was muddy, and slippery in places. Ayla kept the van in low gear, concentrating. It was more of a track than a road, and the rain had washed it out in places.

They topped a little rise, driving over a cattle grid before descending to the property. Her cottage in front of her, the stables to the right. Drawing closer to the house, something didn't look right. There were a couple of random lumps strewn across the grass in front of the house. Ayla glanced at Skye. She was leaning forward, peering through the windscreen too. A gust of wind rustled the lumps, and several feathers swirled into the air.

Ayla stamped on the brakes, her heart racing. She knew what it was lying in haphazard piles on the grass. The chickens! The coop had been open when they left yesterday. Something had killed the chickens! Skye whimpered. 'Mama?'

Reaching over, Ayla patted her daughter's hand. There was no hiding it. Skye could see them too. 'We weren't home to shut the chickens in last night Skye. I'm sorry baby, but it seems that a fox or dingo has killed them.' She tried to sound matter-of-fact.

Skye's eyes opened wide, then she frowned, shaking her head. 'Bad fox.'

'Yes. Very bad fox.' Ayla moved the vehicle forward edging around the carcases, until they lay behind the vehicle. She would get Skye inside, and deal with the chickens later.

They hurried inside, but not before Skye picked up three feathers from the garden path. Ayla grimaced inwardly. What looked like a brown feather was actually blood. She'd wash them after Skye went to bed.

Later, just as the sun was setting, Ayla went outside with gloves and a shovel. She scooped the three dead birds up one at a time and took them to an old forty four gallon drum beyond the stables that had been a make-shift incinerator. She sighed as she lit it. The bodies needed to be burned, the days were warming and they were already smelly. She counted three bodies. Perhaps the dingo, or fox, had taken some away but there were eight unaccounted for. Ayla walked around to the door of the chicken coop, thinking some may still be in there.

They were. Most of them, anyway. Seven chickens were resting in the laying boxes, still very much alive. Ayla laughed out loud. 'My goodness, how did you escape the carnage?' The chickens fluffed their feathers, watching her with their small eyes. Ayla walked out of the chicken shed, closing the door carefully behind her. It was possible they had flapped into the branches of a tree, out of reach of the predators. Regardless how they survived, it would be nice to tell Skye and show her in the morning.

Leaning the shovel against the garden gate, Ayla heard a noise behind her. It was almost fully dark now, just a circle of light emanated from the porch. Stepping inside the yard, Ayla grabbed the shovel, then latched the gate. She heard it again. Small yipping noises, then the howl of a dingo. Peering into the gloom she saw a stealthy shape slink past the closed door of the chicken coop. It was a dingo, it's heavy belly low to the ground. Ayla stepped back. It was a female, heavily in pup. Two smaller shapes followed her into the scrub beyond the stables. And she has two half grown pups from an earlier litter. Ayla wondered where her mate was, she knew that dingoes mate for life and generally move around in family packs.

The missing chicken was explained, it would have been a meal for them. Perhaps they had come back for the others. Ayla pondered it as she stepped inside, closing the door and turning the external light off. It's also possible that a fox killed some of them, after the dingo took their own meal. The dingoes would rarely leave their kill behind, unless the half grown pups had killed them, leaving them on the ground to return to their lair with the pack.

'Mama!' Skye trotted from her room, holding her favourite book. 'Story now mama.' Ayla sighed. She'd tell Skye about the surviving chickens tomorrow, if she told her now she'd want to visit them. And that was not happening tonight.

* * *

AYLA SLEPT BADLY, KEEPING SKYE IN HER ROOM ALL NIGHT. SHE'D heard the dingoes howling, further away in the forest.

They ventured outside just after dawn. Taking Skye by the hand, she told her she had a surprise in the chicken shed. Skye glanced up at her, nodding. She looked uncertain. Opening the door to the coop, they entered together. The chickens were in the laying boxes, but stood, ruffling their feathers, as they walked in. Skye clapped her hands. 'Look Mama, we have chickens.' She counted them on her fingers slowly. 'Seven chickens!' The birds moved off their boxes and Skye reached in, feeling for eggs. 'And we have eggs Mama!' Looking at the chickens, she spoke quietly. 'Good girls, thank you for your eggs.'

There were only five eggs and Ayla wasn't sure if she should leave the door open, but she decided it would be alright just for the morning. She followed Skye inside the house. Skye had an egg in each hand and was walking very carefully.

25

Thursday seemed to drag, not just for Alex, but the whole school appeared to be waiting for the afternoon when many of their parents would come to help build the raised bed for the vegetable garden.

Alex took his class outdoors just after lunch break when Robbie and Harry arrived to drop off the timber, followed shortly by Drum Murray with a trailer load of soil. His students had already measured the area they were going to use. Sam Fraser and Alex hammered garden stakes into the corners and Ruby tied a string-line between them.

The soil was dumped right beside the area and Robbie and Harry had stacked the timber to one side, the boys jostling each other to help. After the men left, Alex found it difficult to get his class to concentrate on anything but the project, so he set them to researching the best combination of plants to suit the area and bees.

If they were excited about building the garden bed, they

were ecstatic about the scheduled planting the next afternoon with Ayla. He smiled to himself as Sam, Ruby and Bobby Bain had a serious discussion about companion planting, culminating in Bobby and Sam drawing their proposed design on the whiteboard, with Ruby annotating the names of the plants and vegetables. He decided to leave it on the board until the next afternoon, when Ayla could see it and make any amendments she considered necessary.

Hearing vehicles and voices outside, he glanced out of the window. There were already five vehicles parked outside and a small knot of adults waiting at the gate. Looking at his watch, it was only ten minutes to bell time.

'Pack up your desks, everyone, I can see that some of your parents are already here, so we'll ring the bell now.' He glanced at Ruby. 'If you please, Ruby.' She shot out of her seat, almost running to the porch, where she rang the old fashioned bell long and loud.

He followed the last child out as the children from the other classrooms emptied in a flurry of talking, laughing and calling greetings to their parents.

Frank from the general store was there, with Drum Murray, Jim Fraser and Wiley Bain. Melanie Evans appeared, her husband Ben was standing back a bit, his phone to his ear. Another vehicle pulled in, local Vet Max Masters. His son Tommy was in the middle classroom but had been enthusiastic about his dad helping out. Three other dads, and two mums arrived, smiling their greetings to him and other parents, their children excited to have them step inside the school grounds.

After initial greetings, and quite a number of children catching their respective buses, Drum and Jim Fraser led the others through to area behind the school garden and equipment shed they'd designated for the project. Alex waited by the gate until all children had either left for home or were with their parents for the working bee. It was a bigger group than he had imagined, and definitely more people than they needed, but it was a great show of school spirit.

Alex was about to head to the project area when the rumble of Ayla's Kombi heralded her arrival. She parked on the other side of the street, raising her hand in a wave before reaching across to help Skye out of her seatbelt. She stepped out, then lifted Skye down, who immediately dashed across the road to him, shouting, 'Hello Teacher!'

Grinning at Skye's happy face he was surprised when she slipped her little hand inside his, and looked quickly up at Ayla, walking toward him. She was dressed in denim bib and brace overalls with a white tee shirt underneath and short gum boots. Her hair hung over one shoulder in a thick braid. Skye wore denim shorts, a pink tee shirt and miniature pink gum boots, her curls pushed back by a bright pink hair band.

'Hi Alex.' Ayla smiled and he felt his heart race.

'Hello Ayla, Skye.' He cleared his throat, attempting to maintain his school-principal-always-professional demeanour. She smiled more broadly and he castigated himself internally, she knew the affect she had on him.

'Quite a turnout.' Ayla stepped through the gate. 'Have the parents decided to plant the entire football field?' She chuckled.

'Not at all. Just a great community here at Barrington School.' It was said tongue-in-cheek and she laughed in delight.

'Of course.' She began to walk ahead of him but turned when another vehicle parked behind the kombi. It was Harry Stewart in his old Landcruiser. He stepped out and quickly strode across the road. Alex frowned. Harry wasn't a parent. Sure, he'd helped Robbie earlier with the timber, but he hadn't expected him back for the working bee.

Skye had turned too, and seeing Harry she dropped Alex's hand and ran towards him, laughing when he scooped her up and sat her on his shoulders, her little hands clutching his hair, giggling as he bounced her a bit. 'Harry's here mama! Harry's here!'

'So I see. Hello Harry.' Ayla smiled at the younger man, raising her eyes to look at Skye, perched up high on his broad shoulders.

Alex watched Harry's face as she did. Then he saw it. The look he gave Ayla was one of adoration. And something else? Lust? Alex didn't like it. Not one bit. But he held his hand out to Harry, shaking it firmly.

'Twice in one day, Harry. Barrington School thanks you.' He was internally gratified when Harry responded with a sheepish lop-sided grin. He knew he'd been caught out.

'Let's head around to the spot. It wouldn't surprise me if Ruby and Sam have already given everyone jobs to do.' He walked ahead, schooling his face into a pleasant smile as he approached the waiting parents and students. He admitted to himself he was interested in Ayla. He hadn't thought about possible competition for her affection. That could wait until school was out.

The parents and students looked at him expectantly, and he found Ayla had moved to stand beside him, near the stack of timber. He was pleased to see most of the kids stopped what they were doing to wave or say hello to Ayla.

'Firstly, thank you all for coming this afternoon.' He smiled at the group. 'This is Ayla. The Bee Whisperer' He looked down, Skye was standing beside her mother now and Harry had moved to stand by Drum, Jim and the other men. 'And her daughter Skye, who will commence school here in the new year.'

'I'm a bee whisperer too.' Skye was standing, legs akimbo, hands on hips, nodding emphatically. He saw Ayla touch her daughter's shoulder, fleetingly, but she had no need. The faces turned toward them were smiling broadly, with many of them saying 'Hello Ayla, hello Skye.' How could they not, she was sassy and adorable.

The group converged and Ayla shook hands or nodded to each of them as he introduced those she hadn't met. She held Jim Fraser's hand for a moment longer than necessary, Alex thought, but smiled at him as she did. He looked like he wanted to say something, but she released him from her gaze and greeted his son Sam, thanking him for getting his Dad to help. Suddenly any tension that had hovered around the group seemed to dissipate and Alex watched as Sam, Bobby and Ruby explained their measurements and the height they planned for the garden bed, seeking confirmation from Ayla. He could see that Jim Fraser and Wiley Bain were particularly pleased at their sons' confidence in their design. Sam in particular, rarely engaged deeply with his schoolwork, but he was animated and excited to be doing this with his father's assistance. The bee project was meeting more needs than Alex had anticipated, and he was thrilled with the outcome so far.

In less than an hour they had the structure built and were ready to put the soil in. Harry stepped forward, glanced at Alex then Sam and his dad. 'I've thrown some old hay in the back of my ute. Thought we might put it at the bottom, then the soil on top, for better drainage.'

'Thank you Harry, that's even better.' Alex heard genuine pleasure in Ayla's voice as she spoke, and his gut churned. But he nodded with the others at this news.

'Two bales, did you say Harry?' This was from Drum Murray. At Harry's nod, he moved into step beside him. Sam and Bobby ran to catch up, and Jim leaned on his shovel, with a grin at Alex.

'I reckon the young lads are going to try to lug those bales in by themselves. It might take a minute.' Jim Fraser laughed as he spoke, watching fondly as his son walked beside Drum and Harry, both tall, broad men, toward the school gate. Jim nodded at Ben Evans, who had helped assemble the structure but hadn't said a great deal. He continued, 'Ben mentioned there might be a bit more we can do in this little area.' He looked at Ben, seeming to seek confirmation. Alex was curious to hear more, and he could see Ayla was too. She had moved to stand with Melanie, and Ruby had taken Skye and Tiffany to the swings but was tuned in to the conversation too.

Ben looked around at the group. 'We think the kids, er students, should have some seating close by, so they can spend time out here as the garden is established. A picnic table and a couple of bench seats could be situated here.' He waved his hand to an area a few metres away, partially shaded by a large gum tree.

'And maybe a small greenhouse. A sort of potting shed, where they can learn to propagate plants later on.' Frank had joined the conversation. 'I think we could have a couple more afternoons this term and really set it up well.' He nodded to Ayla, who seemed pleased and gave him a dazzling smile in return.

Drum and Harry returned, empty handed. Drum grinned

and jerked his head behind them. They turned to see Bobby and Sam, each with a bale of hay, red in the face and panting, yet determinedly carrying them across the grass.

Drum walked to Bobby, helping him lower the hay bale. He handed him a pocket-knife and watched as the youngster expertly cut the twine, pulled it loose from the bale and tied it into a loop. Sam was doing the same with Harry supervising, then Jim jumped into the garden bed and started laying the hay down as Sam and Harry threw it in, spreading it out. Ayla stepped in beside him and did the same with the second bale. Drum, Ben, Frank and Harry were already on shovels, moving the dirt in on top of the hay the moment they stepped out.

Alex felt he hadn't done much himself, and was about to step in, to ensure the soil was spread evenly and to the edges, but Ruby and the kids jumped in, doing it for him. Melanie appeared beside him. 'Too many helpers. But that's a good thing, right?' She grinned.

'You're right Melanie, I couldn't be happier with the support we've had today. It's very heartening.' And it was. Country schools, small communities, they really know how to step up when needed.

The job was nearly done and Ayla had stepped over to him and Melanie. 'This is great Alex, so many people, we've finished in record time. I wish I'd thought to bring something for after-noon tea, to thank everyone.'

Melanie laughed. 'I'm all over it Ayla.' She gestured to a cane basket sitting beside the kids' school bags. 'I've brought home-made muffins and a few bottles of ginger beer and lemonade and paper cups.'

Alex shook his head in disbelief. Ben and Melanie had pulled this together, but the kids had helped by demonstrating their enthusiasm to their parents. Twenty minutes later, he sat in the shelter shed with the parents, enjoying one of Melanie's chocolate chip muffins, as the kids, including Skye, played a noisy game of tag on the edge of the football field. They'd all had a drink and muffin and seemed to have energy to burn.

The conversation flowed, mostly around the project's further development, but also about the timing of introducing bees, and he was amazed as all of them, even Jim Fraser and Wiley Bain, listened as Ayla explained how best it could work. He glanced at Harry briefly, who hadn't sat down, but hovered behind Ayla the whole time. *Oh yeah, he's got it bad.* But he also noticed Ayla smile at Harry from time to time. *Surely he was too young for her. Maybe eight or even ten years her junior.*

Melanie began to pack up her basket and suddenly everyone was on the move, taking their shovels and other tools, chatting as they did. The kids were called, told to get their bags, and he moved to the front gate with all of them, Ruby beside him, holding Skye's hand.

Jim Fraser offered to help with planting the next afternoon, and Frank said Nadia was keen to help too. Within a few minutes Alex was standing at the gate with Ruby, waving as the vehicles moved off. He had hoped Ayla would linger for a chat, but she was over at her car, speaking to Harry who had lifted Skye in and was doing up her seat belt. Alex couldn't hear their conversation, but when they laughed together he frowned.

Ruby touched his hand and he glanced down at her. 'It's okay Dad, they're just friends.' He smiled at his daughter, disappointed in himself that she had seen his reaction.

Harry waved as he strode to his own vehicle. 'Bye Alex, seeya Ruby.'

Ayla had started the Kombi, and after Harry drove off she

leaned out her window. 'Bye Ruby, thanks for looking after Skye! Bye Alex!'

'Bye Ruby! Bye teacher!' Skye waved madly as they moved onto the road. Alex raised his hand, hoping he was smiling and not grimacing.

26

The bee is an exquisite Chemist. **Royal Beekeeper to Charles II**

Glancing in the rear-view mirror, then back to the road, Ayla breathed in sharply. Another chat to Harry to make herself clear wouldn't go astray.

A few minutes on the road and Skye was already asleep, her long dark eyelashes resting on her cheeks. It had been a busy day and she was becoming very comfortable with the school and its community. Her daughter had made friends with Ruby, and Ayla was grateful the older child was so welcoming. After Ruby, her thoughts segued to Alex. Ruby was lovely and he was raising her, mostly, on his own. So a good father. Good teacher. Respected by the school community, and friends with people she admired like Nik and Robbie. But conservative and maybe a bit rigid. Nodding to herself, she stole a quick look at Skye, still sleeping but her mouth was curved upwards, and Ayla wondered what she was dreaming of.

The teacher. Digging deep, she admitted to herself that yes, she likes him. And not just physically. But he represents everything she had shied away from as she grew up. Authority and a standardised education system. Yet for all that, he had incorporated the bee education into his curriculum with ease, so maybe *not* rigid.

And then there's Harry. Definitely too young for her. And the son of a friend. And while she suspects he has some measure of experience with women, and as tempting as his youthful virility is, to go there would inevitably burn bridges in the community and maybe friendships. But the looks he gave her could melt a glacier. In her earlier life, perhaps. But she let her thoughts rest there, as the dip before the Jems Creek Bridge came into view.

Changing down gears, Ayla drove across slowly. The water had receded but there was debris stuck against the upstream side. A mess of branches - Ayla wrinkled her nose - and what looked like a wallaby carcass.

Before turning into the long driveway of the old resort she slowed again, looking at the rolling pastures on either side of the gravel road, dotted with cattle. Further along, the road dipped into a valley with high ridges on either side, and the heavily timbered mountain before her. The slightly charred stables, then the cottage, came into view, nestled into the last of the green valley before the vista rose steeply behind the house.

Skye stirred in her seat, stretched, then brushed her eyes with the back of one hand as she looked through the windscreen. Ayla watched as Skye blinked a couple of times, then turned toward her smiling broadly. 'Home Mama. Home now.'

Hesitating for a moment, Ayla answered quietly, reaching over to take Skye's small hand in hers. 'Yes. We're home. Home now.' Skye nodded, then unbuckled her seatbelt, inching over until she was in Ayla's lap. Laughing, Ayla, unhooked her own seatbelt and opened the car door. The afternoon was cooling, always a slight breeze up in the hills.

Later, after Skye had been fed, bathed and read to sleep, Ayla sat out on the front veranda, her back against the veranda pole, a steaming mug of honey, lemon and ginger tea in her hand. The bees were quiet, settled in for the evening. A flash of white near the stables caught her eye. It settled on the low branch of an enormous gum tree, fluffed its wings, then let out a mournful hoot. The tree itself had been scorched by the fires, but survived, with new growth in its branches and small saplings springing up beneath it. She contemplated them for a moment, wondering if they could be taken out and planted elsewhere on the property. She'd have to google it. Or ask one of the farmers if she saw them at school tomorrow. Maybe Jim Fraser would know.

A series of loud squarks from the chicken shed made her whip her head around, standing as she did. The surviving chickens were clucking and flapping, she could hear them clearly. She set her mug down and walked to the garden gate, then picked up the shovel she'd left leaning against the fence. She stepped carefully, but not quietly, toward the chicken house at the rear of the old stables, peering in the gloom, the crescent moon not providing much light. A dog-like shape paused by the closed door of the coup, then turned to face her for a moment. She caught a quick glimpse of red-brown fur and white chest markings. A fox then. Not the dingo she had seen the other night. The animal turned and trotted toward the creek, jumping it before disappearing into the underbrush of the forest on the other side.

Stepping to the hen house, Ayla checked the door was closed firmly, speaking quietly to the chickens inside as she did, to calm them. She stayed for a few moments, hoping the fox had given up, for tonight at least. Moving back to the house, she left the shovel by the garden gate. On the other side of the creek, a little farther upstream from the place the fox had jumped across, she saw movement. Stealthy shapes. Then the unmistakable low hung belly of the pregnant dingo, the half-grown pups following her, moved along the creek bank on the other side, heading into the forest. All three animals were lean. Perhaps the younger ones weren't efficient hunters yet and the female so advanced in her pregnancy she wasn't hunting successfully. A memory flitted across her mind. The Aboriginal name for a female dingo is tingo? She'd fact-check that. She also wondered if the pregnancy was quite late, she remembered they usually whelped earlier in the year. Shivering a little as the breeze picked up, Ayla retreated to the cottage, firmly closing the door.

Next morning Ayla and Skye walked up to the buildings left standing after the fire two years before. While eight small cabins had been destroyed, two remained in an area close to the creek. And the large structure that housed the commercial kitchen, restaurant and office was still standing. Earlier investigations revealed that a significant power pole had been lost in the fires, so nothing was operational inside. A tarnished brass plaque beside the front entrance had, The Barn, etched into it.

Cute name, she thought. The building itself was large, high ceilinged with massive Oregon beams spanning the interior, creating a light filled main room. It was dusty and smelled smoky and stale.

'Yuk!' Skye wrinkled her nose, looking up at Ayla.

'Let's open all these doors to the side veranda and we'll see if fresh air will help.' Ayla moved to the eastern side, throwing open the first set of French doors. The second set were stuck, so she moved to the next ones, opening them easily. The room held eight timber dining tables and chairs down one side, and a nest of dusty couches of indeterminate colour around a huge open fireplace on the other. They continued past a partition to the large commercial kitchen at the rear of the building. Walk in freezer and fridge, both empty with doors standing open. They must have been cleaned out at some point. Stainless steel benches, large commercial oven and dishwasher and a huge dry goods storeroom led out through a back door to a further room with commercial laundry equipment. Ayla was surprised the equipment hadn't been sold, but perhaps the bank took over quickly and kept it together, hoping to achieve a better price intact.

She turned around in the kitchen again, noting plateware, cooking utensils and cutlery were neatly stacked away. Stepping over to the large stainless steel sink she turned on the tap. It spluttered, then water gushed out, cold and clear. Ayla wondered for a moment at the water source, then remembered it all came from the little creek behind the building that continued on past the house. It was spring fed, fast and clear. Without power, she didn't expect the hot water tap to yield anything but turned it on for a moment anyway. Looking again at the enormous commercial stove and ovens, she noted the gas elements on top. Taking a breath, heart fluttering, she stepped out to the laundry, then to an area behind it. There was a large natural gas tank hidden behind a vine covered trellis. Of course! Closer inspection revealed the gas was turned off, and although she was tempted to turn it on, she wouldn't risk it without having a plumber or builder check it out first.

She stepped back inside. This place still had potential, but her thoughts were not on its previous life as a tourist resort. She had something more granular in mind.

Taking Skye's hand they walked across the creek via a small footbridge, to the two cabins untouched by the fire. The door to the first one opened easily, but the stench had her stepping away from the door, hand covering her nose.

'Euww Mama. Stinky.' Skye shook her head then turned away. 'What smells so bad?'

'Hmm, I'm not sure. Stay here and I'll go in.' Ayla wrapped her scarf around her face, covering her nose and mouth, then entered the building. It was a mess. Animal and bird droppings everywhere, deep marks on the timber floors, curtains in the main living room torn to shreds. The door to the balcony was partly open, and Ayla could see the space had been used by possums and birds. The timber furniture was scratched and chipped and couches ruined. Upstairs, the loft bedroom was less damaged but the bed was beyond help. It needed work, cleaning mostly, walls painted and floors sanded back.

Downstairs again, she opened the bathroom door. It had been firmly closed and apart from a musty smell, was undamaged. The leadlight windows let in a soft light and while dusty and unkempt, the large corner spa tub seemed in good condition. 'Not a complete disaster,' she whispered. She closed all the doors and windows so further intrusion wasn't possible and stepped outside. Skye was sitting on the grass near the door playing a game with leaves and twigs.

'Want to have a look at the other one with me, Skye?' Ayla started up the hill, turning to check if Skye was following. Her daughter shook her head, not looking up from her game.

Opening the door to the second cabin, it was musty and smelled somewhat damp when she first walked in but had been closed securely and no wildlife had been inside. Upstairs she saw a mark on the ceiling on one side where water had come in, from a damaged section of roof. The rug beside the bed had been wet and was the source of the damp smell so she dragged it out to the balcony, locking it outside. Turning around, she could see this one had huge potential and didn't need a lot of work. Smiling, she let herself out and blinked for a moment in the bright sunlight.

Skye wasn't where she'd left her and Ayla felt her throat close up, calling out hoarsely, 'Skye! Skye! Where are you!' She ran back to where her daughter had been sitting, the twigs and leaves still there and looked around frantically. She can't have gone far, Ayla hadn't been out of sight for more than twenty minutes. Twenty minutes. Ayla sucked in her breath, calling again and again as she ran toward the main building, scanning anxiously from left to right as she went. No movement in the forest, perhaps she had gone back to the house to the toilet. But even as she thought it, she knew Skye would tell her first. And there were toilets inside the main building. Ayla ran across the footbridge and into the building, then through the kitchen. No sign of Skye, but she ran to the other end to the bathrooms, calling out as she did.

A splash of colour caught her eye through the open front door and Ayla increased her pace, almost knocking Skye over as she bounded down the front steps, her little girl standing at the bottom. Gathering her into her arms Ayla sat heavily on the bottom step, tears coursing down her cheeks as she hugged Skye tightly.

'Stop Mama, you're squishing me!' Skye pushed against her and Ayla relaxed her hold but wasn't willing to completely let go. 'You're crying Mama! Why are you crying?'

'I couldn't find you Skye, couldn't see you.' Ayla sniffed, then drew in a breath. 'Why did you wander off without telling me? You know you're supposed to tell me!' She knew her tone was sharp, but the fear of losing Skye seemed to push the words from her. Skye pulled away, beginning to cry and Ayla let out a breath. She was safe, they were both safe. She scooped her up again and wiped her eyes. "Don't cry Skye-baby, I was frightened when I couldn't see you. I'm not angry.' She rocked her until she stopped crying.

'I saw one of the chickens and I chased it, but then I couldn't see it anymore. I wanted to put it back with the others so the fox can't get it.'

'Really, there was a chicken up here?' Ayla looked around. It was possible one had escaped the carnage and was roosting away from the others. Skye nodded, her tear stained face serious.

'Come with me, I'll close all the doors up here, then we'll go and have a bath. We need to go to Barrington School to help plant the vegetable garden after lunch.' Ayla stood, feeling the rhythm of her heart slowing from its frantic pace in the minutes she couldn't find Skye. 'If we see the chicken we'll try to get it back with the others, okay?'

27

His students were excited about planting the vegetable garden with Ayla, but it quickly became clear that there were too many children and too few jobs to do. The older students, his class, were doing the planting and he was on the verge of sending the other students and teachers back to their class, until Ayla glanced across. She seemed to take in the situation quickly and called out to him.

'Mr Mac?' He moved closer to the garden bed, Ayla stood on the outside but Ruby, Sam and Bobby were kneeling in the garden, making holes with their trowels and planting. Skye and the rest of his class were handing the small seedlings to them.

He cocked an eyebrow at Ayla. 'Yes, Ayla.'

'We could really use some signage at the end of each row, with the names of the plants and perhaps a picture.' She smiled as she spoke, nodding toward the younger students trying to crowd in and help.

'Excellent idea Ayla.' Turning, he clapped his hands,

gaining the attention of students and teachers. 'We need some signs made, for the end of the rows, with pictures and names. Who can help with that?' Hands flew up and Mrs Brown took her class to the library to gather drawing materials and make a start, while the middle grade class discussed how to attach the signs to the garden bed, before heading to their classroom to work on their project.

Most of the seeds and small plants were in place before the other students returned, and within minutes the garden was finished. He sent Billie Murray to ring the bell, parents were beginning to arrive outside the gate. Ruby, Bobby and Sam were covered in soil, but they'd changed out of their uniforms before they began. He directed them to wash their hands at the outside tap, and smiled as Skye went with them, followed by Ayla.

A few parents walked over to have a look, including Jim Fraser, Drum Murray and Melanie Evans. Sam Fraser rushed to his father's side, grinning. 'We've planted them in rows, see Dad, and the little kids made the signs here.' He was flushed, and proud of his handiwork. 'Ayla gave us seeds and bulbs which we've put between rows, to help attract the bees. We've got lavender over here, and even a few sunflowers at the northern end.'

'Good work son.' Jim glanced at Ayla, 'It's a good project. Practical as well as theoretical.' Alex watched the interaction closely.

Ayla smiled at Jim, then looked at Sam and the older students that had yet to leave. 'We're not quite done yet. Who knows what we still need to do?'

Ruby raised her hand, but Sam spoke first. 'Water them. We need to water them in now, and again on Monday.' He looked at his father for confirmation, receiving a very slight nod. 'And every other day unless we get rain.'

Clapping her hands Ayla beamed. 'That's right Sam. Is there a hose we can we use from the tap over there? Or is it buckets for today?'

Alex stepped toward her. 'Buckets for today. Boys, run over to the storage shed and get two plastic buckets out please.' Turning back to Ayla, he added, 'I'll pick up a length of hose on the weekend.'

Leaving Jim and Ayla to supervise the watering, he walked across to the school gate. Most students had already left, but a couple of parents were chatting by their cars. He waved to them and walked back to the garden area, saying goodbye to Drum and Billie Murray as he did. Melanie Evans and Tiffany were chatting with Jim and Ayla, while Ruby and Sam handled the watering.

'Well that seems to be it.' He grinned at Ayla. 'Let's hope we get some growth soon. I have a feeling these guys will be monitoring it closely.'

Picking up the large wicker basket she'd brought the seeds and bulbs in, Ayla said goodbye, thanking the parents for their help, paying particular attention to Ruby and Sam. He watched as Skye tugged on her hand. 'I'm hot, Mama. Ice-cream?' He loved the way she looked guilelessly up at her mother, wrinkling her cute little nose slightly.

'Alright Skye. We've had a big day and I need to get fuel. We'll go to Nadia and Frank's and yes, you've been such a big help, you may have an ice-cream.' Glancing at Jim, Melanie and Alex, she raised her eyebrows. 'Perhaps I can buy an ice-cream for the other hard workers today?' Did he imagine it, or did Ayla's eyes linger on him?

Sam looked quickly at his father, who glanced at his son, seemed about to say no, then nodded. 'I need to pick our mail up from the general store, we'll get ice-cream.' He clapped his hand on his son's shoulder. 'But Ayla, you're not paying. Sam has pocket money.'

'We'll meet you there.' Melanie took Tiffany's hand. 'I bet you don't have any pocket money?' She laughed as Tiffany shook her head.

'Alright Ayla, we'll come to the store too, but we need to lock up first.' Alex began to walk toward the administration building but stopped when Ayla called his name.

'Alex! May Ruby come with us? You can meet us there.' Ayla handed the basket to Ruby and picked up the extra shirts she had brought, in case any of the kids had forgotten to bring one.

'Okay Ruby, go with Ayla. I'll see you there in a few minutes.' As he spoke he saw a quick look pass between Sam and Ruby. A look and a smile. Oh yeah, Sam has it bad. And maybe Ruby has interest too? Something to keep an eye on.

28

If bees only gathered nectar from perfect flowers, they wouldn't be able to make even a single drop of honey. **Matshona Dhliwayo**

Skye bounced up and down in her seat chanting, 'Ice-cream! Ice-cream!' as Ayla drove around to the store. Ruby giggled and asked Skye what her favourite ice-cream was.

Jim and Melanie pulled into the car park beside her and Skye happily ran into the store with the bigger kids to choose her treat. Ayla strolled in with the others and they chatted with Nadia while the kids opened and closed the lid of the ice-cream display.

'Sam! Stop opening the lid. Wait until everyone has decided, then get them out.' Jim spoke brusquely and they quietened for a moment, before noisily discussing their options again. Ayla looked at him, and he gave her a lop-sided smile. 'My bark is worse than my bite. But with four big lads, I need to be loud sometimes.' Looking at Sam, he sighed. 'At least he still listens, not so much with my older boys now.'

Melanie laughed. 'Tiffany is nine going on fifteen. I think boys are easier Jim.' Their chuckles included Ayla and she looked over at Skye, just as eagerly standing on tiptoes to see into the display, until Ruby picked her up and almost sat her on top of it. Ayla looked quickly at Nadia, about to protest, but she just shook her head. 'No harm, Ayla, they're having fun.'

The teacher's car pulled into the car park, and right behind it the little mail jeep with the Australia Post contractor sticker on the doors. Ayla's heart sank. She was doing so well with these people, please don't let the mail lady make a scene and spoil it for her and Skye today.

'Oh good, Joyce's here. She'll have the mail.' As Jim spoke the children arrived at the counter and Ayla whipped out her card to pay for the ice-creams. Sam pulled a grubby wallet from his pocket, but Ayla raised her hand to stop him. She turned to Jim. 'Please let me get these. The raised garden was Sam's idea and he and a few others have worked really hard to get it together. It's a small token of my appreciation. Very small.'

Roughing his son's hair with his hand, Jim nodded. 'Say thank you to Ayla.' The children chorused thank you as Alex stepped inside and they rushed past him to the picnic table outside to unwrap their treats. Ayla was surprised when Jim spoke quietly to her. 'He's a good lad but hasn't been very interested in school. Seeing him excited these last few weeks has been because of you Ayla, and your bee project. Thank you.' He then stepped to the door, taking the heavy mail bag from Joyce and following her inside. The woman glared at Ayla as she came in.

Melanie led Ayla and Alex outside and they sat at the end of the picnic table, chatting with the kids. Jim joined them, a few envelopes in his hand, as they talked quietly, discussing the recent rain and the height of the rivers around town. Ayla just listened, happy to be in their company, feeling a part of the community.

The spell was broken when Joyce Wilson came outside, walking toward them with her signature rolling gait. Probably a bad hip, Ayla thought to herself. Maybe she has pain and that's why she's always so miserable and negative.

'You!' Joyce stood in front of Ayla, hands on hips, legs apart, looking ready for a confrontation.

Ayla took a deep breath, conscious they were all watching her.

'What is it, Joyce?' She kept her voice even, although she really wanted to wipe the expression off the woman's face. From the corner of her eye, she noticed Ruby take Skye inside, ostensibly to wash her hands and face. She was grateful. Skye didn't need to hear anything this woman said.

'You'll be gone from up there soon enough,' she jerked her head towards the mountains, 'Ben Evans just told me the new owner intends to live there. You'll have to go, and good riddance to the likes of you!'

Alex tensed beside her, and Melanie looked like she was about to speak up, but Ayla touched her arm softly. 'I heard that too. That the owner wants to live there, develop the place.' She sensed the teacher looking at her, but she was focussed on the angry, unhappy woman standing in front of her. Jim looked uncomfortable and rose.

'Wait Jim.' Ayla smiled at him. 'You might want to hear this too.' He sat down. Nadia and Frank appeared now, Nadia looking anxious.

'I know about the new owner, and their plans, Joyce. And it doesn't bother me in the slightest.' Ayla was enjoying the look of confusion on the woman's face.

Joyce was belligerent, rocking slightly on her heels. 'Well, I hope you've got your bags packed and somewhere to go, my girl. You and your brat!' Her words were angry, and ugly. The teacher moved, Ayla could feel his tension. She stopped him with a quick shake of her head.

Maintaining her composure, she spoke again. 'The reason I know this, Joyce, is because I am the new owner. The contract has settled. I was able to move in when it was unconditional a couple of months ago.' For a moment she was tempted to add she was setting up a nudist commune, and as funny as it would be to see the woman's expression, she controlled herself. She didn't want Jim or Melanie, or the teacher, to take it the wrong way.

'You?' Joyce almost spat the words at her.

'Yes. Me.'

Shock registered on Joyce's face, and she stomped back into the store without another word. Melanie grinned and Nadia clapped. 'I knew it. I told Frank two days ago I thought it was yours. Debbie at the café told me about your huge Instagram following, and I put two and two together. Well done! And welcome!' She followed Joyce into the store, just as Ruby and Skye came out.

Frank stood, a sheepish smile on his face. 'I'm happy to hear this Ayla. And I'm sorry I got caught up,' he nodded toward the door of the store, 'in all that nonsense.' He entered the store too, and Ayla was relieved he'd apologised. She glanced at Jim.

'Well I'll be! I wondered.' He held out his hand, and she placed hers in it, laughing aloud as he pumped it up and down. 'So we're neighbours. Good. I'll need to talk to you about fire breaks before the really hot weather hits us.' She nodded, grinning madly. Skye giggled and climbed onto her lap.

Finally, she turned to the teacher. He laughed. Ruby was looking from her father with Sam hovering beside her. Alex spoke. 'So you'll be settling here then Ayla?' He looked like the cat that got the cream. She nodded happily. 'Excellent. Isn't that good news Ruby?' Standing, he placed his hand on Ruby's shoulder. 'We'll see you soon then Ayla. You and Skye.' He turned and pumped Jim's hand. 'Thanks for your help at school this week Jim.' She watched as he walked to his car, followed by Jim and Sam to theirs, all waving as they drove out.

Melanie's face said it all. 'You knew, didn't you Melanie? Because of Ben?' Ayla stood, Skye had taken the ice-cream wrappers to the trash can with Tiffany.

'I did, but only a couple of days ago. Welcome to Barrington.' The smaller woman threw her arms around Ayla hugging her fiercely. 'We need more people like you Ayla, and Skye, and I'm really happy you're staying.'

Ayla knew she was smiling, couldn't help herself. A bubble of happiness rose from somewhere deep within her and she hugged Melanie back, her voice almost breaking with emotion. 'Thank you. Thank you Melanie.' A noise from Skye caught their attention. She was clapping her hands and giggling, her mad curls bouncing on her shoulders.

29

Alex thought about Ayla as he drove home. He wondered how she had been able to purchase the property, how she financed it. And he wondered what her plans for it might be. Ruby echoed his thoughts as he drove, and he admitted he really didn't know much about her. How she supported herself and Skye. Her bohemian clothes, relaxed manner and old kombi van had led him to believe she was only just making ends meet. He had judged her as such, and the thought now embarrassed him. He recalled how savvy she was with her invoicing system. He wasn't on social media himself, so had no real knowledge of her possible *influencer* status, that Nadia had mentioned. So now he had questions, but really, was it any of his business? Shaking his head, he parked outside their house.

'I'll check the water trough for the horses Dad, I'm already out of uniform.' Ruby scrambled out of the car and jogged across to the horse paddock, both horses already walking towards the fence. Alex lifted his satchel from the back seat, then sighed as he retrieved Ruby's back pack too. He almost called her to fetch it herself, then remembered how hard she had worked on the garden this afternoon. How hard she had worked on the whole bee project. Once inside he changed into shorts and a tee shirt, pulled a beer from the fridge, and sat on the porch in the shade, watching Ruby with the horses. In the distance he heard his phone ring, he'd left it on the kitchen table. Taking another sip of beer, he strolled inside. The phone had stopped ringing, he thought it might have been Ayla. Hoped it had been Ayla, but Robbie Stewart's number flashed up at him.

He called the number back, still sipping his beer. Nik answered the phone. 'Hi Alex, I saw your car go by and hoped I'd given you enough time to get inside. Busy week for you?'

'It has been Nik. Busy but good.' He paused, waiting for Nik to tell him why she'd called.

'Would you and Ruby like to come for dinner tomorrow night? Just a barbecue. Lucy wants to bake something special for dessert, I thought Ruby might like to help her.' He smiled as he listened. Dinner tomorrow night with friends sounded perfect.

'That will be lovely Nik. What can we bring?' Alex strolled to the fridge, the phone to his ear, checking to see what supplies they might need.

'Nothing Alex. Just yourselves.' Her voice grew faint, she'd turned away from the phone to speak to someone. 'Hold on Alex, Lucy just asked if Ruby could come earlier in the afternoon on Brute and stay overnight? There's a movie Lucy wants to watch with her.'

'I'm sure she'll want to do that, but she's outside with the horses. I'll get her to message you when she comes in.' He paused. 'Thank you Nik, I'm looking forward to it.'

Putting the phone down he glanced out the window. Ruby was brushing Brute. She was so happy here, maybe tomorrow night would be a good time to ask Robbie if he had interest in subdividing the house and a horse paddock, Alex would love to buy it and really put down roots.

He was on his second beer when Ruby came inside. Flushed and grubby, she was as happy as he'd ever seen her.

'Home made pizzas tonight Rubes, we need to do some grocery shopping tomorrow. And a shower first please, you smell like potting mix,' he leaned toward her, 'and horses.'

'Pizza is great, I'll help you.' She dashed off, but he called after her.

'Ruby!' She skidded back into the room, her socks sliding on the polished timber floor. 'We've been invited to dinner at Nicole and Robbie's tomorrow. I said yes. Lucy wants you to ride over in the afternoon, after homework, and stay the night.'

Ruby looked him for a moment then began laughing, so loud and long that he was laughing with her, although he had no idea why. Finally, she wiped tears from her eyes. 'Daa-ad! Lucy said *after homework*?' she giggled again. 'You're such a *teacher!*'

He stood up, putting an arm around her. 'Okay smarty pants, you've got me. The *after homework* was my addition. But tell me, do you want to? Ride over, have dinner? Cook dessert with Lucy, and Nik said something about a movie too, then stay the night?'

'Yee-ess. It's a no-brainer Dad.' She turned, walking from the room. Then poked her head back around the corner, trying to compose her face into a serious expression. 'After I've finished my homework, of course.' She ran off, giggling.

He shook his head but found himself grinning. Moments like these, laughing together, teasing each other, he'd cherish for the rest of his life. He loved her developing sense of humour. And he'd take teasing over sullen silence any day. Reaching into the freezer, he withdrew two pizza bases, then turned the oven on.

* * *

'Best. Dessert. Ever.' Alex leaned back, patting his still-flat stomach. 'I may have to undo my top button.'

'Eeuw! Dad!' Ruby made a face, but not before he saw her exchange a happy glance with Lucy. The girls had made a triple chocolate cheesecake and served it with fresh cream and vanilla bean ice cream. They'd already had barbecue meats and salad and Alex was grateful he'd asked for a small dessert serving, it was really rich. Harry, in contrast, had devoured a second serve.

Nicole began clearing the dishes, the girls had gone to another room to watch their movie, and Alex stood up to help her. Nicole and Alex washed up the items that wouldn't fit in the dishwasher, while Robbie cleaned the barbecue and Harry left the room, mumbling something about checking the horses and dogs.

They sat on the top veranda, talking quietly and gazing across the paddocks to the shadow of the mountains beyond. There was a half moon and the rains had left the landscape lush and green.

'Another glass of wine mate?' Robbie reached across, the bottle of red wine in his hand.

'No thanks, any more and I'll have to camp here for the night or walk home. I don't think I could fit anything in anyway, food or drink. I'm pleasantly full.' Alex leaned back in his chair comfortably, as Robbie poured the last of the bottle into Nicole's glass.

'You're not doing me any favours here Alex.' Nicole sipped from her glass. 'I'll need a designated walker just to get to the bedroom, I've had more than my share of wine tonight.'

'I'm your designated walker love. Just enjoy it.' Robbie looked at Nicole with such affection that Alex wondered if he should leave now, but he still hadn't spoken to them about the house.

Leaning forward, he cleared his throat. Robbie and Nicole looked at him expectantly. 'You know that Ruby and I are really happy here. Settled in your house across the way. With the horses, and you know, close enough to visit Lucy by herself.' He knew he was rambling but could see Nicole was nodding and smiling. Robbie looked like he was about to speak, but Alex held his hand up, stilling him for a moment. 'I want to ask you something. Well, to consider something.'

Robbie leaned forward to. 'What is it Alex?'

'I'd like to make you an offer. On the house, and the paddock for the horses. We'd like to stay here, at least until Ruby finishes school, but longer I think. It feels like home.' He knew he was rambling again, but in the same moment sensed Robbie had pulled back, and now he wondered if he should have brought it up at all.

'You want to buy my place?' Robbie looked at Nicole, who had set her glass down on the table. They turned in unison at a noise behind them. Harry stood in the open balcony doors. He looked from his father to Alex, than back to his father. He seemed about to speak, but Robbie got in first.

'We're happy you love it here Alex. We love having you here, looking after the place for us.' He looked up at Harry, giving him a slight nod, before turning back to Alex. 'But the house is not for sale. I built it for my family when Harry was born. It will be Harry's one day, when he's ready, for his family. I'm sorry Alex.'

Disappointed, Alex nodded. 'Of course. I understand. I knew you lived there before, but I didn't realise the history. Your attachment.' He stood, held his hand out to Harry, who shook it heartily. 'And it's your inheritance Harry, that's lovely.'

Robbie stood too and shook his hand in turn. Then Nicole stepped over and gave him a quick hug. 'You've become a part of the community in the two years you've been here Alex. You and Ruby. And we love having you so close.' She looked at Robbie, for confirmation Alex thought.

Robbie spoke quickly. 'We do mate. And Harry's in no hurry to move in there.' Robbie playfully tapped his son on the shoulder. 'He's on too much of a good thing over here. Meals, laundry, family.'

'It was an idea. I thought I'd bring it up. But I'm in no hurry to move out, although I'd rather own than pay rent now I've decided to stay.' Despite the conversation not going the way he'd hoped, he was relieved he knew where he stood.

'Actually, we should thank you Alex.' Nicole was now at Robbie's side, holding his hand.

'Really. Why?' He sensed a story.

'Well, Robbie and I had been, um, seeing each other for a while. And he and Harry were having a lot of meals here, you know, helping with the renovations. I wanted to ask them to move in but could never bring myself to say it.' Alex watched Robbie put an arm around Nicole, bringing her closer to his side.

Robbie continued the story. 'Then the Education Department told the school community the new Principal was coming with his daughter, and they wanted room for a couple of horses. The original school master's cottage is tiny, but the previous principal had no family left at home, just he and his wife. So, we had to find a property to secure you in the job.' Robbie kissed the top of Nicole's head. He continued, speaking more quietly, making Nicole dig him playfully in the ribs. 'I desperately wanted to make a home with Nik and knew she wouldn't leave the courthouse. Your imminent arrival was just the opportunity I needed to put it to her.' He laughed.

'So we discussed it then. Harry wasn't ready to live in the house himself. We offered it to the Education Department as your rental, with a paddock for horses as you'd requested.' Nicole reached out, touching Alex's hand. 'Little did we know how well it would work out. Lucy and Ruby are great mates, and we've all become friends.' She sighed happily, then winked at Robbie. 'And it moved us to discuss the thing we'd each been thinking.'

'Great story. I'm happy our arrival drove you to move in here Robbie. It looks like that's working out well for you.' Alex grinned.

'And for me.' Harry nudged his father with his shoulder. 'Much better meals over here. There's only so much steak and potato a man can eat. You know how it is.' He gave Nicole a warm look. 'And Nik offers a same day fluff and fold laundry service, so I'm not moving out any time soon!'

Nicole swatted him with her hand, but the genuine affection Harry gave her was obvious and warmed Alex's heart. He'd seen Harry with Lucy and Ruby often enough to know he was a fun big brother too.

He said his goodbyes and looked in on Ruby, watching the movie with Lucy. It was the original Man from Snowy River movie; he recognised the music. She blew him a kiss and he left.

Driving home he thought about his situation. He was disappointed the house would never be his but felt firm in his decision to stay in the area, which means he needs to buy a home of his own in the next year or so. He'd start looking around in the Christmas break, speak to Ben Evans, see what was available. He was in no real hurry.

30

We all share a common issue. No bees, No life. Save the Bees Australia aims to empower others to create change in their world. Bees and humanity face a major challenge from insecticides, herbicides, industrial-scale monoculture food farming and habitat fragmentation. Together we can tackle these issues and Save the Bees. www.beethecure.com.au

The weekend passed quickly, with Ayla spending early mornings and evenings on her plans for the property. Her ownership was no longer a secret and she wanted to clarify her ideas. Now that she had taken a good look at the remaining buildings, her concept had grown and diversified.

Remembering how little she had when Skye was born, after several years travelling the world, and working just enough to get by, making plans for this property still amazed her. But hard work, passion and an intuitive flair for marketing was reaping rewards and she knew she was in the one percent of working adults able to make a living doing what they love. The time had come for her to make some decisions for herself, Skye and the future of the property. A wrong decision now could quickly undo the last few years of success.

Speaking to her friend at Save the Bees Australia, while Skye napped on Sunday afternoon, helped clarify her thinking and she was about to call Nicole and Robbie when she heard a vehicle outside. Walking out, the phone still in her hand, she watched a dusty Landcruiser park behind her Kombi. Jim Fraser stepped out, along with Sam and two older lads. Ayla walked toward him. 'Hi Jim, Hi Sam. When you said we need to talk about fire breaks, I didn't think you meant this soon!'

'Ayla, hello. Sorry to drop in unannounced. It would be good to have your phone number, we're your nearest neighbours.' He took his hat off as Ayla smiled her acknowledgement. 'But I wanted to bring my older lads over to meet you. And apologise.' He beckoned his sons forward. 'This is Bill, he's my eldest and this is Neil.'

They looked like teenagers, maybe eighteen and nineteen at most, tall and lean in jeans, boots and tee shirts. Both looked a bit sheepish but held out their hands in turn to shake hers. She was as tall as them and shook their hands, while saying, 'Hello Bill, nice to meet you Neil.'

Bill cleared his throat before speaking. Jim stood just out of his son's line of vision, eyes twinkling when Ayla glanced his way. 'We'd just like to say, er, sorry. Neil and me. For, er, watching you at the river that day. We should have turned away, um, more quickly.' He looked at his brother for support.

Neil, his face red with embarrassment. 'Yes, we're sorry Ayla.' Jim cleared his throat, then nudged Neil. 'We're also sorry for, um, for telling people. Well, for telling Joyce anyway, what we saw.'

Ayla waited, to see if they had anything further to offer. Sam had wandered over to the stables but returned now. 'Dad said we're to help you. You know, do some work for you here.'

Taken aback, Ayla looked at Sam and his brothers, then at Jim. 'Oh! Well, er thanks. Um, that's not necessary.' She paused, smiling at the boys for the first time, noting the instant relief on their faces, 'But I really appreciate meeting you and thank you for your apology.'

'As you're staying Ayla, there will be plenty to do around here I'm sure, and we will talk about those firebreaks soon. If you agree, we can take care of your side of the ridge when we do our side.' Jim waved his arm, indicating the general direction of the work. 'The previous owners didn't take the right precautions, believing they were being environmentally conscious, but sadly this approach left fuel building up for years and when the fire came through, hot and fast, there was no time to save all their buildings.' Ayla nodded as he spoke. She knew the dangers too, and in this area at the edge of state and national forest, firebreaks were necessary.

'Thanks Jim. I will take you up on that, helping with the fire breaks. My knowledge is limited, and I appreciate your experience.' She laughed then, 'And the manpower and equipment. So yes, I'll gladly accept help for this.' She turned to the boys. 'But as to any debt you feel you owe me, consider it expunged.' Bill blinked at her, clearly not understanding her meaning. More quietly she added, 'There is no debt. You weren't deliberately seeking me out that day at the river, and I know you weren't there long. And I also understand that in the telling of what you saw, at a property bordering your own, you were concerned with who might be in the area.' She knew she was letting them off, but now she'd met them, she realised there was no malice in their actions, that day or any day after.

'Thank you Ayla.' Neil spoke first, but then Bill echoed his words. 'Thank you Ayla.' As he spoke Skye opened the front door and stepped out, her hair a curly mess, a soft toy under one arm, rubbing her eyes with the back of her hand. When she saw the men, she hesitated, until she caught sight of Sam.

'Sam!' She ran out to the garden gate, climbing on to the bottom rail. 'It's Sam, Mama!'

Ayla picked her up and sat her on top of the gate, holding her steady as she did. Sam had waved at Skye but didn't speak. Possibly embarrassed in front of his brothers. 'Would you and your,' she was about to say boys, 'men like some afternoon tea? I have banana bread freshly made.'

Skye nodded vigorously. 'I'd like banana bread please Mama.'

'That would be lovely Ayla, if we're not interrupting too much, thank you.' Jim waited while Ayla opened the gate.

'It's cool here on the veranda, if you don't mind being casual. Skye and I usually sit on the edge and dangle our legs over.' Ayla took Skye inside to get the banana bread while Jim and his lads arranged themselves in the shade. She returned with home-made lemon and honey iced tea, the banana bread, an assortment of cups and glasses and paper napkins.

They chatted about the property while they ate, Jim explained where the fence line between their properties were. He said he maintained it, to keep his cattle on his side, but if ever she found any on her side, she should let him know. The beehives in the garden, only a few metres away, hummed with activity. She'd pointed out the box with the colony she'd rescued from the school to Sam. He'd stepped a bit closer for a look but stopped when the bees began flying near him.

Skye finished her drink and banana bread and asked if she should lock the chickens in.

'It's a bit early Skye but go and count them. If they're all inside you can close the door, I'll check it later.'

Turning to Sam, Skye explained, 'The bad fox killed some chickens because we didn't lock them in. Now we have to 'member to do it every day.'

'Really? Well, I'll come with you and see how many are there.' Sam followed Skye through the garden gate, to the back of the stables.

'A fox Ayla? Not wild dogs?' Jim stood, placing his empty glass by the jug. 'We've had them over our side. Pests really, they'll take down a newborn calf if we don't watch out.'

'No. Definitely a fox, quite large, I saw it two nights ago.' She decided not to mention the pregnant tingo and pups that had been hanging around. They looked half starved. It was her responsibility to keep the chickens safe. 'It killed some of the chickens the night the bridge was impassable, we stayed in town. But a few of them were quite resilient and kept out of reach, I think.' She chuckled.

Skye and Sam came back, and Jim thanked Ayla for afternoon tea. He handed her his phone. 'Can you put your number in for me please? And I'll send you a message with mine and the home phone number. Julie's away this weekend, her Mum's not well so she's up in Walcha helping her dad. But when she's back, we'll have you over for tea, she's keen to meet you.'

'Thank you Jim, we'd like that.' The boys said goodbye and

climbed into the vehicle. Ayla picked Skye up and held her on her hip as Jim opened the car door. 'And thank you Jim, for bringing your sons to meet me. Now, when we catch up, all the awkwardness has been dealt with.' She watched him get into the vehicle and start it, rolling the window down as he did. 'But I will continue to swim in the river on *my* land, and I prefer to do that clothes-free.' She lifted her chin as she spoke, knowing her tone was somewhat defiant.

Jim looked surprised at her words but didn't comment, glancing instead at Bill in the passenger seat. Bill blushed. Skye and Ayla waved as they drove out. She was heartened by Jim's acceptance. But living next door to the property with tourists coming and going for about thirty years, he was obviously more worldly than some in the area. Unlike Joyce Wilson. She also recognised that he wanted to ensure fire safety, not just for her property, but for his own. A hot fire through her forest could continue to his own farm, burning fences, trees and grass as it went. He was ensuring good dialogue from the beginning. Smart man. But she chuckled as she thought it.

31

With Ruby not due home until lunch time, Alex took the opportunity to drive into town for coffee. And maybe breakfast. The coffee shop was busy, and he glanced around, seeking an empty table. Tourists mostly, but a few locals. He had almost decided to just get a takeaway coffee and pick up a bacon and egg roll from the general store when he heard his name called.

'Alex. Join us!' He glanced around again, then saw Melanie waving from a table near the back. She was sitting with her husband Ben. Alex waved, ordered a coffee, pointed at Melanie's table, then made his way over.

'Hi Melanie, Ben.' He greeted his friends with a handshake and smile. Alex pulled out a chair and sat opposite them. 'I don't want to intrude, happy to grab my coffee and go.'

'Mate. We've just ordered breakfast. Tiffany stayed at Billie Murray's last night, this is a treat.' Ben grinned. 'Join us, we don't often catch up outside of school.'

Alex watched the waitress serve two plates of eggs benedict to the next table and his stomach rumbled. 'I shouldn't be hungry, had a huge meal at Nik and Robbie's last night. But the eggs benedict looks delicious.' As he spoke, Debbie appeared with their coffee order.

'Here you go, coffee all round. You didn't order breakfast Alex; would you like something?' She looked toward the door, then back again. 'No Ruby today?'

'No Debbie, she stayed over with Lucy last night. Cooking breakfast just for myself didn't appeal, so I've come into town, and now I'm crashing Melanie and Ben's *date* breakfast.' He tried to look serious as he spoke.

'Ha! Not much chance of a romantic encounter in here this morning, way too noisy for that!' Debbie gave Ben's shoulder a light push, 'I'm sure they had date night last night. Now they're in recovery mode and Ben looks hungry.' She winked as she said hungry, drawing the word out, and Melanie laughed out loud.

'That's it Deb. The big man needs food.' Melanie was giggling and Alex laughed as Ben looked uncomfortable for a moment, before raising his eyebrows and leaning towards Melanie saying 'give us a kiss love' in a creepy voice. She batted him away, still giggling, and Alex sighed, 'eggs benedict please Debbie.' Debbie nodded, chuckling as she walked away.

'Alex. So funny. But I know you wouldn't say that at the school gate at home time.' Melanie raised an eyebrow, and he shook his head.

'You've got me there. I try to keep my dignity at school as much as possible.'

They chatted for a moment about the success of the bee project, and Ayla. Alex wanted to ask Ben if he knew more about her background, her business, but he sensed Ben wouldn't discuss what he knew, as she was a client, so he decided not to put him on the spot.

He sipped his coffee. 'This is good. Better than city coffee shops. Debbie runs a great little business.'

'She really does.' Melanie spoke, but he saw Ben nodding in affirmation. 'She worked for a few years in Sydney, then London.' She glanced around. 'But it's been extra busy lately, especially weekends. Lots of tourists around with the rivers running so high.'

'And how is your business, Ben? Real estate is buoyant too. Or so I'm hearing on the news.' Alex glanced at Ben, wondering if it was okay to discuss real estate when he wasn't at work.

'You're right Alex. A lot of people are moving to regional towns, especially when they're close to major cities. We've had steady growth for a few years, but it was skewed toward retirees. But now, with working remotely widely accepted by many firms, we're getting younger people. Professionals, some with young families. Small business owners, entrepreneurs. It's gone from being a buyers' market to a sellers' market. We're having trouble getting listings, and when we do they go quickly.' Ben spoke quietly, but Alex listened carefully. It might be harder to buy here than he thought.

'I need to make a time to come and see you, Ben. I asked Robbie Stewart last night if he was interested in selling his place to me, but it's a firm no. It'll be Harry's one day.' Alex paused as Debbie brought their meals. Smiling his thanks, he picked up his cutlery, continuing, 'But I've decided to stay. Ruby's settled and she has six years of High School yet, so I'm keen to buy, rather than keep renting. And I want a place big enough for our two horses.' He was about to say more, but

Melanie looked like she was bursting to say something. 'Melanie?'

'You're staying? Beyond the two-year contract? That's so great Alex!' She was almost bouncing in her chair and Alex watched, slightly amused, as Ben put a steadying hand on her leg.

'We've wondered if you'd stay Alex. A small country school is not for everyone. We were without a principal for two years before you came.' She looked at Ben. 'A lot of teachers left the system because of COVID, and it was hard to attract staff to a small rural school. Even before that we had a series of principals who only stayed for two or three years, depending on their contract, using it as a steppingstone to a larger school.' Ben's tone indicated his pleasure at the news he was staying, but Melanie's face said it all, she was beaming at him.

Alex swallowed, they were touching on familiar territory here. The last three years had been challenging for him too. He'd left the system, home schooled Ruby and undertaken remote curriculum development from home. He'd been thrilled when the rules changed, and the opportunity came up at Barrington. But it wasn't something he was willing to discuss, not everyone shared his views. 'I like it here. The community, the town. And Ruby loves it. She's settled. Being a single Dad, I need to take her into account. Running this school gives me plenty of time with Ruby. I don't know how I'd manage in a bigger school with a larger teaching cohort. My hours would be longer and that would impact the time I have for her.' He took another mouthful, thinking for a moment. Ben and Melanie continued their breakfast, waiting, as if they knew there was more he wanted to say.

'It's this place. It's a lifestyle. The school community is

strong, helping whenever I put the call out. I've never been supported so much in my role, and like I said, it helps me be better, I think. Better Dad. Better principal.' He could hear the emotion in his last few words, but he meant it. And somehow, he didn't mind Ben and Melanie knowing. He watched them nod.

'You're a good fit here Alex. You and Ruby. Right from the start.' Ben picked up his coffee, raising it slightly. Alex laughed, picked up his own coffee and 'chinked' with Ben, then Melanie.

'Thank you Ben, that means a lot. It's been great to see how well the parents have accepted changes to the curriculum, like the bee project for example. They trust my judgement.' He grinned sheepishly. 'At least, I hope that's what it means.'

'Ha ha. It does Alex.' Ben laughed. 'Choosing a project that the kids can relate to, in their own environment is brilliant though. I don't think any parents would be against that.'

Melanie set down her cutlery, then looked at Ben. She'd only eaten half her meal. Ben picked up her plate, replacing it with his empty one and proceeded to finish her breakfast. Alex chuckled. Such a married-couple thing to do.

'Just Joyce Wilson. But that was more about Ayla than the project.' Melanie frowned slightly. 'I like Ayla. I don't know her full story and Ben, if he knows,' she elbowed him in the ribs, 'isn't telling. But there are more people around like Joyce and I'd like to make sure we're supporting Ayla.' She looked at Ben again and Alex sensed an unspoken agreement passed between them. Alex watched her take a breath. 'I know from experience how stories can spread in small towns, whether there is any truth in them or not. I thought, at one time, that it would be easier to leave and start over somewhere else.' She looked at Ben, her love for him plain to see. 'But I stuck it out, and a few people rallied around, supported me. Ben, of course. And Angus and Rose Hamilton. And Debbie.' She drew another breath.

Alex nodded, although he didn't know what had happened to Melanie in the past, he sensed a deep hurt and felt privileged she was comfortable showing him her vulnerability.

'Thank you Melanie. For telling me that. And I agree about Ayla. I want her to continue the bee program at school, for the rest of the term at least. But more than that, I'd like her to settle here too.' He stopped, wondering if he should say any more, but Melanie had opened up, so he added. 'I'd like her to stay, because I want to get to know her. And I'd like Skye to start school next year and then they'll both be part of the school community. But you're right Melanie, some people may not be accepting of her differences. I personally think she has an enormous amount to offer the community.' He leaned back, picked up his coffee, realised it was empty and set it down again. He wondered if he'd said too much.

Ben spoke quietly. 'And I know, from experience,' he winked at Melanie, 'that friendship is the foundation of all these relationships. And Ayla is a smart girl, and business savvy, but she thinks outside the box and not everyone will understand her. Even us. But we don't have to understand. We just need to be her friends and support her. And that's all you're getting from me on the subject. Anything else needs to come from Ayla.'

32

It was the bumble bee and the butterfly who survived, not the dinosaur. **Meridel Le Sueur**

After Skye was settled for the night, Ayla made a few calls, thinking about Nicole's accommodation and her original idea to offer a haven for women in need. Ayla hadn't shared her plans for the resort with her new friends and now, getting to know the region better, her ideas had developed. She called her Aunt Susie in Sydney. Not an aunt really, but her godmother and her mum's best friend. Not just that, but a social worker, working with women's refuges, homeless shelters, food hubs and several related organisations. Ayla often wondered how she did it, always upbeat despite all she saw. But her aunt had told her many times that creating a better outcome for just one person made it worthwhile and inspired her to continue, often in the face of adversity. And Ayla knew she had touched many hundreds, possibly thousands, through the work she did, largely unnoticed and rarely remarked upon.

The conversation with her aunt was uplifting. Better than that, Ayla could tap into her network, offering Nicole's accommodation as a next step to, initially, a couple of women with children that were ready to leave a city women's shelter and were happy to head to a country town. She had set the wheels in motion and would call in to Nicole's on Monday to help her prepare. Her first guests would arrive in two weeks.

That done, she turned her attention to her own ideas. Her business at her old home in Victoria needed to be moved to Barrington, as she'd sold the property and the contract had settled in time for her to complete the contract in Barrington. Ayla had delayed moving her business up, as her production manager was settled in Victoria and wouldn't come north. But now Ayla had less than eight weeks to relocate her business. She had plans to develop her product range, all honey and beeswax based, and her meeting with Council confirmed that the commercial kitchen at the resort could be accredited for her purpose. With a couple of months to get the property ready, move her stock and equipment up and find some staff, even two or three part time, she was on schedule.

* * *

Ayla parked to one side of Nicole's house, again admiring the beautiful stonework of the building as she led Skye to the front door. The two dogs, Scout and Minnie, wandered along the veranda and Ayla no longer felt nervous around them, reaching down to pat Scout as Skye flung her arms around the younger dog's neck, before running along the veranda with Minnie trotting behind her.

Nicole opened the door before she could knock. 'Ayla, lovely, you have the best timing, I've just boiled the kettle.' She turned to Skye, now running back, the dog beside her. 'Would you like to come in for a biscuit Skye?'

Ayla watched, amused, as Skye thought about it. The biscuit must have been tempting but she shook her head, her fingers now lightly brushing Minnie's head, the dog sitting at her feet, tongue lolling. 'Can I stay out here and play with Minnie? Please?'

'Of course you may.' Nicole leant down, patting Minnie for a moment too. 'I think we'll have our morning tea out here on the veranda, then you can play with Minnie, and if you feel at all hungry, have a biscuit too.' Ayla laughed aloud as Skye nodded vigorously, before charging to the other end of the veranda and back, the dog behind her the whole time. Scout wandered across the front lawn and lay in the shade of the gnarly old golden ash tree.

'Ayla.' Nicole touched her shoulder lightly. 'You can wait out here too, if you like.' She tilted her head toward the rattan patio setting to the left of the front door. 'I'll bring out the teapot and biscuits, won't be a moment.'

'Thank you Nik.' Ayla chose a chair and leaning back she watched Skye scamper about on the lawn with the two dogs. Minnie had presented her with a grubby old tennis ball and Skye sat by Scout, one arm across her back, throwing the ball which Minnie bounded after, returning with it in her mouth then dropping it in Skye's lap. Skye laughed and clapped her hands each time, saying 'good girl Minnie-dog, good girl!'

Nicole returned with their tea things on a tray, pouring and making small talk as she did. Skye ran over, her eyes on the plate of biscuits. Ayla wondered if she should take her in to wash her hands before she took one, but Nicole laughed, handing Skye a biscuit, who broke a piece off and gave it to Minnie before running back to the shade of the tree. In an undertone she said to Ayla, 'You know her hands are all over the dogs, it won't make a scrap of difference if you wash them now.'

'You're right. She loves the dogs. I never thought we'd be *dog people,* but here we are.' She took a biscuit herself. 'Anzacs, yum. Did Lucy make these?'

'Do you think I don't bake, Ayla Forrest?' Nicole chuckled as she bit into one. 'But you're spot on. Lucy baked these yesterday.'

'You've taught her well.' Sipping her tea, Ayla was about to tell Nicole about Aunt Susie, and the prospective arrival of guests, but Nicole sighed, a small smile playing around her mouth as she watched Skye.

'The baking started when we left my ex-husband, Lucy's step-father. I was home schooling her; she had become so shy and introverted and wouldn't speak to anyone but me.' She took a deep breath and Ayla reached out, touching her friend's hand for a moment. 'I was recovering from that last brutal bashing and Lucy.... Well, Lucy had become good at staying hidden, making herself invisible. But that last time, he'd really hurt me, I was bleeding.' She touched the scar on the right side of her face and Ayla swallowed, emotion washing over her. Anger, outrage at what Nik and Lucy had been through, and admiration for their bravery. 'Lucy leapt from her hiding place behind my desk and threw, no, *hurled* a large candle in a glass jar at him. It hit his shoulder, didn't really hurt him, but at the same time she began to scream.' Nicole shivered. 'She screamed and screamed and didn't stop. He looked at her for a moment. I was terrified he'd hurt her, then he just turned and left the house. A neighbour arrived, she'd called the police and an ambulance, but Lucy, she just kept screaming. I held her, tried to comfort her, but my face was bleeding. Over both of us. It was deep. It was in that moment I made the promise. That we'd leave. That we'd never go through this again. I promised her I'd never let a man back into our lives, our home.' She wiped a tear from her cheek. 'But Robbie. And Harry. They helped us both heal. And Scout,' she glanced at the dog, who, upon hearing her name, got up and walked across, laying at Nicole's feet. 'Scout drew Lucy out from the shadows. The boys, this place, the horses.' She sighed again, then threw her head back and laughed.

'I really got off track then! But now you know it Ayla, the worst of it. But the best of it, apart from moving here, was the cooking. Like I said, I was home schooling her, and we spent a lot of time watching various shows together. Mostly renovation programs and cooking shows. A *lot* of cooking shows. And Lucy really lit up, watching them, talking about them. So, we began baking, trying to reproduce recipes we'd watched, and she loved it. But more than that, she was good at it. And it gave her confidence. By the time we moved here, she was baking without my help.' She leaned toward Ayla, her face now relaxed and happy. 'And it's a blessing we met Robbie and Harry. Not just for the obvious reasons, but all that cooking ...' she patted her flat tummy, 'could have been a disaster. But those men, they sure can put the baked goods away!' She laughed aloud and Ayla laughed with her, delighted Nik had found happiness and that Lucy had overcome some of her trauma. Ayla had always found her to be quiet, yet confident. Mature beyond her years too, but she was obviously happy and doted on Robbie and 'big brother' Harry. She'd heard Lucy call Robbie *Cowboy Dad* which had seemed cute and quirky, but she sensed Robbie had become a father figure Lucy could rely on.

'Thanks for sharing that Nik. You had mentioned the trauma before, and I wondered about the scar, if that's how you got it. You're a strong woman, and resilient, I admire that so much.' Taking another sip of tea she waved to Skye, who had now walked across to the horse paddock, where several had appeared near the fence. 'Stay on this side of the fence Skye!' She turned, waved, then climbed on to the bottom rail of the gate, reaching up to pat the nearest horse. Ayla waved back.

'Nik, I told you I'd put some thought into your accommodation here, in the house. My Aunt Susie, she's my godmother, is involved in social work and various programs in Sydney. We've spoken at length. I didn't want to tell you until I'd spoken to her, and she has two women who are ready to move from a women's refuge. They desperately need to free up the beds at the shelter, but she also needed to be sure she's sending women who *want* to come to the country, who want more than a refuge, but are ready to find a community and hopefully re-settle.'

Nik was beaming, but a tear slipped down her cheek, which she wiped away quickly. 'Really? Ayla that's perfect. Two women. That's brilliant. Do you know much about them? When will they be here?'

'I don't know much, but Aunt Susie has your number and email and she's going to brief you, as much as she can, later today. We're hoping they will travel together, they know each other, and arrive on the train in two weeks. I thought we could both go and meet the train; we'll need two cars. One has two children, one at primary school and a toddler. The other is younger and has a child about Skye's age ready to start school next year. That's all I know for now. I hope that's okay.'

Ayla stood. Skye was sitting on top of the gate now. 'Skye!' Her daughter turned and waved. 'Get down Skye! Come here please.' Ayla felt her chest tighten. There were several horses milling around at the fence, if Skye fell, she'd be under their hooves. She started to walk across, quickly, but not wanting to startle Skye or the horses. Then, seemingly from nowhere, Harry appeared. He was standing in the paddock with the horses, and reached out to Skye, lifting her into his arms. Ayla slowed down, watching, as he carried her from horse to horse, letting her pat each of them in turn. She couldn't hear what he was saying but Skye's happy giggles rang out clearly. Harry turned, saw Ayla, and raised his hand. She waved back, watched for another moment, then returned to Nicole.

'He's good with her. She'll be fine. He's a natural, like his father. Horses, dogs, children.' Nicole spoke with a quiet pride and Ayla clearly saw her love for Harry reflected in her eyes. Ayla watched Harry and Skye for another moment. Skye was on his shoulders now and he was cavorting across the lawn to them. Her breath caught for a moment. Harry? What did she really think of Harry?

33

Alex glanced at Ruby, before turning into their driveway. She hadn't said a word on the way home from school and she'd rebuffed several attempts to engage her in conversation. In fact, she'd been quiet all week, the only time she had become animated was when Ayla and Skye came on Monday afternoon and again today. Something had happened at school during the week, and he guessed it had to do with young Sam Fraser. He'd noticed Ruby glaring at him several times and she completely ignored him when Ayla took the class to check on the school garden. He also saw that Sam appeared confused by her enmity. Alex sighed. He felt a bit sorry for Sam. Most of the time women confused the heck out of him too. Like Ayla today. It was nothing she did, or said, but Alex felt she'd pulled back a bit, created a subtle distance between them. With students milling around he hadn't been able to talk to her much and wondered if he had only imagined it. But no, now that he thought about it, she had exuded her usual warmth to all the children but didn't appear to extend it to him. Not that he could say or do anything himself in the school environs. Skye had been her usual bubbly, friendly little self though. He told himself she was just being professional, ensuring no further gossip began, but in his heart he knew it was more than that. Disappointment clutched at his heart for a moment, then he rallied. Ruby's well-being was more important, and he needed to focus on her in the here and now.

Alex decided he'd wait for a bit, see if Ruby opened up, perhaps he could get her chatting while they prepared dinner, but she went straight to her room, and after little more than a minute or two was out again wearing shorts and tee shirt. He expected her to come to the kitchen for a snack, but she rushed outside, calling to him over her shoulder that she was checking the horses. While her anger wasn't directed at him, Alex knew she had something on her mind. Maybe she'd work through it herself.

He called out to Ruby an hour later, and she finally came inside. They made pizzas together; their usual Friday night meal and he asked her if she wanted to watch a couple of episodes of Ted Lasso on television. He thought she might say no, or ask to go to Lucy's, but she seemed a bit happier by the end of their meal and even offered to make some dessert to eat in the lounge.

'Let's get the dishes done first Ruby, I hate dealing with it in the morning, then we can relax.' Alex nudged her with his shoulder, and she smiled at him brightly, almost too brightly, and agreed.

As he handed her the last soapy plate to dry, she spoke. 'Dad, are dingos protected in this state?'

'I think so, why do you ask?' Alex frowned. He recalled they were protected on Fraser Island in Queensland, and in some areas of Victoria. But New South Wales? 'We should look that up, Rubes.'

'Can I have your phone Dad? Just to google.' She hung the tea towel on the rack and took his phone, tapping quickly. 'Oh! Dad, they're not protected in New South Wales.' She looked up at him, eyes swimming with tears. He took the phone she handed to him and read aloud *the dingo is the only native mammal that is not protected in New South Wales.*

'I didn't know that Ruby, but why is this upsetting you so much?' He waited quietly while she gathered her thoughts. He could see her struggling with emotion.

'The boys were talking about it at school. Killing wild dogs. But I think they really mean dingoes. Culling them, Sam said. His brothers have been shooting them at night. Sam and some of the other boys say they're a pest and they kill lambs and little calves and chickens and such.' She was sobbing now. 'But it's not right Dad. It's not right to kill them. Then they told me they shoot kangaroos too.'

Alex pulled her into his arms, rubbing her back as he spoke. 'We don't think it's right, but we're not farmers, Ruby. Kangaroos compete with their stock for grass, and if dingos are killing lambs and calves, then they're doing it to protect their livelihood.'

Ruby pulled, back, the phone still in her hand. She wiped her eyes with the back of her hand. 'Read this dad. It says here that dingoes are a predator of kangaroos, wallabies and rabbits. So, if they didn't shoot the dingoes there'd be less animals eating their pasture and crops. I'm going to tell Sam that.'

'There's more.' She was indignant now, flushed with passion for her subject. She tapped the phone, then read aloud, 'it says here only two percent of wild dogs killed are actually dogs. The remainder are dingoes according to DNA, behaviour and features. They are territorial top chain predators that assist the eco system by culling feral pigs, cats, rabbits and more. They mate for life and live in families rather than packs.' She looked up, eyes shining.

'That's a good counter-argument Ruby.' He was happy she was fact-checking and developing her own opinion. It might not be popular at school, or in the community generally, but he'd always encouraged her to stand by her beliefs.

He smiled as she continued. 'Sam says I'm a city slicker and I don't know anything about farming. He laughed when I said I'd like to be a horticulturist. It made me really mad Dad. Just because I'm from the city doesn't mean I can't be a horticulturist, or an apiarist like Ayla. You don't have to be born on a farm, do you?'

'You can be anything you want Ruby. I know you love it here, in this town, having a home with our own horses in the paddock. I didn't know you were thinking about making this a career choice, and I'm proud you're investigating options. It's called thinking outside the square.' Alex patted her on the back, relieved to see her nod in agreement.

'Thanks Dad.' Ruby opened the freezer, withdrawing a tub of double choc chip ice cream. Alex handed her two bowls and watched as she served up a few scoops for each of them.

Sam wouldn't see it coming. He chuckled.

34

---

*If you want to gather honey, don't kick over the beehive. **Abraham Lincoln***

itting up, heart pounding, Ayla checked her phone. Almost midnight, she'd only been in bed an hour, but something had drawn her from slumber. She held her breath, listening, sure a noise had woken her. Nothing. Getting out of bed, she used her phone to light her way across the hall to the other bedroom. Skye was sprawled sideways across the bed but sleeping deeply. Ayla gently moved her to the centre of the bed and pulled the blanket up, still listening as her bare feet whispered from the room to the kitchen. It was dark, just a sliver of moonlight. A shiver ran up her back. Something wasn't right, she could feel it.

Stepping out to the veranda she realised the night wasn't really silent. The creek was home to a frog orchestra and closer to the house cicadas were emitting a high-pitched whine. Standing for a moment, to allow the sounds to settle to a degree that she could recognise individual noises, she heard a dingo howl. Beyond the stables, but closer than the ridge. Further away, where the forest rose steeply, she heard an answering bark. She waited, perhaps the dingos had woken her.

About to head back to bed, the unmistakable sound of gunshots rang out. Two quick ones, a pause, then three more. Ayla drew her breath in sharply. It sounded close, on her property. Or possibly near her boundary with Jim Fraser. Moving into the house, Ayla closed and locked the front door, before checking on Skye again. She contemplated carrying her into the main bedroom, but she might wake, and it served no purpose. Ayla was now sure it was hunters. Either the Fraser lads or others who had come down from the State Forest area. She pictured the pregnant tingo and her pups. She hadn't seen her for more than a week, but she was close to whelping.

SUNLIGHT CREEPING THROUGH THE BLIND WOKE HER. SHE RUBBED the back of her hand across her eyes. Sleep had taken a while to return the night before, and she took a moment to stretch before standing. Barely out of bed, Skye ran in, her arms raised for a cuddle. 'Morning Mama!' Ayla picked her up, holding her warm little body close.

'I'm hungry Mama!' Skye wriggled, and Ayla set her down, watching with amusement as she ran across to her room. Ayla wrapped a sarong around her waist, leaving the singlet on that she had worn to bed. In the bathroom, she brushed her hair and tied it in a high ponytail, then wandered into the kitchen to put the jug on. She'd make herb tea, with honey. Skye reappeared, wearing denim shorts and her favourite pink tee shirt, the one with the pocket in the front.

'Want to collect the eggs now Mama! Eggs for breakfast.' She nodded as she spoke and Ayla chuckled to herself. They'd collect the eggs and she'd scramble them. Breakfast sorted.

They sat on the bench outside the front door, it was an old church pew, to pull their boots on. Holding Skye's hand, they walked to the garden gate. Ayla walked; Skye skipped. It was clear she had not woken in the night.

They found five eggs, enough for breakfast, and were carrying them back carefully when a distant rumble had Ayla looking along the driveway. She could clearly hear a vehicle approaching but couldn't see it. Turning, she realised the sound was coming from behind the house, on the other side of the creek. Placing the eggs in an upturned hat on the bench seat, she took Skye's hand and walked through the garden toward the back gate. She'd walked this way a few times, foraging for wild lemons, but the track was rough and steep. She knew it led into the state forest eventually, but anyone using it this close to the house was trespassing on her property. Glancing down at Skye, she wondered if she should have left her inside the house. No, they'd stay together. She held her hand firmly and walked to the gate, the sound of the vehicle in low gear driving over rough terrain seemed to echo around her. She held herself tall and straight, prepared for confrontation.

The vehicle appeared on the narrow track. An older model

white Landcruiser ute. She couldn't see the face of the driver, a man in a hat.

He stopped the vehicle, waved through the windscreen, opened the door and stepped out.

'Harry!' Ayla was astonished. Harry was the last person she expected to see driving through her property this early in the morning.

'Ayla!' He grinned, walking toward them. 'Hello Skye.'

'Hello Harry!' Ayla could see Skye was pleased to see him, but she was keeping her own thoughts to herself.

He took his hat off as he approached. Ayla didn't welcome him as warmly as she might have, still concerned with his appearance on her property, uninvited. 'What are you doing here Harry?'

She watched him stop and register the tone in her voice, his grin now reduced to a sheepish smile.

'Oh, yeah. I was with Bill and Neil Fraser overnight, culling dingos and 'roos.' He continued, seemingly more confident. 'They told me you were having a problem here too, with dingos. So, we've removed a few overnight.' He glanced at Skye, making sure Ayla knew he was choosing not to say *kill* or *shoot* for her daughter's benefit.

'So, the gunshots I heard around midnight, that was you?' She tried to keep her tone friendly, but she was seething inside.

'Yup, that was me, and the lads.' He was pleased with himself; thought he was doing her a favour.

'So hunting, shooting native animals, that's a thing you do often?' She couldn't hide her antipathy any longer.

'No, not often. Um, Dad's never been one for it.' He looked down at his boots for a moment, then up again. 'I got talking to Bill in the pub on Friday night, he said he'd been over here and met you, and, um, mentioned the chickens had been killed and well, I decided I'd come too.'

'Firstly, my chickens were killed by a fox. It's been lurking around at night ever since.' She watched his expression change. He had genuinely expected her to thank him. 'And yes, I've heard the dingos nearby, but they haven't bothered me here.' Her gaze moved to Skye, who had wandered across to the beehives. 'And Skye loves seeing the kangaroos and wallabies.' She looked him in the eyes now. 'Honestly Harry, I didn't expect you'd be running around at night like Rambo, shooting animals. The Fraser boys, well, I understand they might be protecting their stock. But you?' She shook her head.

'I'm sorry Ayla. It seemed like a good idea at the time.' Now he gazed back at her, moving closer to the fence where she stood with one arm on the top rail. 'If I'm honest, it was more about coming up here, seeing you.' He took a breath, and now Ayla understood. 'When Bill said, you know, at the pub, how gorgeous you are, well, I got annoyed. I knew he'd seen you before, at the river.' He added quickly, 'But he doesn't mention that, not since the first time really. I just, I don't know, I didn't like him thinking about you, living so close, and I just invited myself to come up for the hunt. You're right, it's not something I would normally do.' He scuffed the ground with his boot.

Ayla took a step back. He was young, she'd give him a break. But whatever earlier attraction she had felt for him had been erased. Not by his words, or even his actions, but by her realisation that he lacked the maturity she wanted in a partner, lover. His feelings for her were a crush, plain and simple, and she would make it clear, as gently as she could, that it was going nowhere. But to his credit, he was honest, and she wanted to ensure they could be friends.

'It's alright Harry. I understand. Why don't you drive around to the front of the house, just follow this track.' She pointed to the west. 'It will bring you right around.' She watched him nod, he seemed relieved. As he opened the car door, she called out. 'Harry?' He paused. 'Then come inside and have breakfast with us.' She flashed him a friendly smile and he grinned back.

'Thanks Ayla. I'm starving!' He started the vehicle and Ayla called to Skye, taking her by the hand, they walked back to the house.

She scrambled some eggs, fried up tomatoes and mushrooms and served it on home-baked toast. While she was cooking Harry asked if he could have a look at the damage to the back part of the house, and how she had repaired it.

Over breakfast Ayla talked to Harry about some of her plans for the place, and that she had already asked Robbie to quote on repairs and renovations to the other buildings. Robbie had organised for the electricity pole to be replaced, and with power reconnected to the main buildings she'd be able to run her business from there. She hadn't thought of doing anything to the house, initially, it was big enough for her and Skye.

'I can see that Ayla. But your repairs at the back aren't insulated. It's alright now with the warmer weather but come winter you may not be able to use the living area at all. 'I'll be here, helping Dad, if you give him the go-ahead. I can fix the back of the house, in my own time, using recycled materials, if you'll let me.' He took his empty plate, and Skye's, to the sink, began washing up. 'Lovely breakfast, thank you.'

'Let me speak to Robbie again, I was going to drop by tomorrow before I go to the school. It's a good idea. But Harry, I'll pay you for your work.' She nudged him with her shoulder, so he moved away from the sink, and she washed her own plate. He picked Skye up and swung her around, making her giggle.

'You'd best go now Harry. Are you going to tell Robbie and Nik about your, ah, hunting trip?'

Setting Skye down, Harry turned to her. 'Of course. I know I've stuffed things a bit with you Ayla, but I'm always honest. Too honest sometimes, I think.'

'You can never be too honest Harry. And I appreciate your friendship. I'm honest too, and you're a bit of a hunk Harry Stewart,' she chuckled as she spoke, 'but you're not on my romantic radar. You're definitely in my friend zone.'

'That's not a bad place to be Ayla. I'll take that.' He scooped Skye up again. 'Are we friends Miss Skye?' Ayla laughed as Skye clapped her hands, then gave Harry a noisy kiss on the cheek, nodding happily.

* * *

WORKING IN THE GARDEN LATER THAT MORNING, AYLA HAD AN odd sensation that something wasn't right. She looked toward the creek crossing, and up the track Harry had driven down earlier. Higher, in the sky, one of the eagles from the ridge to the west was circling. Perhaps that's all it was. She dug her shovel into the earth of her vegetable garden again, chuckling as Skye mimicked her with a smaller shovel. A shadow passed overhead, and she looked up. There was a second eagle now, circling with the first, their languid movements bringing them closer to the ground with each rotation. She stood, watching. It was fascinating to see them so close, their wingspan had to be more than two metres. Magnificent.

One of them circled higher for a moment, then drew its

wings into its side and plummeted toward the earth, it's trajectory only two or three hundred metres from her yard. Ayla, pointed it out to Skye and they watched, fascinated, as it seemed to break it's dive toward earth by turning its body, so its mighty feet were now extended downwards. It disappeared, hidden by the forest.

'Where did it go Mama?' Skye pointed to the second eagle, circling higher now, roughly over the location of the first one. The first one reappeared, something small and tan in its talons, it flapped its powerful wings, rising toward its mate, then flew west, a lifeless body dangling from its claws.

'What is it Mama? What did the eagle catch?'

Ayla drew a breath, her hand on Skye's shoulder. 'It looked like a dingo. One of the young ones I've seen here before.' She followed the eagle's flight, one had landed on the spot she knew their nest clung to the side of the ridge, the other soon joined it.

Picking up her shovel, she made a quick decision. 'Let's go and have a look up the track, where the eagle picked up the dingo.' Skye nodded, and they walked through the garden gate, to the creek. Ayla carried Skye across, then taking her hand, with the shovel still in her other hand, they walked along the steadily ascending track. In moments they were within a canopy of trees, the track rising and winding before them. Ayla knew it was an old logging track, cut into the side of the hill. On one side the trees and foliage grew from the ground several metres above their heads and on the other side the hill dropped away to a ravine with a creek at the bottom. The same creek they'd crossed near the house.

They turned a corner, and several crows were pecking at a carcass, lying on the edge of the track. 'Shoo! Shoo!' Ayla rushed at them, waving her arms and they took off, only to land a few metres away down the side of the hill. Stepping closer, Ayla saw it was a young dingo, half grown. Probably one of the two she'd seen in the last few weeks with the pregnant dingo.

'Euww, Mama!' Skye held her nose, shaking her head.

'I know Skye. I'm going to move it into the grass at the side here.' She picked the pup up with the shovel and laid it down in a grassy patch. It was dead, the crows had already opened its soft white belly with their vicious beaks. But that wasn't its only injury. A bullet had ripped right through its small chest and Ayla took a deep breath. Bloody Harry and the Fraser boys! They'd been right down into her property with their guns.

Standing, she was about to step back when she heard a small sound, a tiny whimpering. She peered into the under-growth. There was a large tree stump down a bit further, and signs of digging around its base. She wondered if it was the dingo's den. If it was injured, or cornered, it could attack and she began to back away, thinking of Skye, and her own fear of dogs.

The crows had gathered around the dingo pup's corpse again and she shooed them away, wondering if she should bury it, or let the crows have it as that was nature's way. Another group of crows had gathered a bit further up the track. What was the collective noun for crows? She smiled grimly, ah, yes, a *murder* of crows. Taking Skye's hand she walked toward the feasting birds, then stopped.

'Oh no!' It was the tingo, her body lifeless. She began to turn away, Skye kept waving her hands at the crows and was getting upset. Taking a last look, she saw that the tingo's belly was lean, although her nipples protruded. She'd whelped then. Ayla had no idea when, she'd seen her pregnant a week or more before. Turning away sadly, leaving the crows to their meal, they began to walk home. She glanced at the body of the pup as they drew closer, then heard something, a tiny whining noise, almost like a kitten, from the direction of the tree stump down the slope.

'Stand here Skye, I'm just going down to that old tree.' Skye looked uncertain but nodded. Ayla slid down the few metres to the tree stump on her backside, still carrying the shovel. She couldn't risk tumbling down to the ravine. Steadying herself against the old tree, she could see the trunk of the tree was there too, but completely overgrown with vines and other vegetation. It must have fallen, hit by lightning perhaps, many years ago. She knelt in the bare patch of dirt to one side of the stump and peered into a shallow depression, under the old tree trunk. She couldn't see anything, it was too dark, but she heard the whining noise again and hoped she'd found the tingo's home and not some other animal. She reached in, somewhat gingerly, and her hand touched fur. The animal was tiny, and she managed to get her hand around its small body, withdrawing it from the burrow. It was a dingo pup, but lifeless. She laid it gently beside her and reached in again. Her hand connected with another little body, but this one was warm, and moving. She withdrew it. A tiny pup. She knew it couldn't be much more than ten days old.

'Mama! Come back!' Skye's wails hurried Ayla along. 'I'm coming now Skye.' She reached in again, felt the back of the hole. Empty. Lifting the little pup, she gently slid it inside her singlet. It wriggled against her chest, and she chuckled. Taking the shovel, she crawl-climbed back up to the track where Skye stood. She was close to tears. Moving into the centre of the track Ayla knelt and opened the neck of her shirt for Skye to look down.

Skye clapped her hands, her face glowing. 'A little dog!'

'A little dingo.' Ayla stood. 'But Skye, he's been without its mother since late last night, so I'm not sure if he will survive. But let's take him home and see what we can do to help him.' Skye nodded and skipped ahead, down the track toward their house.

35

Monday arrived with a cool breeze coming down from the mountains, but by mid-morning the sun had appeared, and the wind softened. Most of the students had removed their jumpers and were keen to head out to the playground. Ayla was due any minute and Alex stayed in the classroom, setting up her easel and reorganising the desks.

He heard her kombi arrive and strolled out to the school gate. Ruby was there with a couple of younger kids. Ayla waved as she got out of the van, Skye climbing out behind her. Ayla reached back in, lifted a small rattan basket out and gave it to her daughter, before opening the back of the van. Alex nodded at Ruby, indicating she could run over and help Ayla, but he was fascinated by Skye. She walked across to him, carrying the little basket very carefully in her arms, like it was filled with something precious.

He opened the gate for her, and she beamed up at him. 'Hello Teacher. Mister Mac.' She held the basket out to show him. 'We've brought Bandit to meet you.' He leaned over to look in the basket, then raised his eyebrows, looking up just as Ayla appeared.

'Is that what I think it is?' It looked like a puppy, but something about its features made him wonder if it was a dingo pup. He reached in, patted the little dog gently. Its eyes were open, and it nuzzled at his hand.

'If you think it's a dingo pup, then you're absolutely right.' Ayla spoke firmly, making him feel she was ready for a confrontation. She wouldn't get one from him.

'Ruby!' He called to his daughter, now back in the school gate with a small box, filled with jars. Ruby set the box down and stepped closer. He placed the basket on the ground, and she kneeled in front of it.

'Oh! It's a puppy! She petted it for a few seconds, then looked up at Ayla, her mouth a wide 'o' shape. 'It's a dingo, isn't it?' Ayla nodded in confirmation. 'Where on earth did you get it? Is it even old enough to be away from its mother?'

'His mother was killed. By hunters two nights ago.' Ayla picked up the basket, but he saw the look of horror, and anger, on Ruby's face. 'We really didn't know if he'd make it. We've been feeding him small amounts of milk every couple of hours and this morning he had a tiny bit of raw mince. He's a fighter. I wasn't going to name him, just yet.' She looked at Alex and he nodded his understanding. In case the little dog didn't make it. 'But this morning, he was so cute and looking for his food, I told him he was a bandit because he'd stolen my heart already, and Skye decided Bandit should be his name.'

'Come into the class, we'll get you set up.' Alex picked up the box Ruby had set down. 'Bring Bandit too Skye.' He walked toward the classroom, Ayla fell into step beside him, the children trailing behind, marvelling at Bandit. More kids headed across from the playground.

'I'm sorry Alex, I couldn't leave Bandit at home. He needs to be fed. And we're going to drop by the vet after this, to have him checked out, see if he needs worming and if there's anything more we should be feeding him.' He saw her glance over her shoulder. 'I hope he survives; Skye adores him already.'

'It's fine Ayla, no problem here. Ruby was upset last week because Sam said his brothers were going to hunt some dingoes and kangaroos. We looked it up, dingoes aren't protected in this State. Ruby is making it her mission to convince Sam, and therefore his brothers, that not culling them will be a better outcome for their farms.' He shook his head as he spoke, then noticed Ayla looking at him. Her expression had changed, she seemed impressed. As much as he liked that, impressing her had no bearing on what he said next. 'Would you mind if we took a bit of our bee program time this morning to talk about dingoes? I'd like the students to see little Bandit here, to understand their history.' Ayla was smiling, nodding in agreement. 'But I should add, it might be a two-way conversation, because young Sam Fraser is sure to support his brothers' actions.' And he knew Ruby would have a strong counter-argument.

'Great idea Alex. And I totally understand that for the Frasers, and other farmers in this area, dingoes and kangaroos can be pests and a threat to their livestock. But having a conversation in class, encouraging the kids to see both sides, is great.' She touched his arm, adding 'thank you.' Her touch, such a small thing, made his heart swell and he really wanted to touch her too. Not touch her. Hold her. Hug her. Then he realised she was waiting for a response, and to cover his moment of confusion he looked at his watch, then turned to Ruby. 'Ring the bell Ruby, please.' And walked ahead of Ayla into the classroom.

The lesson passed quickly, the students enjoying the dingo discussion, and they all had a chance to pat the little animal, until Ayla said maybe they should let Bandit sleep and they'd feed him before they left. Sam Fraser was red-faced, defending the culling of dingoes and kangaroos, and Ayla and Alex made sure they didn't suggest that Sam's brother had killed Bandit's mother, although he was sure most had guessed. A few other boys, and a couple of girls, spoke up about the damage kangaroos did to the pasture and crops and that dingoes would take down newborn calves and lambs. Ayla, with Ruby's emphatic support, discussed native wildlife in the area and where the dingo was in the food chain. She also mentioned the wedge-tail eagles had taken a young dingo to their nest. Alex was left with a strong sense that Ruby's argument had hit home. Interesting.

Ayla and Skye, with Bandit, visited the other classrooms, then left as the bell rang for lunch.

THE NEXT TWO WEEKS PASSED QUICKLY FOR ALEX. AYLA CAME TO the school three times and the bee program was really engaging the students. He had to start a watering roster because the kids in his class started arguing about whose turn it was to water the garden. They could see growth on some of their plants, especially the lavender and cherry tomatoes. She brought Bandit each time and he was getting stronger, now out of his basket and walking around, nosing into corners and coming to Skye when she called him. He'd been reading up on dingoes and it seemed they were easier to train than domestic dogs, if their trainer bonded to them from a young age. It was fascinating.

He knew Ayla was doing work up at her place and he was hoping she'd invite him and Ruby up. He really wanted to learn more about her business. He'd even started an Instragram account, using @mrmac as his handle, so he could follow her. He'd mentioned it to Ayla, and she'd raised her eyebrows and nodded, saying 'I know.' Then he'd felt like he was stalking her, so he followed Debbie's café and The Courthouse too, plus a few other local businesses and events, including Ben's real estate agency and @startoverinbarrington which was all about relocating to the area and @ithappensinbarrington an events business, both operating out of Evans Real Estate offices.

Spending time with Ayla wasn't difficult, she happily dropped by the school whenever he asked, but getting to *know* her was harder. He wondered if he should just invite her and Skye to dinner on the weekend, maybe ask them to stay over. But thoughts of them in the house, overnight, led his imagination in a whole other direction and he needed to be aware of how this might affect Ruby. And Skye.

Friday mid-morning, as the kids filed out of class for recess, he heard Ayla's Kombi arrive. Alex strolled to the school gate, waiting as Ayla lifted Skye from the car. The little girl, with Bandit in her arms, immediately ran across to him and he bent down to speak to her and give Bandit a pat.

'Hello Skye.' He loved the way she bounced on her toes, always excited to see him. Or maybe just to be at the school, he thought, watching her peering beyond him, most likely looking for Ruby.

He straightened as Ayla approached. 'Hello Ayla, what brings you here today?'

'I'm catching up with Nik today.' He watched as she paused and seemed to be considering her words. 'We're picking up some arrivals to the area, they're coming in on the train this afternoon.'

Alex raised his eyebrows, sensing there was more to come. 'They will be staying at Nicole's, um, downstairs accommodation.' Then he knew. Nik had shown him the accommodation downstairs when Robbie first finished it, explaining she hoped to offer refuge to women in need. He wasn't sure of Ayla's involvement, but he nodded his understanding.

'That's good news Ayla. Not that there are women needing the accommodation, but that they have Nicole's place to come to.'

Ayla seemed to relax, then spoke quietly. 'Oh good, you understand. Alex. There are two women coming, with three children between them. Two are school age. I wondered if there was something I can give them, regarding enrolling here.' He watched as she nibbled her bottom lip. 'And if there is, can I enrol Skye for next year too?'

He was surprised. He thought she knew Skye was not only expected at school next year, but that he very much welcomed her. 'Of course, Ayla.' He glanced down at Skye for a moment. 'We're very pleased to have Skye attend here.'

He saw Ayla take a deep breath, so he waited. 'Skye isn't vaccinated, Alex. We aren't vaccinated.'

He raised his eyebrows, his heart seemed to beat faster, but he steadied himself and asked in his best school-principal manner. 'Against COVID?'

Ayla nodded. 'Is it going to be a problem here?'

Alex grinned. Ayla's expression changed to confusion for a moment, then understanding. 'You too?'

Now he nodded. He spoke quietly. 'A conversation for another day, but yes. Me too. And Ruby.' Her expression was now one of relief. 'But tell me, has your, er, status, caused problems in the past? You know the rules have largely changed now.'

Ayla exhaled, nodding again. 'I had her name down for school at our last place, and somehow her vaccination status became public knowledge and parents we'd become friendly with stopped inviting her to play with their children.' The anguish this had caused her was clear, and he was horrified she'd had to deal with that sort of negativity, but his own experience had him nodding in understanding. 'I just didn't want it to happen here too.'

'You needn't worry Ayla. There are several children here, also unvaccinated. It's not an issue. I won't let it be an issue.' He opened the gate, ushering them in. 'Come over to the office, I'll get Jenny to give you the paperwork.' The warmth of her gaze almost undid him. He would do the same for any parent and student, but doing it for Ayla gave him a buzz, and a bit of confidence.

'So, you'll be at Nicole's this afternoon, with her guests? Once they've been settled, would you like to stop by, have dinner with Ruby and me?' He tried to make the invitation sound casual, friendly, but his stomach had tightened, waiting for her response.

They were standing outside the library now, Skye had skipped over to the vegetable garden with Bandit in her arms, seeing Ruby there. Children ran by, chasing each other. He had to tap Tommy Masters on the shoulder as he sped past, two girls chasing him. 'Slow down Tommy Masters. You too Billie. Tiffany!' He watched them slow down until they thought he was no longer looking, then take off again, laughing as they ran. But Ayla had said something, and he'd missed it, so he returned his focus to her.

'Sorry Ayla. I was distracted. What did you say?'

'Yes. I said yes, Teacher. We'll come for dinner. What can I bring?'

'Just yourselves Ayla. Friday night is pizza night at our house, we make our own.' He said this with some pride, he knew the pizzas they made were good. She laughed; the sound did something weird to his solar plexus. He loved hearing her laugh. Loved the thought that he'd made her happy, even if just in this moment.

'Home-made pizza sounds wonderful, thank you. See you then.' She hesitated. 'Um, we'll have Bandit with us.'

'Of course!' He laughed. 'No show without Bandit!' He looked at his watch and turned away. 'Ruby! Ring the bell please.' Turning to Ayla, he nodded at the building. 'Let's get this paperwork for you.'

36

The hum of bees is the voice of the garden. **Elizabeth Lawrence**

Nicole looked nervous and excited. Ayla felt a bit the same. 'Should we take the girls? There's enough room. Or do you want to leave Skye here with Lucy?' Her aunt had given a potted history of the arrivals, as much as she could. Julia was in her mid-thirties with two-year-old Kristal and twelve-year-old David. She was escaping her partner, the father of Kristal. Avery was younger with a little girl, Jacinta, about five years old. She had been sleeping rough after losing her job and came to the shelter when Jacinta became ill with a virus. She'd indicated she was keen to make a fresh start and wanted to find work.

'I think we'll leave them here, if you're sure Lucy is okay to watch Skye for me? And Bandit.' She grinned. 'I don't want to overwhelm them.' Ayla checked her watch. 'We should go.'

'Okay.' They were sitting in Nicole's kitchen, Lucy and Skye were out on the lawn playing with the dogs. Bandit was wobbling around on the grass too, and Ayla was amazed that Minnie and Scout treated him just like any other puppy. Once outside, Nicole spoke to the girls. Lucy nodded solemnly when asked if she could watch the younger child, but Skye jumped up and down shouting in a sing-song voice, 'Lucy-time, Lucy-time, Lucy-time!' which made them all laugh.

The train station was old-fashioned with beautiful sandstone on the outside and what used to be a tearoom inside. Sitting on the platform seats, Ayla told Nicole that she was heading to Victoria for about ten days, to ensure her business and stock was packed up and ready to be trucked up to Barrington on her return. She spoke about some of her products, and her methods for making them. She had plans to use the two remaining cottages as staff accommodation, if needed, but she would employ locals too, if anyone was interested in learning small-scale organic manufacturing. The stock Debbie had introduced at the café had sold out several times over, but Ayla wasn't sure if locals, or tourists, were buying it. A question she should ask Debbie.

'It's a big trip for Bandit, to Victoria and back. All that car travel. Would you like to leave him with us? Lucy will take care of him.' As Nik spoke, the train whistle blew on the other side of town. They stood.

'Really? You'd have him?' Ayla was doubtful. It was a big ask, but the puppy was doing well and had been to the vet. She knew that travelling with the little dog may be problematic, having to stop more often for food and toileting.

'Of course. It's no problem at all.' Nik linked her arm through Ayla's. 'That's settled. Leave him with us tonight.' She turned; the train was slowing for the station. 'You could leave Skye with us too, if you like.'

Ayla grinned at her friend. 'Not this time, but it's nice of you to offer, and I know she'd love it, another time. But we have friends and family to catchup with, they'd be disappointed not to see her.' She squeezed Nicole's arm briefly. 'Thank you, I really mean that.' She giggled. 'And be careful what you wish for.'

Nicole chuckled with her. Standing there, watching the train pull in, Ayla felt lighter. Nicole had already become a friend; someone she could rely on. She felt a little buzz of happiness in her chest.

About to say more, the train heralded its arrival with a whistle blast, then pulled slowly up to the platform. The women stood, watching as passengers alighted. Mostly locals, Ayla thought, returning from Sydney. And a few tourists. From a carriage near the back two women stepped out, one holding the hand of a little girl and the other carrying a toddler. The little girl was carrying a doll and held a small backpack. Her mother carried several supermarket bags. Nicole leapt forward.

'Avery? Julia? I'm Nicole and this is Ayla.' Ayla smiled warmly at the women and their children. She glanced behind them, looking for the older boy, David.

'David's not coming. Didn't want to leave school and his friends. His father is going to have him.' Julia must have noted the concerned look that passed between Ayla and Nicole. 'His father's not the problem, he's remarried.' Her face softened as she looked at her daughter. 'It's Kristal's dad that's gone bad.'

'Can I help you with your bag?' Ayla smiled at Avery, quite

tall like herself, but very thin. She watched her hesitate for a moment, then pass over the worn backpack she held. 'And you must be Jacinta?' The little girl turned away, burying her face in her mother's shoulder.

Nicole exuded motherly warmth, although she wasn't much older than Julia. 'Let's get you home and settled, it's not far.' She walked ahead with Julia who carried Kristal on her hip.

Avery fell into step with Ayla, briefly moving her child from one hip to the other. Ayla knew it was too soon to offer to carry the child. 'Thank you.' Ayla looked at her. Avery spoke with a quiet determination. 'Thank you. I just need a chance. A chance to get work and get on my feet. Make a home for us. Me and Jacinta.' She looked around as they reached the vehicles. 'I like country towns. My grandparents lived in one like this, but further south, near the Victorian border. I always liked going there.'

'That's great, Avery. Barrington has a lovely community. And if you're serious, there is work to be found.' Ayla was thinking of the café, how busy Debbie was. 'What sort of work have you done in the past?'

'I started a floristry apprenticeship, was almost finished when I got pregnant with Jacinta.' She looked down. 'They wouldn't give me time off for doctor appointments and sacked me when I went anyway. Since then, I've had odd jobs, doing any work I could get, but then we both got sick last year, and I couldn't afford the rent.' She looked away, then turned back, her face brightening. 'I love plants and gardening, but I'll do anything. Cleaning, washing dishes. Anything. I just want to get on my feet.' Ayla could hear sincerity in the younger woman's voice and wondered if she might be a suitable candidate for her own business. Once she had rested and was getting good meals.

She was tall but looked under-nourished. Jacinta, on the other hand, was a chubby little girl and Ayla wondered if Avery had missed meals to ensure her child had enough. A good mother then.

'I think you'll find work here Avery, you have a great attitude. But don't rush, let Nik look after you for a couple of weeks, get settled and then look around.'

Nicole turned to them. 'I've got a toddler car seat in mine, Julia, you and Kristal can ride with me. Ayla has a booster seat.' She turned to Avery. 'She has a little girl the same age as Jacinta.' The women nodded. Julia seemed tired and a bit overwhelmed, but Avery was hanging off their every word. Ayla silently thanked her aunt, for sending these women to them and for finding ones ready for a fresh start.

Avery didn't speak much on the way to Nicole's and Jacinta didn't speak at all. Ayla pointed out a few landmarks, but mostly drove in silence, letting them take in their surroundings. When they pulled up in front of the old courthouse, Avery gasped. 'This? Is it a school or something? It's huge!' She seemed impressed and terrified at the same time.

'It's Nicole's home, she lives upstairs with her family and has accommodation for you and Julia and your children downstairs. It was a courthouse during the gold rush years, and it's been beautifully restored. Come on, I'm sure you're keen to have a look.'

She could see Julia was also overwhelmed. It was a magnificent building. Jacinta perked up when Lucy and Skye came out to greet them. Lucy saying a shy hello and Skye bounced straight up to Jacinta saying 'I'm Skye, I'm five and I'm going to school next year. What's your name?'

'Jacinta.' The child whispered it, but when Skye took her

hand saying, 'Come and meet Bandit and Minnie and Scout', the other child ran with her to where the dogs sat by the front steps.

Ayla looked over Julia's head to meet Avery's gaze. Avery grinned at her, wiping a tear away with the back of her hand while nodding her head at all she saw. Ayla had to glance away; afraid she'd cry too.

Julia was impressed, but a bit harder around the edges, less willing to admit it. They followed Nicole inside, Ayla carrying the few possessions they'd brought with them. She set the bags down in the living area as Nicole showed the two rooms, telling them they could choose.

Julia looked taken aback for the first time. 'A room each? And all of this?' She waved her hand around the comfortable living area and kitchenette. Just for us?' Julia looked at Avery. Avery grinned back.

Turning to Nicole, Julia focussed on her intently. 'This? For us. At no charge. Are you for real?'

Nicole blushed. 'I've been through something too.' She hesitated. 'I just want you to feel safe here. I hope it helps you get on your feet and that when you're ready you will choose to find a place nearby and stay in the community. I'll be here to help you settle in, answer questions.'

'You take the bigger room Julia. Jacinta will sleep with me anyway.' Avery turned around. 'This is lovely Nicole. Really lovely. Thank you so much.' She looked at Ayla. 'I hope I won't need to be here too long, that I find work and a place to live. There are others,' she looked at Julia again, 'who could come here that need it more than me. Than us.'

Julia nodded. 'She's right.' Then she grinned. 'But I'm planning to have a bath every night that I'm here! Aves, did you see the size of the bathroom?' They oohed and aahed and stepped into the bathroom together, giggling. Ayla moved closer to Nicole. Leaning down she whispered, 'You've done a good thing Nik. A really good thing.' Ayla saw Nicole nod, tears in her eyes.

'We'll let you settle in, and I'll send Jacinta in to you.' Ayla laughed at Avery's expression. 'I might have trouble tearing her away from Skye and the dogs.'

'She'll come. She's a good girl.' Avery followed them to the door, calling Jacinta, who ran to her without hesitation.

'Get settled. I've stocked the kitchen with basic pantry items, so you can make a cuppa. There's fresh milk and eggs and bread and my daughter Lucy baked some mini muffins for you. And I've baked a shepherd's pie for your dinner. I'll give you a tour of the whole place tomorrow, if you like.'

More thank yous and Nicole and Ayla walked back to Ayla's car. 'We're having dinner with Alex and Ruby tonight.' Ayla opened the door and lifted Skye into her seat, with Bandit snuggled in her arms. 'And on Sunday we're heading to Victoria to tidy up my business down there. I won't be back for about ten days, so I hope you will be fine here.'

Nicole hugged her. 'I'm sure we'll be fine. And I have your aunt's number if I need help or advice. I'll let them settle in, then by the time you come back I hope we'll have some routines established.' She glanced back at the house. 'I'd like to make sure they've got access to fresh food, and lots of it. Avery looks half starved, and Julia is thin too.'

'You're right Nik. Help them settle. A few days of rest, hot baths and good food is a great start. And follow that up with the possibility of opportunities and a future for them and their children. I can see they're both good mums.' Ayla sighed. 'But there may be setbacks too. We don't know much about them. So be aware and take care of yourself and Lucy. And those big men of yours.'

'I will Ayla, thank you. I mean it. This has been a dream of mine.' Nicole stepped back as Ayla got in and closed her door, winding the window down as she did. Moving back to the open window, Nicole added, 'And enjoy your evening with Alex and Ruby. You know he has a thing for you, right?'

Ayla nodded. 'I know. I'm not sure what I think. He's not the type I'm usually attracted to.' She shook her head for a moment. 'No, that's not right. He is built like a man-god. But I'm wondering if we have more in common than I first thought.' She grinned at Nicole. 'I may have been a bit quick to judge the *teacher*.'

Nicole laughed out loud. 'You may be right Ayla Forrest. And where are the men you're usually attracted to right now?' Nicole raised her eyebrows, but her tone was light.

'Maybe you're right Nik. They're certainly not here.' Ayla laughed and drove away, waving out the window as she did.

37

'Ah, you're here for the famous McIntosh home-made pizza.' His eyes met hers but then he smiled at Skye. Alex was surprised when Skye held her arms out to him. He picked her up.

'I like pizza. I can help.' She put her small hands on each side of his face and gave a confident nod of her head, her words quiet but serious.

'All right then, teamwork it is. Hop up here and you can choose your own toppings.' He placed her on a stool at the kitchen counter, momentarily lost for words. Ayla seemed to sense it and said they should wash their hands first; Skye had been playing with Bandit and Lucy's dogs. They explained they had left Bandit with Lucy and Nicole, to care for while they were away.

Alex was slightly disappointed. 'You could have left Bandit here; Ruby would love to look after him.'

Ruby nodded, then nudged him with her elbow. 'So, you'll

know where to find me after school every day Dad. I'll be over at Lucy's playing with Bandit.' He nudged her back. 'You might have to beat me to it.'

Alex and Ruby prepared the pizza bases and had the toppings in small bowls, arranged within easy reach for Skye, and Ruby who was perched on the next stool.

Ayla lifted her grocery bag from the kitchen bench, taking it across to the sink. 'I'll make a feta and avocado salad to go with it if you'd like.'

He didn't want to admit that he and Ruby usually didn't have salad with their pizza. 'Great. My salads are generally a bit basic. Thanks.' He watched her work quickly, making a delicious looking salad. At the same time, Ruby was helping Skye make her pizza. He stepped over when he heard Ruby question Skye's choice of toppings.

'Olives? Really Skye?' Ruby screwed her nose up. Skye hesitated, then plucked an olive from the bowl and popped it into her mouth, making 'mmmm' sounds, then giggling when she finished it. Alex loved olives himself, but rarely bought them because Ruby wasn't keen. He'd suspected Ayla would eat them so had picked some up today, but he hadn't thought Skye would be so adventurous.

'Hey Ruby, maybe you should give olives a go too. Skye loves them!' He chuckled as he spoke, aware Ruby was shaking her head.

Ayla was behind him; he was sure her breast touched his arm as she reached across to place the salad on the counter. He glanced at her but couldn't read her expression. Being this close to Ayla, in such an intimate setting, had his senses tightly wound, wondering, and hoping, he'd get a chance to express how much he liked her.

The oven was ready, so he loaded the pizzas in, fitting all four on two shelves. Ruby slid off her chair and began laying plates on the dining table, Skye following her about, keen to help. He leaned his back against the counter, Ayla, beside him, chatting together as they watched their daughters. A couple of times Ayla touched his shoulder briefly with hers, and each time he felt a zap of excitement run the length of his body. He tried to contain it, maintain his old-fashioned-school-principal image, but he sensed she was aware of the affect she had on him, and was having fun pushing his buttons. What he really wanted to do, was go all cave-man and kiss her. No, more than that. He wanted to touch her. Everywhere. Explore every last inch of her glowing skin, run his fingers through her hair, feel her long legs wrapped around him. He shook his head, trying to clear that image from his imagination, before he embarrassed himself.

She chuckled beside him. 'What is it Teacher? You're shaking your head.'

He looked into her eyes, and the rest of the room, the girls' chatter and movement, vanished. It was just him and her. Ayla. Beautiful Ayla. Strong and wild Ayla. She held his gaze and he saw her eyes darken, widen. She was telling him something. He knew she felt it too. A pulling sensation was drawing them together.

The oven beeped.

'Pizzas are ready Dad.' Ruby rushed into the kitchen and taking a set of oven mitts she expertly opening the oven door.

'Here Ruby, I'll help you.' He picked up a potholder and lifted two pizzas out. Ruby already had the first two on the large wooden board. Using the pizza cutter, she expertly sliced them up, then slid the pieces on to platters, carrying them to the table. Skye was kneeling on her chair, and grabbed a piece as soon as the platter was placed in front of her.

'Hotsy totsy!' Skye let the piece fall on her plate, before blowing on her fingers, then waving them around.

'Wait a moment, Skye, it's straight out of the oven! Have some salad first.' Ayla served a small helping of salad onto Skye's plate, then passed it to Ruby. Alex wondered if she'd eat it. She was getting better with vegetables but had only started eating avocado recently. He smiled at her as she served herself, nodding to him as she did. She didn't want Ayla to think she was a picky eater; he could tell Ruby wanted to impress her.

Dinner was fun. Skye tried to get Ruby to eat an olive. Ruby took the one Skye offered, hot from her pizza, and held it gingerly between thumb and forefinger. 'What do I get if I eat it?' She looked at him, then Ayla, as she spoke. He was about to tell her she'd get a nice taste, but Ayla spoke first.

'What would you like Ruby? Is there a prize you have in mind for eating an *olive*?' Her tone was teasing but for a moment he wondered if Ruby would get upset. She would if *he* said it.

'Mmm.' She looked from him to Ayla, the olive held just in front of her mouth. 'I'd like you and Skye to stay the night. I promised Skye that next time she came I'd give her a ride on Brute. If you stay, that could be tomorrow morning.'

He hadn't expected that. He looked quickly at Ayla, who winked at him before looking at Skye. She was bouncing on her chair, clapping her hands, saying 'yes, yes, yes, yes!' Then 'Eat it Ruby, eat it!'

'Well. We could do that. If we're invited, of course.' He couldn't believe his ears. She wanted to stay. For the night. Just like that. His wildest dreams ....

'Daaad!' Ruby still held the olive. 'Quick! Invite them!'

'Um, of course. Ayla, Skye, would you like to sleep over tonight?' He felt light-headed.

'Thank you Alex. But only if Ruby eats the olive.' Ayla was laughing, Skye was bouncing, and Ruby opened her mouth and popped the whole olive in. She chewed for a moment, eyes closed, nose wrinkled. Opening her eyes as she swallowed, she reached across to the platter, where a few pieces of pizza were yet to be eaten. Taking a slice with olives, she picked it up and put it on her plate.

Ayla laughed out loud. 'You can eat that whole piece Ruby, but we're only staying one night!' Alex laughed too and suddenly they were all talking. About staying over, riding Brute, finding something to wear to bed. He leaned back in his chair, watching. Ayla glanced at him a few times. He marvelled at how relaxed she seemed. He felt like a boy about to go on his first date.

Somehow they finished dinner and Ruby took Skye to find a tee shirt to wear to bed. He had spare toothbrushes in the bathroom and grabbed towels from the closet. Their guest room had a double bed, already made up.

Ayla took Skye for a shower while he and Ruby washed up.

When they returned, Ruby had a deck of Uno cards on the dining room table. 'It's still early, can we play some cards, all of us, before bedtime?'

Skye, now wearing one of Ruby's tee shirts that came to her knees, ran to the table and climbed on to a chair, clapping her hands. 'Yes. Uno. Yes please!'

38

If bees disappeared off the face of the earth, man would only have four years left to live. **Maurice Maeterlinck.**

Laughing, Ayla joined them at the table, while Ruby shuffled and dealt the cards. The teacher sat beside her, and she could feel the warmth of his thigh, touching hers, under the table. Her concentration was poor, and Skye won the first hand, then Ruby, then Skye again. At one stage the teacher had more than twenty cards in his hand, which made them all laugh, and after Skye won the last game, Ayla said it was time for a story and bed.

Ruby jumped up, 'I'll read her a story. I have lots of books in my room.'

'Are you sure? She always wants 'just one more' so be careful, you'll be reading all night.' Ayla laughed as Skye shook her head. 'No Mama, I'll let Ruby stop when she wants to.' But she was already beside Ruby, holding her hand.

'Come and say goodnight then.' Ayla held out her arms and Skye squirmed into them, kissing her loudly on the cheek. 'Good night Mama, love you.' Ayla held her close for a moment, then whispered in her ear, 'love you too Skye-baby.'

Skye ran around to the teacher, climbed onto his lap and kissed him noisily on the cheek. 'Goodnight teacher, love you too.' She watched as he held her child for a moment, saying 'Goodnight Skye.' As the girls ran from the room, he looked across at her, his eyes dark with emotion.

'She's a beautiful little girl Ayla.' He stood suddenly, heading to the kitchen. She gazed at him as he moved around the kitchen. It was too early for bed, and she really wanted some time alone with him, just to talk.

He returned. 'I've put the jug on, would you like a hot cocoa? I didn't offer you wine with dinner, I'm sorry. Didn't think of it, I don't often drink during the week.'

'Cocoa would be lovely. Actually, I don't drink at all. Alcohol that is.' His explanation pleased her. Hot chocolate made, they moved to the lounge, settling on the sofa, their bodies just touching, as they sipped. Ayla sat cross-legged; her body turned slightly toward his. She wanted to ask him so much, wanted to climb inside him and discover all his stories. But he beat her to it.

'Tell me about yourself Ayla. Your story. I'd love to know more about you, and Skye, and your journey.'

39

The goodnight hug and kiss from Skye nearly undid him. Her spontaneous 'I love you' touched his heart and he knew he had tears in his eyes when he glanced at Ayla after the girls left the room. He'd gone to the kitchen to compose himself. There was something about this woman that moved him. Her fierce independence combined with a wicked sense of fun and completely natural mothering style had seeped into his heart. Even Ruby's response to Ayla and Skye surprised him. Yes, Ruby had always been loving and mature in many ways, but he hadn't thought she'd so happily welcome them. Perhaps he had underestimated his daughter.

And Ayla is sexy. So bloody sexy. And she knows it and is completely comfortable. But with the two girls in the house, he knew they could do little more than share a few hot kisses. And talk. He really wanted to know her story, her ambitions and desires. He stopped for a moment, one hand resting on the tin of cocoa. What he really wanted to know, was there any chance they could have a future together. It was obvious they lived quite different lives, but she'd already said she wanted Skye to start school here. It was too soon to even think of such things, but that's where his head went.

All these thoughts buzzed around in his mind as they moved to the sofa together. He could hear the murmur of voices from Ruby's bedroom. Still reading, enjoying each other.

He watched her face as she spoke. So animated and passionate, yet not all her story was easy.

'I hated school, hated being cooped up, and I know now that I learn in a more hands-on manner. I hated reading back then, but I think it was because I didn't like *having* to read. I read a lot now. If something interests me I love reading and researching.' She looked at him as she spoke, and he felt the pain of her next words deeply. 'I hated the school system. Teachers. Distrusted them all. And my parents tried, especially my mum, I went to private schools, but you know, I just didn't fit the mould. It was always a struggle for me.' He reached out and took her hand, rubbing his thumb gently against her palm as she continued. 'So, I left school early, did some TAFE, you know, Mum insisted on employable skills. Got a Cert Three in Childcare, but I don't like the government system. TAFE was better than school, and I discovered it was easier to learn if I was really interested in the subject, if it was practical, if I could *do* something. Then I started travelling. Um, social media, facebook and Instagram, were becoming popular and I had a keen interest in photography. So I travelled, I took photos and shared them, and I learned stuff.'

He wanted more. 'What stuff?'

She laughed, a deep, throaty, happy yet somehow sensual sound. 'I nannied for a year in San Francisco, studied photography and did a healthy cooking course, started learning more about the Steiner education system. Travelled through South America and learned conversational Spanish. Worked my way around via WWOOF.'

'Woof?"

'W.W.O.O.F. World Wide Opportunities on Organic Farms and developed an interest in permaculture and bees. Then to Europe, did a beekeeping course in Denmark, travelled down through Europe to Spain. Did a belly dancing course there.' She laughed again and he had to control his response to an image of her in a belly dancing skirt and little else. He nodded, urging her to continue.

'I came back to Australia for about six months a year, working in Steiner kindergartens, saving for my next trip. Travelling was amazing, and I was hooked. I rode a motorbike, by myself, through India for a couple of months. Ended up in Mumbai, in a poor section of the city, when my bike broke down. I'd paid eight hundred Australian dollars for it, so it didn't owe me anything. I wheeled the bike to the nearest house and knocked on the door. I offered them the bike. Maybe they could fix it or sell it for parts. I was leaving in six days; I was happy to give it away.' He was fascinated, her stories were amazing.

'They were Hindus and they invited me in. Their daughter was getting married, it's a three-day event there. They invited me to stay, attend the wedding. They gave me a sari, painted a bindi on my forehead.' He was about to ask, but she anticipated his questions. 'The red dot.' She had a faraway look on her face, remembering. 'I could never have paid for that experience, I was just there, at the right time. I'll remember it always.'

He had leaned forward, hanging on her words. She fascinated him. But the moment was interrupted by Ruby.

'Hey Dad, Ayla. Skye is asleep in my bed. We read five books.' She giggled.

Ayla began to get up, but Ruby held up her hand. 'She can stay there Ayla if it's all right with you. It's a big bed. If she wants you in the night, I can bring her in.' Ruby looked pleased and he was happy when Ayla nodded, saying 'thank you Ruby, you've given Skye the best time.'

Ruby stood for a moment, looking at them. 'Well, good night then. I'm going to bed now.' He glanced at his watch; it was nine already.

'Goodnight Rubes.'

Ayla stood and in one stride had her arms around his daughter and held her close for a moment. 'Goodnight Ruby. You're a really special girl.' Then she kissed Ruby on the forehead. He saw a series of emotions cross Ruby's face – surprise, pleasure, happiness. She seemed to glow in the warmth of Ayla's embrace. He felt emotion surging through him, tears in his eyes again.

Ayla returned to the sofa and turned to him. 'Now you, Teacher. Tell me your story so far.'

HE MOVED CLOSER TO HER. 'WHAT'S TO TELL? YES, I'VE travelled a bit. A gap year tour with the lads from school. You know, Germany during Oktoberfest. All I remember from that trip is a lot of drinking, smelly youth hostels and hangovers. But it's a rite of passage.' She chuckled, so he continued.

'Then uni. I'm not sure when I decided to become a teacher.

I knew I wanted to teach primary school, you know, when you have the chance to make a difference in their lives. I met Sasha during those years. She studied commerce, was keen on accounting or banking. We travelled together before we got married, back-packed through the United Kingdom and Europe.' He thought about those times. They'd argued a lot on that trip, he wondered why they ended up getting married. He had wanted to see architecture and history, while she had been interested in fashion and parties, meeting up with other young people.

'I got my first post as a teacher in the western suburbs of Sydney. Sasha got a job with one of the big banks in the city, began working her way up the ladder.' He paused, thinking about it again, before adding. 'I think we were growing apart. I wanted a quiet life, a home and a family and Sasha wanted to be in the city every Friday and Saturday night. I realised I was losing her. We'd been together so long. So, I proposed.' He looked down, Ayla was holding his hand, listening intently. He tried to laugh, but it came out as a grunt. 'It's what people do when they run out of things to talk about. They get married.' Ayla nodded, her eyes warm and understanding.

'It was a big wedding, city hotel, the works. She was Bridezilla, but I was happy, went along with everything. It was the first step to building a family together.' He looked into her eyes. 'The only good thing that came out of it, in the end, was Ruby.' He lowered his voice, even though he knew Ruby would be asleep now. 'A few years into the marriage Sasha kept putting off starting a family, and again, we were drifting apart. Then suddenly, she was pregnant. I know it was an accident, Sasha forgot to take the pill for a couple of days after a big night out. But I was happy. Once she got used to the idea, she was too, and we grew closer again, planning for the birth. I accepted a transfer to a school in Newcastle and Sasha got a part-time bank job. We bought a small house.' He stood, stretched. 'Would you like anything else to drink Ayla?'

'No thank you. I'll just use the bathroom and check on the girls. But I want to hear the rest of this please.' Ayla rose in one long-limbed graceful movement. He followed her to Ruby's bedroom door. With the hall light on they opened it a crack. Ruby was asleep on her side, her back to the door. Skye's little bottom was pushed into the small of Ruby's back, her dark curls fanned out on the pillow. Ayla stepped in quietly, pulling the covers up a bit. He watched from the door.

Stepping into the hall, she closed the door quietly, then leaned close to him, kissing him gently on the lips. 'I'll be back in a moment.' She walked down the hall to the bathroom, and he returned to the couch, his lips tingling, his body taut with desire.

He reached for her when she sat, but she shook her head, smiling. 'I want to hear the rest of your story. What happened to you and Sasha?'

'It was good for a few years. Sasha was a good mother, but she couldn't wait to get back to work, even part-time. Said she needed to talk to grown-ups. We shared caring for Ruby, but it wasn't until she was about four, and Sasha was again working full time, long hours, often late at night that I realised that most of the time, it was just Ruby and me. Even on weekends Sasha had places to go, people to see. Her ambition drove her, and while I never doubted her love for Ruby, she was happy to leave her day-to-day care to me. I didn't mind, I adore being her dad. But Sasha was slipping away from me again. I wasn't exciting enough, ambitious enough.'

Ayla nodded. 'Then?'

'Then I realised Sasha had someone else. Someone from work. At first she denied it, tried to hide it. But I called her on it. We agreed to divorce, Ruby was almost seven. I honestly thought she'd live with Sasha, and I'd have weekends and holidays. It broke my heart thinking about it. But Ruby decided. She flatly refused to live with Sasha and her new man. Sasha gave in quickly. Too quickly.' He shook his head ruefully. 'So here we are. Sasha has married again. Not that guy, there were several before she re-settled. And she has another child, a little boy, Rory. Ruby loves her little brother, but she hates going to stay now they've moved to Melbourne.'

'And you've never, er, re-partnered?' Ayla raised an eyebrow. 'You're a catch Alex McIntosh. You can't tell me there haven't been single teachers, or single mums for that matter, bringing you casseroles and offering to iron your shirts.' She was laughing at him, but he got it. It was funny.

'There was someone, for a while, but Ruby hated her. She didn't try hard enough. Ruby was just testing, looking for someone to love both of us. She fell short. We all knew it.' He sighed and looked at her closely. 'Then the last three years were a struggle for me. I think you know why. I left the school system and taught Ruby at home, doing contract work, mostly curriculum development. It was very isolating, for both of us. The rules changed and the Barrington opportunity came up, and well, I grabbed it with both hands. I wasn't sure if we'd stay, in the beginning, but now I couldn't imagine living anywhere else. We love it here.'

'Those years were isolating for us too. Hearing you mention it, earlier, surprised me. Yes, I've been drawn to you, but there are some barriers that would keep me at arm's length.' She turned to him with her lips parted, eyes shining, and it was all he could do not to kiss her right then and there, but he sensed she wanted to say more. 'Teacher, you knocked that barrier down today, and well, here I am.'

He didn't need to hear more. He reached for her. Ayla melted against him, and he felt his passion stir. Years of pent-up emotion threatened to explode. He kissed her, nibbling her lips for a moment, until she gave a small sigh, and deepened the kiss, pulling him onto her on the couch.

He ran one hand through her thick hair, the other beneath her, then he trailed his fingers down to her breasts. His mouth followed and she arched her back. Her arms around his waist clutched at his back, then she slipped one between their bodies, rubbing his erection through his jeans. Like teenagers they continued, clothes on, to kiss, rub and nibble for what seemed like hours. But the thought of the girls waking, walking in on them, stopped him. He drew back. 'Ayla.' He almost groaned her name. 'We have to stop. The girls.'

She nodded, sat up. 'Yes. Yes we do. Of course.' Her beautiful eyes looked at him with so much emotion. Not just lust, although there was that, but something deeper. He'd touched her heart. He knew it. More reason to wait, he thought.

Her next words took him by surprise.

'We're like teenagers tonight, keeping our energy in our genitals.' He chuckled; he'd thought that himself. She picked up his hand, placed it over her heart, then laid hers against his heart. He knew it was racing. Gazing into his eyes, she spoke softly. 'Breathe with me. Breathe together and we can move the energy higher.' She leaned into him; her lips brushed his lightly. She placed her mouth on his, and he inhaled the warmth of her. His eyes were locked on hers. He'd never felt so connected to a woman. He breathed into her, watched her drink his breath, his essence. In his mind he followed the air inside her, became one with her body. He breathed her back inside him and she was right, the energy had moved higher. It settled in his chest, and he suddenly felt vulnerable. He pulled back, then leaned forward and kissed her gently, still looking into her eyes. Her lids were half closed, her mouth turned upwards in a dreamy, sexy smile. It was all he could do not to start all over.

'Come with me, I'll get you a tee shirt to wear to bed.' He stood. She rose from the sofa to her feet in a single graceful, almost fluid, movement. Leading her by the hand, they went to his room.

40

Swallows have disappeared, bees are dying out because of pesti-
cides that should have been banned long ago – it's a scandal.
Brigitte Bardot

A generous room, with heavy, dark timber furniture. Very masculine. It smelled faintly of him. She'd noticed he didn't favour aftershave or cologne. Clean-man scent. So much sexier. Something about those male pheromones were a real turn-on. His pheromones. Ayla inhaled deeply. She wanted him. She never did this, not with Skye in the house. She was so careful. But this man, this teacher, he'd rocked her world. Strong, yet kind. A loving father. She watched as he pulled a neatly folded tee shirt from a drawer and handed it to her.

She shook it out, it was big, like him. It would swim on her.

'Thank you teacher.' She smiled seductively as she turned and walked to the door. 'I'm going to take a shower and go to bed. Goodnight.'

He stood there looking at her. She had to turn away from the raw desire on his face. She almost laughed as he visibly gathered himself together and said goodnight.

Standing under a just-warm shower, Ayla thought about him as she slowly washed her body. Imagined him touching her there. And there. She wanted him, her desire so strong and her skin sensitive, still tingling from his touch, that waves of pleasure radiated through her body as the water cascaded over her. The shower should have cooled her down. Arching her back for a moment, she sighed, it had the opposite effect.

Standing in the guest bedroom, she pulled the tee shirt over her head. It just covered her bottom. Ayla stepped into the hall, the light on in case Skye woke in the night, although she could have told them Skye *never* woke in the night. She could sleep through anything. His bedroom door was closed, no light showed beneath it. Ayla hesitated, then opened it quietly. She knew she was silhouetted by the hall light.

He rose on one elbow. His chest was bare. Such a large, strong chest. And arms. 'Ayla.' He whispered her name. She moved into the room, closed the door. A bedside lamp came on. 'Ayla.' He said her name again, this time it came out as a groan. She drew the tee shirt over her head, standing proudly, letting him see her. Wanting him to see her. He drew the covers back; he was naked too. She let her eyes rove from his head to his thighs, then looked into his eyes as she slipped into the space he'd created. Wordlessly he gathered her in his arms, and holding her tight, kissed her deeply.

He raised his head for a moment. Looking into his eyes, she

whispered one word. 'Teacher.' Then she pulled his head down, claiming his mouth with hers.

* * *

THE TEACHER WAS BUSY MAKING BREAKFAST, AND SHE WAS setting the table, when the girls got up. Skye ran to her, and Ayla picked her up, hugging her tightly. 'I slept in the big bed with Ruby all night long!' Skye was happy and excited. Ayla glanced at Ruby. She'd walked into the kitchen with her dad. Ayla saw the shoulder nudge Ruby gave her father, and the way she reached for the toaster and began helping. They're a good team, used to each other. Warmth washed over her.

'I'll get Skye dressed.' She'd wriggled out of Ayla's arms and was climbing on to a high stool at the kitchen bench and frowned at her words.

'No! I help Ruby.' Ayla stepped toward her, but Ruby leaned over, tweaking Skye's nose, 'you need to be dressed to have a ride on Brute after breakfast Skye.'

'Okay.' Skye immediately slid off the stool and ran ahead of Ayla to the guest room.

* * *

THEY WERE READY TO LEAVE, IT WAS ALMOST LUNCH TIME AND SHE had to pack the car up tonight for an early start tomorrow, for their road trip to Victoria.

'Thank you, Alex and Ruby, for a lovely night, and for breakfast and your riding lesson.' Ayla leant in, kissing Alex on the cheek, then gave Ruby a warm hug. Skye was reluctant to leave, she'd cried when Ruby lifted her from the saddle, but when Ayla gave her a nudge, she thanked them both with a smile.

Ayla lifted Skye into the car, then turned to Alex, including Ruby in her smile. 'Maybe you'd like to visit us when we get back from our trip south, I'd love you to see our place,' she looked at Alex directly, before adding, 'up close.' She was delighted when he chuckled and reddened at the same time. Ruby looked at him curiously.

'It was entirely our *pleasure*, anytime.' He grinned at her, and she felt her own face grown warm at the way he said 'pleasure'. Cheeky. She saw Ruby glance at her and back to her father, a small smile on her face. She chuckled internally. The teacher might have some explaining to do.

41

Thoughts of Ayla, naked in his bed caught him several times throughout the day, and at one point while hanging out the washing Ruby asked him what he was grinning about. It was too soon to read anything into the previous night, as much as he wanted to, so he avoided answering, choosing instead to occupy Ruby with chores, and then a horse-ride along the river.

He saw Robbie at the general store the next morning who explained that he was working up at Ayla's while she was gone. He'd organised the replacement of the power pole, so the commercial building would have power restored, and he was cleaning and repairing the two cottages. Harry was working with him, and staying up there at night, doing some additional work on the back of Ayla's house. It sounded like this was going to be a surprise for Ayla and he found himself wondering what he could do for her while she was gone.

'You know we have two, um, guests and their children

staying with us? From Sydney.' Robbie spoke quietly as they walked out of the store, each with coffee and newspaper in their hands.

'I heard. It's only been two nights, but how are they settling in?' Alex was curious and he wanted to ensure they knew how welcome they were in the school community.

'They're good. The two little girls are lovely, but very quiet. Julia and Nik seem to have hit it off, so that's great. Avery says she's keen to find work. I've asked if she'd like to spend a day or two at Ayla's, help clean up the old guest accommodation, before we start on repairs. There's a bit to do in the main building first, while I've got the electrician there, but Avery can clean, and haul out the furniture, sort out what's damaged and what can be repurposed. It depends on whether Julia will agree to look after Avery's little one, it's not safe to have her up there with all the work going on.' Robbie was now leaning against his car door.

Alex nodded. 'Is there anything I can do? Up at Ayla's while she's gone?'

'No mate, we're up there while you're at school.' Robbie grinned. 'You trying to impress her? How was your dinner on Friday night?' He nudged Alex. 'I saw she stayed over. Anything to report?'

Alex swallowed, and although he knew Robbie was teasing, he felt himself flush. Robbie raised his eyebrows. 'So that's how it is. I didn't realise. Mate, I wish you well there.' Robbie's tone had changed from teasing to sincere.

All Alex could manage was, 'Early days Robbie. Early days.'

* * *

His phone vibrated just as he was mounting Cal, returning from the river with Ruby. 'Wait a moment, Ruby, I'll just check this.' Alex pulled the phone from his pocket. A text from Ayla.

Safely here. A day and half driving.

He answered quickly.

That's great. Much to do there?

Not as much as I thought. Should be back in a week.

Anything I can do for you here?

Check with Nik, maybe you can meet Julia and Avery. But I'm all good, Robbie and Harry are working at mine this week. Thank you. X

The kiss made him feel bold. He waited for a moment, then typed quickly and pushed send.

Can't wait to see you both. Travel safely. X

Brute's reins in her hands, Ruby had sidled up to him. The little love heart emoji appeared on his last message. He felt unaccountably pleased.

'Is that Ayla, Dad?' Ruby was looking at him directly. She could see his last message, the kiss and the heart emoji.

'It is, Ruby.' He took a breath. 'They made it down to Victoria and should be back in a week.'

'Good.' Ruby mounted Brute and he threw himself into

Cal's saddle, turning toward home. 'I know you like her. And I don't mind, Dad. She's lovely. I like Skye too.'

He was about to reply but Ruby nudged Brute into a trot, and he took a moment to catch up with her. He felt he should say something, and he didn't want to lie and deny he had feelings for Ayla. So, he told Ruby what he'd said to Robbie earlier. 'It's early days Ruby. But yes, I like her. And Skye.'

* * *

Alex called Nicole when they returned, asking if he could meet Julia and Avery when they were ready. Nik told him that Avery had already completed the enrolment form for school for Jacinta, and she said she'd bring her down next week, when Ayla was back. Julia said she'd come too, to see the school grounds and the vegetable garden the kids had planted, even though Kristal wouldn't start school for almost two years. He heard the happy tone in Nicole's voice and again thought about how Ayla had touched the community he had grown to love.

42

If we lose bees, we may be looking at losing apples and oranges. We may be looking at losing a great deal of other crops, as well, and other animals that depend on those crops. **Annalee Newitz**

T ired, her eyes gritty from the long drive, Ayla slowed down near the general store. Almost midnight, it was closed. She knew it would be and wondered again why she hadn't stopped for fuel in Raymond Terrace. But Skye had been asleep, and she had pushed on, sure she would find a service station open along the way. Looking at the fuel gauge, she probably had enough to get home. But not enough to get back down the mountain. Taking a deep breath, she wondered if she should pull in at Robbie and Nicole's, stop for the night. But they had Julia and Avery downstairs, and it would mean waking everyone up.

And that's how she came to be parked in front of the teacher's house. She killed the engine, wondering if she should wake him and risk waking Ruby too, of if they should just sleep in the car. At that moment, the front light came on and the teacher was silhouetted in the doorway. Skye stirred.

'Home Mama?' It was barely a question. But he was there, opening the passenger door quietly as she opened her own. He gently scooped Skye into his arms, closing the door with his elbow, and carried her inside. Ayla grabbed their canvas overnight bag. She had packed one, thinking they may have stopped sooner at a motel. She hurried into the house behind him, down the hall to the guest room. He already had Skye on the bed, her shoes off, but straightened and stepped back, letting Ayla take over.

Ayla looked at her daughter, her eyes closed again, her lashes dark against her soft cheeks. She contemplated undressing her, but decided she could just sleep in the leggings and tee shirt she had on. Pulling the covers up, she turned and left the room. She needed sleep herself.

Alex was in the kitchen, boiling the jug. He opened his arms, and she stepped into them, relaxing against his shoulder as he held her.

'You're exhausted Ayla. You've driven all the way through.' His words were quiet but sounded like a reprimand somehow. She pulled away, wanted to explain, justify her actions. In the same moment, she realised she didn't have to. Her decisions were her own.

'I was fine, Skye was asleep. It was easier to keep driving.' She explained anyway but knew her tone was defensive.

He ignored her tone. 'It's alright Ayla. I'm happy you stopped here. I'm making chamomile tea, with honey, and you can go straight to bed, if you want, or have a shower.' His words were soothing, gentle. And he did sound happy to see her and pleased she had stopped.

'Yes, a quick shower. Then bed.' She stepped back into his arms. 'Thank you.' She wondered if she should add that sleep really meant sleep, and not a romp in the sack. As nice as that would be, she was too exhausted. He walked her to the bathroom, handed her a large towel, then left the room quietly.

Five minutes under a warm shower refreshed her, and she stepped out, grateful for the lack of questions. Alex hadn't overcomplicated her decision to stop. Returning to the kitchen wearing a tank top and boxer shorts, she took the cup he handed to her. Warm chamomile and honey. Perfect.

Two sips and he took her arm, leading her wordlessly back to the hallway. Wrapping his arms around her, he whispered. 'With Skye? Or in my bed? I know you need sleep, but I'd love to be near you, hold you.' Her heart sped up at his words. No pressure. No questions. Just acceptance. She walked to the guest room, peeked at Skye, sound asleep and in starfish position in the middle of the bed. He looked over her shoulder.

'I think Skye has decided for us. Come.' Leaving Skye's door ajar, he led her to his room, pulled the covers back and took her empty cup as she folded herself into his bed. She heard him running water in the sink in the kitchen and thought she'd wait for him and kiss him goodnight. The least she could do.

43

He returned in less than five minutes. She was asleep. He smiled to himself as he climbed in beside her, placed an arm across her waist and let himself drift off to sleep. It was the second time they'd shared a bed, but it felt comfortable, easy, like they had been doing it for years. He didn't think he'd ever enjoy sleeping alone again.

* * *

HE'D BEEN TO THE BATHROOM, BRUSHED HIS TEETH, AND NOW THE gentle fingers of pre-dawn light crept through a gap in the curtains, touching his shoulder, before stealthily roving across Ayla's neck, her ear, her face. He watched her lashes flutter against her cheek for a moment, before she stretched languidly, rolling on to her back, casually throwing one long leg across his. She smiled, eyes still not open, then turned her face to him.

'Good morning teacher.' Her eyes opened slowly; her tone was sultry, seductive. There was no other word for it. He hardened immediately. She knew. It was obvious she knew. Leaning closer, she kissed his lips softly, then rolled away, sitting up on the edge of the bed in one seamless, fluid movement. Looking at him over her shoulder, she stretched her arms up, then stood.

'Bathroom.' Not quite a whisper. He nodded as she moved to the door, naked, then rolled on to his back. Glancing at his phone, he saw it was only five. Ruby would sleep until half six, at least. He wasn't sure about Skye. He wondered. Was there time? He'd let her lead the way. She might want another hour or two of sleep.

She returned, closed the door behind her. 'Skye won't be up for a while. Ruby?'

He understood her meaning, although she was speaking in shorthand.

'Half six. Usually.' He watched, as she nodded. Like the last time, she stood there naked, unselfconscious, completely natural. No vanity either. Just comfortable in her own skin.

Throwing back the covers, he made room for her. She lay down facing him. 'Kiss me.' Her breath was fresh, minty. He silently congratulated himself for brushing his own just before she woke. He leaned over her, took her bottom lip between his teeth, nibbled gently. She sighed. 'More.' Damn, he wanted to pace himself but lying here, his skin touching hers, he was filled with heat and lust and didn't know if he could take his time. She wriggled, now almost under him. She deepened the kiss, moaned quietly, carelessly draped one long leg around his hips. 'Now, teacher.' It was a demand, one he quickly met.

Their coupling was quiet, with their daughters were just

down the hall. But there was a wild intensity he hadn't experienced before. She gave him everything and demanded the same. For once he stopped thinking, analysing, and just gave in to his desire. He kissed her deeply as he plunged into her, over and over, then rubbed his stubble against her chin, down her neck and to her breasts. She arched, pulling him deeper, clenching around him. So much heat. He was lost in the moment and hoped she was nearly there, because he couldn't hold back. Didn't want to. Abandoned all sense and came with a shudder, murmuring her name in her ear as he did. She bore down against him, once, twice, then he felt her orgasm. Powerful, complete. Their limbs slowly melted into one another, and he rolled on to one hip to take his weight from her body. Her arms relaxed; he'd been vaguely aware of her raking his back with her nails. Now she rolled toward him, both on their sides facing one another. She kissed his mouth softly. 'Nice work teacher.'

He chuckled, brushed her hair away from her cheek. She nuzzled his hand for a moment, sighed, then closed her eyes. 'Sleep Ayla. It's early.'

He lay there, watching her. She was asleep in moments, one hand under her pillow, the other on his shoulder. He could watch her for hours. It was after five-thirty, he'd let her sleep until six, then they'd better shower and dress before the girls woke.

* * *

'DAAAD!' HE WOKE WITH A JOLT. RUBY WAS OUTSIDE THE bedroom door. He was surprised she hadn't just opened it, but maybe she'd found Skye alone in the guest room and figured out Ayla was with him. Ayla stirred, looked at him. He was already running through his mind the words he would say to Ruby, to explain.

'You're frowning.' She sat up, reached around, smoothing the crease he could feel between his eyes.

'It's just. You know. Ruby. Telling her.' He was muttering, but now pulling on shorts and a tee shirt. The whole room smelled of sex. He watched Ayla stand and pull her shirt back on. She stepped to the door, opened it a little, slipped into the hall and closed it again. He strained his ears.

'Good morning Ruby.' Her voice was pleasant, friendly.

'Hello Ayla.' Ruby sounded less certain. 'You must have arrived late last night.'

'We did, it was late, and I need fuel. Had to stop.' Ayla laughed and he heard warmth in her next words. '*Wanted* to stop. I hope you don't mind Ruby?'

'No.' Ruby still sounded uncertain. 'But, um, is Dad awake? Um, we all slept in. Will I just make some smoothies for breakfast?'

They were moving further along the hall. He hesitated at the bedroom door, took a deep breath.

'Smoothies will be perfect. I'll have a super quick shower then get Skye up. Your dad is awake.'

He waited. Cowardly he knew, but he wasn't keen to face his daughter. He heard the shower running, and the blender in the kitchen. Taking a deep breath, he walked quietly into the room; Ruby was pouring the drink into glasses.

'Morning Rubes. Great idea, smoothies. We're, ah, a bit late.' He waited for her reaction, but she was focussed on the blender.

'It's okay Dad. I get it.' She looked up, half smiled, then he saw tears in her eyes, and he rushed forward, enveloping her in his arms.

'Ruby.' He wanted to say more but she shook her head and drew back from him. Looking up at him, a tear slid silently down her face. 'I'm not upset. I'm happy Dad. Happy for you. For us.' Then she gave him a lop-sided grin. 'You need to shower. You stink. And we're really, really late.'

He'd been holding so much tension that he threw back his head and laughed out loud at her words. 'I am happy Ruby. And I love you. So much.' His smile was echoed in her face, and he turned, strode down the hall and opened the bathroom door. The shower was still running. He stepped in as Ayla stepped out. He kissed her quickly. 'You're amazing.' She raised her eyebrows, touched the beard rash on her neck. 'So are you.'

Showered and dressed in record time, he returned to the kitchen to find Ayla and the girls finishing their smoothies. Skye held up her arms, and he picked her up, hugging her briefly. 'We slept at your house.' She nodded emphatically.

'Yes, and I'm so happy you did.' He set her down and took the drink container Ruby handed to him. 'Your breakfast Dad. We'll have to get lunch from the general store today. It's almost time to ring the bell.'

Two minutes later he was in his car, idling behind Ayla's van as she waited for an oncoming vehicle before turning onto the road. The vehicle slowed slightly. It was Joyce Wilson, the mail contractor. He saw Ayla wave to her as she went past. He looked at Ruby, who was chuckling.

'What?'

'Your secret's out now Dad.' She pointed to his expression as he drove on to the road, turning off to the school as Ayla pulled into the general store. Frank was standing at the bowser.

Alex looked at Ruby. 'Definitely no secret. Now.' And they exchanged a complicit look as he pulled up at school as the bell rang.

44

The bees always seem to have a way of gently reminding me of the interconnected nature of life, they have a very special way of bringing the right people together at the right time. @embodybee

Ayla thought again about Nicole's words to her last time they'd caught up. *The men you're usually attracted to, where are they now?* The words, the concept, had preyed on her mind. She'd always trusted her own judgement, in everything. And when she broke it down, the men she'd allowed into her life had been, well, like her. A bit wild perhaps, off-grid in more ways than one, many of them travellers, or wanderers. Unsettled. And that had been fine, and fun, for many years. But she had Skye now, and she'd changed a bit herself. Needed to be settled, grounded. She wanted to consider a move from Yin-Yin to Yin-Yang. Perhaps.

Alex was settled and grounded, and she had told herself, from the beginning, that he wasn't her type. Yin-Yang. But she had judged quickly. It was what he represented, and the education system he worked in. She was a Steiner education convert herself, eschewing the government system. Physically, he was built like a god. No problem there. Emotionally he was conservative. Or was he? He had taken a risk last night, with the girls so close. He'd dropped his school-principal-conservative-dad persona to be a surprisingly good lover. The first time she had slept with him she knew he held himself back, waited for her pleasure before achieving his own. That was lovely. Considerate. But she had pushed him last night, to let himself go, abandon any pre-conceived notions he had about being a good lover, and just feel. Meld with her body, her mind, even her soul. She had been amazed; his response had touched her heart. She had turned a switch on in him and he had matched her, more than matched her, in passion, energy, depth. Her head spun.

He was subtle too. Yes, he was a state school principal, but he had pushed for the bee program, and was constantly trying to adapt the curriculum to the needs of his students, even allowing a discussion in class on dingoes: to cull or not to cull. And now she knew he shared some of her beliefs. When he believed in something he took risks, but he was also clear-headed and strategic. It was something Ayla was trying to improve in her own style, especially with her business. Yes, passion is fabulous, and she has confidence in her instincts. For products, marketing and people. But sometimes she lets her own prejudices, formed by earlier experiences, colour her judgement. She loved his relationship with his daughter, and he was generous in his affection to Skye.

Ayla sighed. A big decision. She couldn't afford things to go pear-shaped, she was putting everything into this move, settling here in Barrington. But she'd give it a go. See where it led. There'd be hiccups, she was sure, but instead of walking away like she had in the past, she could choose to stay, and fight for the relationship, if necessary. If he was worth it. He could be. Worth it.

* * *

PULLING UP IN FRONT OF HER COTTAGE SHE WAS EXCITED TO SEE several vehicles there. Robbie and Harry, an electrician, a plumber and even Nicole's car. She helped Skye out and looked toward the main building. The large power pole had already been replaced. Taking their bags and the groceries she'd picked up in town, she hurried inside, keen to head up to the main buildings to find Robbie. And the truck with her business equipment and stock was coming today, possibly just an hour or so away.

She opened the door to the cottage and felt a breeze, then heard music playing. Skye ran in front of her, to the living area at the back of the cottage. Harry and Bill Fraser were out there. They'd removed her makeshift wall, replacing it with timber framing, vee-jay panels on the inside. They had set in glass and timber French doors, like the ones in the main building, and on either side, timber framed windows. Harry and Bill were outside, standing on what looked like a whole new back deck. Ayla couldn't believe it.

'Harry! Hello Bill.' She stepped toward them, grinning while she took in the work they'd completed in only a week. Harry pulled his phone from his top pocket and turned the music off. She could see a small speaker sitting on an esky to one side.

'Ayla! Hi, I wasn't expecting you until tomorrow. We'd hoped to have this almost done.' Harry stood tall. She could see he was proud of the work they'd done.

'It's wonderful Harry.' She stepped out to the veranda, Skye behind her. Harry bent down and picked Skye up. Ayla pointed. 'Where did you get the doors, and these windows? They're just like the ones in the guest accommodation.' Ayla turned around. The veranda was wide, timber cladding already installed on the outside wall.

'That's the thing. We cleaned up around the cottages up there the very first day. Avery came up and she and Bill were tackling the worst one, while Dad I got started on the good one. As they pulled out the ruined curtains and furnishings and so on, they saw a pile of rubble under the cottage, covered in an old tarpaulin. They decided they'd pull that out too, thinking it was rubbish for the dump.' He stopped, looked at Bill, who was grinning. Ayla was laughing too, waiting to hear what came next.

Harry paused, and she nudged his arm. 'Come on Harry, I'm dying to know more!'

'Under the tarp was a hole, well, a depression really, lined with more tarp. It was filled with windows, doors, cladding, vee-jay, even roofing beams. Pretty much all the materials to build another cottage.' His eyes crinkled and he juggled Skye to his other hip.

'Oh! Really? I've never looked underneath. How fabulous! And the materials are in good condition, so you've used them here?' She was shaking her head at the wonder of it.

'Mostly good condition. There was one broken windowpane. But that's not all Ayla.' She raised her eyebrows. 'The same materials supply was under the second cottage. We've pulled it all out, it's in the stables, it's all good stuff. It's been protected from the weather and the fire didn't reach it. But Ayla, you have enough materials to build a third cottage up there, if you can get Council approval. And still have enough to add an extension on here, if you want to.'

'Oh gosh! That's brilliant Harry!' She impulsively reached over and hugged him, then took Skye into her own arms. He flushed. She looked at Bill. 'And you too, Bill, thank you.' She hugged him too and he responded awkwardly, blushing furiously. She chuckled. She was pumped.

'I'm going to walk up and find Robbie. And Avery. Wow! I'm so excited.' She began to turn away. 'Oh, Harry, there's a truck coming with my business equipment and stock. Can you send it up to the main building. I'm hoping we can move stuff straight in, rather than here at the stables.'

'Sure Ayla. The stables are full anyway. We'll come up with it, help to unload. You're going to love what we've got done up there too.'

Back in the kitchen, Ayla grabbed the brownies she'd picked up at Debbie's that morning, packing them into a basket. They walked up the hill to the main building. She stopped at the front doorway. The room gleamed, the floor shone, furniture was polished. She could hear noise from the kitchen end, so they walked down there. Standing in the doorway she saw Avery on her knees, scrubbing the coolroom. The stainless-steel benches shone, and Robbie stepped in through the back door, Nicole right behind him.

'Ayla! You're back!' Nicole walked over, hugged her and took Skye's hand, pointing to the basket in the corner where Bandit was now standing, wiggling his rear end in excitement. Skye ran to him, scooping him into her arms. Avery stood, wiped her knees briskly. 'Hi Ayla.' Ayla just stood for a moment, her pulse racing. She hadn't expected they'd achieve so much in a week. She felt her eyes fill with tears. She looked at Robbie, opened her mouth, but no words came out.

He stepped close, put his arm around her shoulders. 'We've had a lot of help. It's been a good week.' He walked her back into the main room, pointing as he went. 'They set the new power pole in on Monday, and we had power that afternoon. Avery has been amazing, she's a hard worker. She has cleaned everything, got the smell out of that first cottage too. And you've probably seen Harry?' He didn't wait for an answer. 'Avery and Bill found the building materials. We've used a small amount on your house, but there's plenty left. It's in the stables.' Ayla nodded, her emotions now under control. Robbie was calm and practical and, she thought, enjoying her surprise.

'The electricians have reinstalled power here and to the cool room and freezer. And they're just checking the connections to the two cottages. They need furnishings, but they're ready to use. Water is on too.' They walked back to the kitchen.

Avery stepped across to the commercial dishwasher, lifted it, and pulled a steaming tray of clean crockery out. 'Everything works Ayla.' Ayla nodded, feeling overwhelmed again.

Nicole took the basket from her hand. 'Put the urn on Avery, we'll make some tea, it looks like Ayla has some of Debbie's brownies in here.'

Everyone began talking at once, then Skye ran in from the main room, Bandit still in her arms. 'There's a big truck coming Mama!'

Ayla clapped her hands and spun around, almost running

to the front door to direct the truck. She needn't have bothered, Harry was riding in it, directing the driver to the rear of the building. Running right through to the back of the main building as the truck backed the rig in expertly, she sat Skye by Bandit's basket. 'Look after Bandit while we unload, I don't want anyone stepping on him.'

THEY UNLOADED THE STOCK INTO THE LARGE STOREROOM AT THE back of the building, then stopped for morning tea. But after half an hour they started again, getting all the equipment out, bringing it through to the main building. And there was furniture too, that had been in storage. The driver was keen to get going, he had a two-day drive back to Victoria.

Later, it was just Nicole and Ayla. Skye carried Bandit back to the house with Harry, he'd done some work on the chicken coop and she was keen to see it.

'I can't believe it Nik, so much completed in just a week. I honestly thought it would be months to get to this stage.' They were on the side veranda of the main building, drinking herb tea. The Barn. She called it that in her head so she thought she'd keep the name.

'Many hands Ayla. Avery has been a huge help. She's a hard worker and wants to show you what she can do. She was talking about herbs and vegetables too and she's keen to discuss the possibility of a job. Robbie is paying for her time now, and he says she's been worth it. She'd have worked unpaid, grateful for the home we've provided, for a chance to show what she can do, but Robbie wouldn't hear of it. And Julia is looking after Jacinta, so Avery is paying her too.' Nik sipped her tea. 'And Bill Fraser has been here every day, he's a good labourer and gets on well with Harry.'

'And you Nik? You're here too.' Avery smiled over the rim of her cup.

'Not every day, but I helped clean the cottages once everything was out.' Nicole glanced away for a moment. 'And I'm happy to do it.'

'And Julia, how is she coping?' Ayla asked gently.

Nicole sighed. 'She's missing David. She's asked him to come up and have a look, but he's not keen. He seems happy with his dad. I'm not sure if she'll stay, but we had two lots of guests in our stable accommodation this week, and I asked her if she'd help with the housekeeping, change the linen and clean when they checked out. I usually do it myself or pay a couple of locals to come and do it. She was brilliant and loved that she could earn and have Kristal with her. And she liked looking after Jacinta too. But she's had a few dark moments, so we'll see.' Ayla nodded. She'd expected ups and downs. But she was impressed with both women, it was a big change for them. And Avery, she'd make time to talk to her. Perhaps she could offer her a job. Maybe more than a job.

45

No one had commented on his late arrival at school, and he didn't offer an explanation. The morning flew by. He didn't have time to think about his night with Ayla. Or about Ruby and Skye and if there were changes afoot. And what shape they may take.

But at lunch time he drove around to the general store to pick up sandwiches for himself and Ruby. He asked Nadia for a coffee while he was there. She seemed a bit quiet, but he was tired himself, so paid for the goods and returned to school.

He was pleased when the day ended. He was hoping to speak more to Ruby about Ayla staying over, and he had essays to mark. But he also wanted to speak to Ayla once Ruby went to bed. He knew that two nights together didn't make a relationship, but he wanted to hear her voice, and make plans to visit her. Mid-week if she'd let them come up, or on the weekend. He knew Robbie had been up there all week. He'd even asked on Saturday morning if he needed a hand, said he could come up and do some labouring, but Robbie said he had Harry, Avery and a couple of the Fraser lads. Alex was curious, he wanted to see the place up close. And he wanted to see Ayla.

They had an early dinner. He'd broached the subject with Ruby, and she'd been vague, making a yuck face. 'You don't need my permission, Dad. I like Ayla, and Skye. I want you to be happy.' She'd gone to bed to read, and he had cleaned up in the kitchen, then messaged Ayla.

> How is it up there? X

>> Brilliant! Robbie and Harry are amazing. And Avery and Nik and Bill Fraser.

He was disappointed she hadn't returned the kiss, but told himself not to overthink, she had a lot going on.

> Anything I can help with? Ruby and I could come up after school one night. X

>> I'm not sure. Yes, maybe. We might need some groceries and I'm not sure I'll come to town this week. X

He was heartened by the kiss. But he didn't want to sound needy either.

> Just message me your list, we can pick up what you need. Any night is fine. X

>> OK thanks. I'll get back to you. Probably tomorrow. Goodnight. X

Goodnight. X

He should have called her. She sounded distracted. But he hoped she'd follow through and send him a shopping list, then he and Ruby could go up there. Maybe stay the night.

* * *

RUBY WAS MAKING THEIR LUNCH NEXT MORNING WHEN HIS PHONE rang. She handed it to him. 'It's Melanie Evans.'

He raised his eyebrows and took the phone. 'Hi Melanie.'

'Hi Alex.' She paused. He was about to speak, when she continued. 'You might have a problem.'

'Oh?'

'I don't like being the one to tell you, but it's best you're forewarned.'

'Forewarned? About what?'

'There may be parents asking questions when you get to school today. Joyce Wilson saw Ayla leaving your place early yesterday, and she has been telling anyone who will listen, including parents, that you're having an affair with the 'the nudist hippie', her words Alex, not mine. She's made it sound like you've been involved for a while and that paying her to do the bee program is a conflict of interest. There's more, that your wife left you because of this and so on. None of it is reasonable, but she's had a grudge against Ayla from the start. There was even a comment about Skye's, er, possible heritage that was very nasty. Ben had some calls last night, he's tried to hose it down, but you know, it's the ugly part of small towns. Gossip. And unfortunately, as the school principal, you have to be above reproach.' She sighed.

'Damn! I did not expect this. Yes, we saw Joyce drive by yesterday, but really?' He was frustrated, and suddenly nervous. And angry that anyone would use Skye to make a point. Or Ruby for that matter.

'Thank you for calling Melanie. I'll warn Ruby, this may be hard for her, and we'll be at school shortly.' Now he understood why Nadia may have been quiet. And he'd thought she was on Team Ayla. But Joyce had the mail run, and the ear of a lot of people on this side of town. Perhaps she was making it awkward for Nadia.

He called Ruby to the car. He thought of glossing over it as they drove to school, then decided she was mature enough to know the facts. He relayed Melanie's conversation to her. He didn't mention the bit about Skye. Ruby was quiet for a moment.

'It doesn't make sense Dad. Some kids at school have parents who aren't married. Like Billie Murray. Harriet isn't her mother, or even her step-mother. And Tiffany's dad isn't her real dad. Robbie and Nik only got married this year. What's the big deal?' He was pleased she understood. And was on his side. And Ayla's.

Parents were milling around at the front gate. Not as many as he thought. He was pleased to see Drum Murray, Ben and Melanie there. And Joyce Wilson was there, but she had a grandchild at the school, so he couldn't send her away. He sent Ruby straight inside, then stood at the gate. Maintaining his composure, he turned toward them.

'Is there something you need?' He didn't look at Joyce but let his gaze rest on other faces. Frank was there, standing beside Joyce.

'You're our principal. You can't be knockin' off that chit from up the tops.' Joyce jerked her head toward the mountains, her tone was rough, ugly.

'My personal life is not open for discussion. I will never,' he paused, looked at them all again, 'do anything to jeopardise the school community. I have not and will not. If you have a genuine complaint, put it in writing.' He nodded at Ben, Melanie and Drum, then waited. The group around Joyce murmured together and began to move off.

Joyce turned, hands on hips. 'We will. Put it in writing. And we'll send it to the School Board too. You'll be out on your ear; you mark my words.' Joyce nodded as she spoke and moved away with her small band of followers.

Ben stepped over. 'You have witnesses Alex. I don't know if she'll follow through, or what grounds she can give, but be prepared. It may get worse before she's done.'

Alex nodded. He thanked them for the warning, for their support, and stalked inside. During the day some of his students were a bit quiet, and he saw Ruby was angry and upset after the lunch break. He tried to catch her for a moment.

'Rubes?'

'It's okay Dad. It's just talk. I blame their parents.'

'Is it Sam Fraser again?'

Her face was surprised, and she gave him a wan smile. 'No Dad, not Sam. I had to stop him from punching someone. He's on our side.'

'Gosh Ruby. Tell me, I'll handle it.' He tried to put his arm around her, but she stepped away.

'I've got this Dad.'

He had to trust that she did. The next day was no better, but there weren't any parents waiting for him. One family with two

children, Joyce's grandchildren, kept their children home the
rest of the week.

* * *

Still want to come up for a visit? x

It was Thursday morning and he hadn't heard from Ayla
all week. He had bumped into Nicole, and she'd said it was
chaotic up there, that Ayla had product orders to fill and had
been working day and night, but she had Avery helping her. He
hadn't talked to her about the blow up at school, wasn't sure if
she knew and didn't want to add to her stress, or workload.

Sure. Tonight? Want me to get
groceries? x

He was keen to see her. He'd tell her what was happening,
but only in person.

No. Just come up. Bring Ruby. Stay
over, we have room. X

He thought she sounded chirpy. He was pleased for her.

Can't wait xx

He told Ruby in the car. 'Cool.' Was her only response. The
chatter at school had been less yesterday. The kids seemed to
be over it. He hoped the parents were. And Ayla was booked to
give a lesson on Friday afternoon.

There was a letter on his desk when he arrived, from the

Education Department. Not unusual at this time of year. He'd asked for a teacher's aide for the middle grades for next year.

He opened it quickly; just one page. He scanned it, then sat down, shocked. It was a one page 'please explain', focussing on a complaint that he had procured employment for a sub-contractor, Ayla, and was also in a relationship with that sub-contractor. The inference being he had misappropriated school funds to pay his lover. He rested his head in his hands for a moment. Anger built in his chest, and he fought to tamp it down. He must remain calm. And think this through.

46

We have to admit that the natural pharmacy of bees is incomparably more effective than the entire modern chemical and pharmaceutical industry and we have a lot to learn from them. **Valery A. Isidorov**

The first week of production in the Barn was probably the busiest she'd ever experienced. Almost out of a lot of stock items, Ayla worked harder than ever before to get the on-line orders ready to be shipped out at the end of the week. But the newly installed power had allowed her to set up her business system in the office at one end of the building, complete with label printer for orders and enough internet service to keep her website and socials up to date.

The range of bee-based health products – various honey and beeswax products including the Miracle Balm she made for Save the Bees Australia, giving profit from each tin sold back to them – had run low and she had needed to go into production sooner than she'd have liked. She had quite a store of beeswax candles, but her Chicks Vapour Rub and healthy honey products had almost sold out. Her honey range was now iconic, whipped with herbs and natural medicines and she was struggling to keep up with demand. Avery had been a blessing; she had come up with Robbie every day and had quickly taken over packaging the products. Ayla had asked her if she'd be interested in a job, and she was keen but was worried about leaving Jacinta with Julia every day. Not that Julia wasn't great, and enjoying the work, but Avery wasn't used to leaving Jacinta all day. Ayla had some thoughts on that too but wasn't ready to share.

Harry and Bill had almost finished the extension on her house and Robbie had completed repairs on the two cottages. There was still some painting to do, and she needed to figure out furnishings. Her original vision had expanded.

One thing that had never changed, however, was her plan to make the eight-hundred-hectare property into a bee sanctuary. The tiny and deadly Varroa Mite had recently breached the shores of Australia. Disastrous to honeybee colonies, government agencies were exterminating hives in an ever-expanding circle of infestation in a seemingly chaotic and ill-thought out Varroa Mite management plan. Ayla was working with Save the Bees to save the bee populations and had relocated her own hives to the area just in time to avoid destruction in Victoria. Hers were free of the infestation, but many beekeepers had not been so lucky. No bees, no pollination, no one eats. The message was simple, and clear, but still rogue apiarists, and farmers in some cases, had been moving infested hives into areas formerly clear of the disease for mono crop pollination. The very thought made her anxious, and angry. It was possible that commercial producers would begin to introduce chemical treatments but looking at Varroa in the rest of the world, it becomes resistant to the treatment and stronger poisons are employed in the hives. By making her bee sanctuary treatment free, using only natural remedies, some bees would die but those that survived would create stronger genetics over time.

But getting the first batch of orders out, with just Avery helping, had kept her too busy to dwell on the problems in her industry. On top of that, she was quietly excited about the Alex and Ruby coming to stay over. She wanted to show him what she had done so far and share some of her plans. His reaction would help her move forward with him. Or not. He didn't have to share her dreams, but he needed to understand them, if they had a chance together. And she wanted to spend more time with Ruby, make sure she was alright, assure her she wouldn't lose her dad.

Alex and Ruby drove in just after Robbie, Harry and Avery drove out. They would have met on the long driveway in. Ayla had told Skye they were coming, and she was excited about sharing her room, and big bed, with Ruby. Ayla would let Ruby know she could sleep on the sofa if she wanted, would give her the choice, at least.

Skye sped ahead to the garden gate and ran straight to Ruby when she stepped out. She was laughing and talking, tugging on her hand, chattering about the chickens and Bandit. Skye almost ignored the teacher in her haste, and he just winked at his daughter as she was led across to the chicken house. Ayla strolled through the gate, feigning nonchalance when really, her heart had sped up at the sight of him. In shorts and a tee, his long legs tanned, he looked even better than he had naked in his bed. She shook her head slightly, telling herself to let that image go until later.

He stepped across to her, leaned in, then seemed to have second thoughts. But his hesitation was brief. He wrapped his arms around her, pulling her hard against his chest, speaking quietly into her ear, 'So good to see you Ayla. Thank you.' His words warmed her. Still in his arms, she leaned back to meet his eyes. 'We're happy you're here.' She kissed his lips briefly, then stepped out of his arms. Sliding her hand into his she led him to the chickens, then the four of them walked on to the stables.

There were four stalls, a tack room, a workshop area and a large bay at the other end for hay and feed which had been fire damaged. Harry had plans to repair it. There hadn't been horses in them for years, and the stalls were full of building materials, but Ayla knew it was a solid building and she was lucky to have the storage space. It was Ruby's response that surprised her.

'Ayla! Proper stables. And yards, and a horse paddock over there too. Oh gosh, did they have horses here when it was a resort?' Ruby, Bandit in her arms, ran from stall to stall, then into the tack room. Poking her head out, she beckoned them. 'There are saddles in here, and bridles. And horse rugs and helmets and even riding boots! Did they just walk out and leave this stuff?' Her face was flushed with excitement.

'Um, yes. I think that's exactly what happened. There's furniture in the two cottages that didn't burn down, and the main building, the Barn,' Ayla pointed up the hill, 'still has dining furniture, kitchen equipment, even crockery and cutlery.'

'Wow! You could have horses here Ayla.' Ruby stepped out of the tack room. 'Although the saddles and bridles need oiling and some of the leathers have been chewed by something.' She screwed her nose up then and they laughed.

'Horses!' Skye had been listening intently. 'Can we have horses Mama?' She took Ayla's hand shaking it a bit. Ayla saw the Teacher shake his head slightly at Ruby, who made an O with her mouth, then nodded.

'Not yet Skye, but yes, I think so, later on you can have a horse, or maybe a pony.' Ayla knelt to answer Skye directly.

'When I'm six?' Skye bounced a bit, then put her hand on Ayla's cheek.

'Once you've started school. We'll start looking for a pony for you. Robbie and Harry might be able to help us.' Ayla stood up, taking Skye's hand. 'Come on, let's show them the main buildings, before it gets dark.'

Skye let go and ran ahead with Ruby. Ayla and Alex followed. 'Do you ride Ayla?'

'I have done. When I was younger. I'm not confident, or knowledgeable. But there are people here who can help.' She looked at him, then. 'Maybe you, and Ruby, can help?'

He seemed to think about this. 'Maybe we can. Perhaps you can get a horse too, something quiet to begin with, and we can all ride. I understand you're on the edge of the State Forest and National Park here, so many places to ride.' He grinned at her. 'And as Ruby so clearly pointed out, you have stables, yards and a horse paddock.'

'Hmm. I hadn't thought beyond having someone teach Skye. But yes, perhaps. It's not something I have a particular passion for, but to do it with Skye, well, that's worth some consideration.'

Ayla watched Alex's reaction to the Barn, her office already set up and the products stored in the kitchen and cool room. 'Amazing. This is amazing.' Then she took him to the cottages, now empty and ready to paint.

'This must have been quite spectacular in its day. These are beautiful.' Skye and Ruby had run upstairs in the first one, then down again, with Ruby exclaiming, 'Wow! This bathroom is better than ours at home!' He admired the large spa bathtub, giving her a look as he did.

Ayla chuckled. 'There's an identical bathroom down in our little house. They must have put it in when they built these.'

'How very clever of them.' Was all he said.

The girls ran back down the hill, Skye was taking Ruby to see the beehives. She was particularly keen to see the colony Ayla had rescued from the school.

Ayla and Alex took their time. He held the young dingo against his chest. 'What are your plans for the cottages, Ayla?'

'It's good you ask that. My ideas have shifted, a bit. Originally I was going to use them as accommodation for international workers, or WOOFers. But now I'm thinking about offering one of them to Avery as part of a job package. She could live here, have her little girl with her; we can have Jacinta, and Skye, with us when we're working. She can borrow my car to drive into town when she wants to and maybe she can buy her own at some point. If she says yes, we'll try it. If it works, maybe I'll do the same with the cottage. Offer it as a haven for a woman, or women, who need a fresh start. I need more staff, I can get some locals to come in, but this could work too. Maybe to Nik's to settle in, get used to the local area, then here if they want work and don't mind being a bit further out of town.' They were nearing the house, and she really wanted his thoughts on this. It was the first time she'd said them aloud.

'You're an amazing woman, Ayla. The way you think, and your generosity of spirit and your entrepreneurial mindset. You can create your own community here. A safe haven. Bees, women, children.' His face was full of admiration, although his words were crystal clear too.

Her heart beat a little bit faster. 'Maybe single-dad-teacher-and-his-horse-mad-daughter too?' It was too soon to discuss such a thought, but the words slipped out. She knew he rented his place from Robbie. Would he live up here? Could he live up here?

He stopped, they were at the garden gate and the girls were just a few metres away. Wrapping his strong arms around her he said, 'That's entirely possible Ayla. Let's talk about that a bit more. Later.'

She kissed his mouth, hard. Then led him through the garden to the rescued colony. His words left her tingling. In a good way.

47

Relaxing on the new back deck, mugs of honey cacao tea in their hands, Alex and Ayla chatted quietly, while the evening darkened, and the frog and cicada orchestra began to warm up. Skye was asleep already and Ruby was at the kitchen table writing a report for class on the rescued colony of bees. She had taken photos with his phone and was putting a presentation together for school the next day.

'I see why you love it here Ayla. It's beautiful and peaceful, and pristine. That little stream at the bottom of your garden is crystal clear, no wonder there are so many frogs, I read somewhere that frog life is an indication of a clean environment.'

'It is amazing to think I own this now. Well, not own exactly, I have a mortgage, but it's not large. If the fire hadn't destroyed the business here, as it was, I would never have been able to buy in. Getting so much land, in this location, is magic.' She turned to him as she spoke, and he loved seeing her expressions; passion and conviction and gratitude, underlining her words.

'Was it a risk for you, Ayla? Not financially, but emotionally? Moving to another state, uprooting your business, recruiting new employees, starting over?' He was genuinely interested. Moving here had been a risk for him too. Had it not been for COVID, he may never have considered it. It had worked out for him. He frowned then, thinking about the letter he'd received from the School Board. He would tell Ayla. Later. He didn't want to spoil the moment.

'Perhaps it was a risk, but Alex, I don't think that way. I generally don't analyse everything, I'm driven by instinct, I think.' She gazed out into the night, her words soft. 'Developing my business, taking on social media the way I have. Instinct. In fact, I'm a bit of an introvert.' She nudged him with her elbow, and chuckled. 'I know I seem confident, and out there, but really ...' She hesitated.

'But really?' He let his tone match hers. Soft. But he was keen to hear more.

Taking a breath, she continued. 'If I believe in something, have passion for it, then I just seem to follow through. Once I decide, have clarity, then I'm one hundred percent invested. My online community seem to get me. When I tell them I've made something I love, I believe it. So do they.' She sipped her drink, then set it down beside her chair. 'There were times, well moments in time, that I felt low. I had a relationship fail, before. I was heart-broken. At first I tried to suck it up, put on a brave face, engage with my peeps online. Then one morning, I just wasn't feeling it. I cried just getting out of bed. So, I filmed myself. Bared my soul. It was cathartic, just expressing my sadness lifted me enough to get up and get on with my day. I needed to do it for Skye. Then later, about mid-morning, I watched the bit I'd filmed. I cried again but decided to post the video.' Watching her speak, her eyes glistening, he knew she was back there in that dark moment. 'I'd had comments previously from my community telling me my products lifted them, in some way, or that my words and videos and posts did. So, I wondered what their reaction might be to me, sharing my pain. The video wasn't long, but it was raw and real.'

Her hand was in his now, he'd reached across to take it as she spoke. His thumb was rubbing the back of her hand and he'd never felt closer to her. 'And their response?' He asked the question, but already knew what her answer would be.

'So much love and support, for me, for Skye. For my business, my mothering. It was beautiful. And some shared their own pain, and the community rallied around them too.' She laid her head back, looking up. He followed her gaze. Millions of stars, bright and clear in the night sky. 'If online support can lift someone, like it did, imagine what physical support can do? There have been times I've felt lonely, just me and Skye, but I have a chance now, here, to offer support to others who may be going through something. Avery and Jacinta to begin with, but Alex,' Her face was brighter now, excited by possibilities and he felt his own mood match hers. 'Alex, I have the materials to build a third cottage and to add on to the house here a bit. Another bedroom, second living space. And I've spoken to Council. The property was previously approved for ten cottages, I don't even have to apply to Council to build, they just need to inspect them before they're inhabited.'

'I'm so impressed Ayla. I had no idea, when I met you, that

you had a business like this. You've worked so hard, and your instincts are good.' He shook his head in wonder, with a feeling bubbling away in his chest. He considered it for a moment. He was proud of her, proud of what she had achieved.

She laughed then. 'Don't get me started Alex. There's more.'

'More?'

'I have plans for a weekend Honey Festival. With local music, produce and art, make it an annual event and use proceeds to support the Bee Sanctuary. But also, as a driver for tourism, good tourism. I'd have it in Barrington or even here at the property. Share the bounty of the bees. There are so many wonderful businesses in the area. Debbie's café is amazing, there's a new event planner, I'm wondering if we can work together on the festival.'

'I love the idea. Gosh Ayla, you're an absolute breath of fresh air. We're so lucky to have you here.' He hesitated, should he tell her about the problem at school now? He didn't want to spoil the moment. And the reality is, it's his problem to solve, not hers. He just hoped the fallout wouldn't compromise her in any way.

'Hey Dad?' Ruby stepped out on to the deck. 'I've finished the report, can you look at it please?' She seemed shy, uncertain in front of Ayla perhaps.

He stood, wrapped an arm around her. 'Of course, Rubes. I'll look at it now.' He glanced at Ayla, but she was standing too, bending to pick up their mugs from the floor. He followed Ruby inside; she'd been working on her laptop. Ayla murmured something about checking on Skye.

He finished reading, made a couple of minor suggestions and told Ruby it was brilliant. It really was. Ayla returned, hovered near the table. He looked at Ruby. 'Is it okay if Ayla reads this?' Ruby nodded, shy again. He realised that Ayla's opinion was important to his daughter than even his, but he had faith that Ayla would be generous with her response. He wondered if Ruby would become a bee activist too.

He washed their cups at the sink, leaving Ayla to sit with Ruby. As she read, Ayla asked Ruby questions. 'Where did you get this information, and this piece here.' Ruby responded. 'Save the Bees website has so much information Ayla, that's where I got most of it. But also from you, when you were showing us the beehives. See, I've used your words here, and here.' As Ayla put an arm around his daughter's shoulders, he stepped closer to hear her words. 'You're already a bee activist Ruby, and this report is excellent. Really clear, the kids in your class will understand it, but full of information that you've fact-checked. You should be proud of this Ruby, I know I am.' He saw Ruby lean into Ayla for a moment and he was touched beyond words.

* * *

THEY WERE UP BEFORE THE GIRLS, MAKING TIME FOR THE THIRTY-minute drive down the mountain. Alex had lain in bed before dawn, still tingling from their earlier love-making. Slow and tender, they had explored each other thoroughly and he had marvelled at the beautiful contours of her body. Lean and graceful, yet strong. He had led to begin with, but she had become demanding at some point, and he was happy to follow her direction. He'd held back, ensuring she orgasmed, before allowing himself to let go. They'd slept, then sometime in the wee hours a dingo howl had woken them. They'd gone out to the deck, naked, and listened, leaning into each other. Back in bed she'd thrown a leg over him, enveloping him, then riding him hard and fast. He gave in, stopped thinking, and just let himself *feel* her. All of her. She made love with such abandon, her face reflecting her emotions. He knew, as she bore down on him, then covered his chest with her breasts, that he could love her. Did love her. Early days, but he had never felt closer to a woman.

They showered together, giggling as they soaped each other up. He admired the large oval spa tub in the bathroom, but they'd not had time to use it. He told himself there'd be other times. Many times. Dressed and in the kitchen when Ruby and Skye appeared together, still in pyjamas. Skye was bubbly and excited to find Ruby in her bed when she woke up. Skye put her arms up, and Ayla picked her up, held her close and told her good morning. Ruby said good morning, gave him a hip bump, then headed to the bathroom.

It was early, but a breakfast of home-made bread, scrambled eggs and fresh tomatoes and he and Ruby were ready to leave. They'd call in at home first, so Ruby could get into school uniform. It was Friday and Ayla and Skye were coming to school in the afternoon to do another bee talk, and Ruby was going to present her report to the class then.

Standing at the garden gate, he kissed her quickly while Skye and Ruby ran off to check for eggs and let the chickens out.

'Ayla, there's been a, um, hitch. It may come up when you're at school this afternoon, if parents turn up.' He hated telling her, it was spoiling the mood. But he didn't want her to be blind-sided.

'A hitch.' She raised her eyebrows.

'A complaint to the School Board. About my, er, our, relationship.' Her eyebrows rose higher, but a faint smile played around her lips. She probably thought he was being overly conservative again.

'What does *our relationship*...' He watched her pause, then say it again. She seemed to like saying it. A bubble of pleasure enveloped him for amount. 'What does *our relationship* have to do with the School Board?' Now she had a small crease between her eyebrows, and he was tempted to lean forward and kiss it, but the girls were coming back so he needed to be quick.

'I've been sent a *please explain* letter. Basically the complaint suggests I've misappropriated school funds to hire you for the bee program, that we were in a relationship prior to the contract.' He sighed. Ruby was helping Skye carry the eggs inside, but she glanced at him curiously as she went by.

'Well, that's not true.' Ayla had her hands on her hips. 'We've only just started seeing each other.' She gave him a cheeky grin. 'I'm not even sure I *liked* you, when you hired me.' That made him chuckle. He knew that too.

'The thing is, it's my word against the complaints. And the department.' He took her hands in his, bringing them to his chest. 'I understand if you'd like to cancel coming today, there may be fallout. I really don't know.'

'Joyce Wilson?' He nodded. Not willing to say more, Ruby was now back at his side.

Ayla leaned across and hugged Ruby. 'Thanks for coming. Skye and I loved having you here.' Ruby nodded, hugging her back quickly. She waved to Skye; Ayla had picked her up.

Ayla called out as Ruby opened the car door. 'I'll see you

this afternoon. Can't wait to hear your presentation.' Ruby grinned, waved and got into the car.

He looked at Ayla. 'So, you'll still come?'

'Pfft. Of course.' He kissed her lips quickly, tweaked Skye's nose making her giggle, and walked to the car, his heart pounding. He had serious feelings for this woman. For Skye too.

48

In ancient times honey was known as Food of the Gods. They were right to worship the bee and viewed honey as the medicine it truly is. But they didn't understand it was the female bees foraging nectar and transforming it into honey. Alchemists of the sun and her flowers. Honey is really Nectar of the Goddesses. @embodybee

By the time Robbie, Harry and Avery arrived, Ayla and Skye were in the Barn, getting ready to load the orders into her van, for posting.

Robbie and Harry set off for the far cottage, they planned to polish the timber floors today and do a first coat of sealer. Ayla asked them to have Bandit with them, she didn't want to take him into town today. When Ayla drove down to Barrington she'd pick up some sample paint pots for the walls. They'd paint the inside of the Barn too, hopefully she could make a start on the weekend.

As they loaded the parcels into the vehicle, Ayla asked Avery if she'd consider a job, flexible hours, if it included accommodation in one of the cottages.

'Really? Do you mean that Ayla?' Avery stood stock still, a package in her hands, looking at Ayla in amazement. Work here? Live here too?' Then her face fell. 'But Jacinta...'

Laughing, Ayla pointed to Skye, laying on the floor of the main building with an assortment of dolls, immersed in a game of her own making. 'Company for Skye, and they will start school next year. They can play in here and help us with our work. I've always worked with Skye by my side.' She grinned. 'It's tricky sometimes, but there's two of us to watch them. And I'll likely get some more help in, part-time.' Avery's face lit up, she shook her head in disbelief, then wiped her eyes with the back of her arm. 'Flexible hours too Avery. Just because you'll be here all the time, doesn't mean I'll expect you to work all the time. And you can use my car to go to Barrington for supplies, see Julia, get to know the locals...' Avery nodded, lost for words. Ayla kept working, sure that Avery might have a question or two.

'Can I help paint the cottages, you know, if I'll be living there?'

'Of course. Much quicker with two of us.' Ayla stood, stretching her back. The back of the van was full.

'Um, Ayla, I know you've got a vegetable garden down at your house, but could I maybe start one up here?' She walked across to the French doors on the eastern side of the building. 'There's an area there that may have been a vegetable garden before the fire. See.' She pointed. Ayla knew exactly where she was looking, she'd thought the same thing herself. 'We can grow some of the herbs you have to buy in now. Rosemary, mint. And I can plant ginger and garlic.' The enthusiasm in Avery's voice brought an easy smile to Ayla's lips.

'I love this idea, Avery. Yes, definitely. Would you like to make this a project, something you can oversee?' Avery nodded; her eyes wet with unshed tears.

'Want to drive in with us today, help get this lot,' she gestured toward the rear of the van, 'to the post. Then we can check paint samples.' Another idea popped into Ayla's head. 'We can collect Jacinta on the way back, you guys can stay the night if you like, and we can paint a bit tomorrow.'

As they drove down, they talked about it some more. Avery had no furniture for the cottage, but Ayla had a few bits and pieces she could provide, that had arrived with her business stock.

'You can take a sofa and a table and chairs from the Barn, there's plenty there. And you can use the commercial laundry, and the coolroom and freezer too. You might want to get a little bar fridge later. The bed frame from the cottage is fine, but you'll need a mattress. Pretty sure it's a queen size bed.' Ayla chuckled. 'Oh, and there's a lot of linen, you know, sheets and towels and so forth in the laundry storeroom. So yep. Just a mattress and you're set.'

'I can't believe this Ayla. Meeting you and Nik. You've changed my life. Jacinta's life.' She gazed out the window as she spoke. 'You know, they told me at the shelter, the social services people, that there's funding for study, and job skills. Maybe as an employer you can get some funding to support my work too?' Avery gazed at Ayla.

'Gosh, I'm sure you're right. I didn't think of it for myself, but yes, we should check this out online, see what we need to do.' Skye had been dozing between them but woke when the van slowed to turn into the general store.

'And Ayla?'

'Yes.'

'If there's help for study, I'd really like to do a course on horticulture, or permaculture. Sustainable food growing. I've always been interested, just didn't think I'd have a chance until Jacinta went to school, at best.'

'Brilliant idea. You can use the main computer in the office.'

'I think they even help fund a laptop.' The excitement in Avery's voice made Ayla's heart swell. She would like to know Avery's story, hoped she would share it when she was ready, but loved that she was grasping every opportunity to change her circumstances with both hands. Her response gave weight to Ayla's dreams.

She pulled in close to the general store. It was a post office too. There was another one, a bigger one, in the centre of the town, but Ayla thought she'd see if Nadia wanted to process her parcels on a regular basis. Could be good for the store.

They strolled in. Nadia gave them a friendly hello.

'Hey Nadia. We've got some parcels to post. For, er, my business. A lot of parcels. Would you like them to come through here or should I take them into the main post office in town?' Ayla hesitated. Frank had appeared from the back room.

'Oh, post them from here. It's good for us. We get a lot of incoming post but not a lot of outgoing.'

'Alright. Do you have a side door we should use, or just bring them through the front?' Avery was already heading back to the van; Skye was holding her hand.

'Through the front.' Frank spoke gruffly, and she saw Nadia frown at him.

'Okay, thanks.' She walked out to the car. They had the parcels segmented into postcodes in large plastic tubs. Avery carried one in; Ayla grabbed another. She needed to think about getting a trolley. These were heavy.

'Is this it?' Nadia had started to sort through them. 'Oh, properly labelled and in postcode order. Excellent Ayla!'

'No.' Ayla laughed. 'There's seven more tubs.'

'What? No!' Nadia laughed too and started to step around the counter. She looked at Frank.

'I'll give you a hand.' He was less gruff, his surprise obvious. At the back of the van, he scratched his head. 'Wow. A lot of postage. How often will you have this much?'

'This is two weeks' worth, but half this every week. And the business is growing.' Ayla couldn't keep the pride from her voice.

'Wait.' Frank held up his hand. 'I'll get a trolley.' He was back in moments, loading three tubs onto the trolley at once. Ayla and Avery carried in a tub each and Frank went back for the last two. As he did, Joyce Wilson pulled up in her jeep. She walked to the back of the van, Ayla couldn't see or hear the conversation and was about to walk out, but Nadia put her hand on her arm. 'Let Frank deal with this.'

A few minutes later Joyce left, and Frank came in with the last of the parcels. He turned to Ayla. "We can set up an account for you Ayla, so you can print your own postal labels. You just need scales; the price is worked out on weight. You'll get a commercial rate, save a bit.'

Ayla bit her lip. She'd had an account set up in Victoria, and she owned scales. But she nodded and thanked Frank and asked if he could help get her set up. In the end Nadia did it while Frank dashed outside to serve fuel to a customer. Ayla could see he was deep in conversation, waving his hands toward the van and the store. She caught Nadia's eye, she smiled wanly. 'You're full of surprises Ayla Forrest.' It was kindly meant, and Ayla nodded.

'Avery has been a great help. She's going to be working with me. But I might need some part-time help too, if you know anyone?'

'I do actually. Leave it with me.' By the time Frank came in the parcels were sorted and they were ready to go to the hardware store for paint samples. They waved goodbye and giggled as they drove out.

'You're clever Ayla. They are thrilled to get your business. I don't know how post offices work, but I'm sure the volume of parcels you'll put through there will really help.' Avery grinned.

'I don't know how it works either, but you're right. I've been accidentally strategic.' She slapped her hand on the wheel, laughing loudly.

'What's funny Mama.' Skye's tone was plaintive, she'd been a bit left out. 'I'm hungry.'

Ayla looked over her head to Avery. 'We can go to Debbie's café, then the hardware store. Then we'll drop Avery home to Jacinta and pick them up again after we've done the bee program at school. They're going to stay the night.'

Skye clapped her hands and bounced a bit in her seat. 'Can Jacinta sleep with me?'

'Not this time Skye. You can sleep in my bed and let Avery and Jacinta have yours tonight.' Skye clapped her hands again, she never passed up an opportunity to cuddle in Ayla's bed.

* * *

THE CAFÉ WAS BUSY, ALTHOUGH THE LUNCH RUSH SHOULD BE JUST about over. Debbie was at the coffee machine. She waved them through to the table at the back. She joined them in minutes. Ayla introduced Avery and they ordered a light lunch. Skye was already drawing.

Debbie returned with their drinks and looked directly at Ayla. 'I need a word.' Ayla nodded. Debbie seemed serious. 'You may have heard already that there's been a *stupid* complaint made against Alex.' She glanced at Avery, then back at Ayla.

'It's okay Debbie. Avery knows I'm seeing Alex.'

Debbie brightened. 'You are? That's great news, he's a good bloke. Good dad, great principal.' She drew a breath. 'So that bit is true. Okay. Maybe I'm speaking out of turn. But it seems someone,' she rolled her eyes, 'has suggested your employment at the school is somehow inappropriate, as if Alex would ever do anything dodgy!'

'Alex told me this morning.' Ayla knew her eyes were twinkling. 'After breakfast. When he and Ruby left to go to school.'

Debbie slapped her hand against her leg. 'Brilliant. That's brilliant. Congratulations!'

'But I'm sure you, and the school community know we'd never met before I came to catch the bee swarm. The relationship bit is new. But Debbie, how did you hear? What did you hear?'

'Joyce was in this morning, with some of her cronies. I think she's taking a *posse*,' Debbie giggled as she said posse, 'to the school this afternoon when you're there. Maybe right at the end of the day. I'm not sure, but I think she may have someone from the School Board coming. I don't know what she's told them to get someone all the way over from Taree at short notice, so it bothered me.'

Ayla nodded. 'That's ridiculous.' She looked up, there were two people waiting at the counter. 'You go Deb, I'll think about this.' Debbie rushed back to the counter.

'What will you do Ayla? Will you still go to school this afternoon? Or will you being there make it worse for Alex?' Avery sharpened a pencil for Skye as she spoke.

'Oh, I'll still go. But maybe I'll have my own *posse*.' She grinned at Avery. 'Interested?'

'Yep. And Nik. And Robbie and Harry if they're home.' Avery was on board. Ayla had already realised Avery was smart, just her circumstances had been difficult.

Returning with their sandwiches, Debbie sat down, a coffee in her hand. The café was quieter now. 'What are you thinking Ayla?'

'I'm thinking a pro-Alex-Macintosh-school-principal posse to be there this afternoon too. I know you're working, but Avery and Nik will come. Maybe Nadia too and Robbie and Harry.' Ayla was thinking aloud. 'I think Jim or Julie Fraser would come. Maybe Drum Murray, but I don't know him well.'

'Of course. Drum and Harriet. And I'll call Melanie. She and Ben will go and maybe Max Masters, the Vet, his little boy Tommy goes there too.' Debbie stood. 'I'll make some calls. Cathy can look after the café. I'll get Jamie to pick me up, we'll come too. The School Board person can't ignore all of us.'

Ayla looked at Avery. 'We've got a plan. I hope it's a good one.'

'It can't make it worse for Alex, for them to see the support he has. Hopefully it will make this Joyce person look a bit silly.'

'I don't want to hurt her, make things worse, but I'm not sure what the ramifications are for Alex if the complaint is believed. I'm happy to give the funds back, break the contract, do the schoolwork for free but that doesn't address him employing me in the first place, if they believe we've colluded in some way.'

49

Let the wise man live in the flower of his village, like the bee, gently taking flowers' honey, but not harming the blossom and its colour and scent. **Buddha**

Alex checked the clock. Ayla would be here in fifteen minutes. He clapped his hands, getting the class to move to the library. Ayla will speak to all students at once, then Ruby would give her presentation. Sam Fraser had also prepared something, and Ruby said they'd present together.

The other classes were moving to the library, when Jenny came out of the office, a young woman in a navy skirt and heels accompanying her.

'Alex.' Jenny called him over. 'This is Ms Warner. From the School Board in Taree.' Jenny raised her eyebrows.

Alex smiled and shook the woman's hand. 'Alex Macintosh, nice to have you here.' He knew why she was there. 'Would you like to speak to me in my office or join the school in the library for the last lesson. We have Ayla Forrest, the Bee Whisperer, joining us. We've been doing a segment on bees this term, since finding a wild swarm of honeybees at the school.'

The woman hesitated, although she seemed friendly enough. 'I'll join you in the library Mr Macintosh. We can speak after, if you like.'

'Perfect.' He saw the blue van pull in. 'Here's Ayla now. Perhaps you'd like to go into the library, Jenny can show you the way.'

'Oh, I'd like to meet Ayla. The Bee Whisperer.' The woman walked towards the school gate. Skye ran over carrying some posters. Ayla strode across behind her, more materials under her arm. Alex noted she was dressed in denim bib and brace overalls, a white tee and white canvas shoes. Little Skye was wearing a denim skirt and pink top, pink clogs on her feet and her hair still in the ponytail that Ruby had done for her in the morning. Cute.

Ayla smiled at the woman. 'Hello. I'm Ayla, this is my daughter Skye.'

'Jessica Warner, nice to meet you. Can I carry something for you?' Alex was surprised at the woman's warmth, but then, if she was here to assess the situation, she needed to keep an open mind. Good. A Landcruiser pulled up, Jim and Julie Fraser stepped out. They walked across, shaking Alex's hand. He introduced them to Ms Warner.

'We've come to see Sam's presentation Alex; I hope you don't mind.' Julie chuckled, turning to the other woman. 'He's never volunteered to do a project before, or to speak to the class.'

'Something we have to see, in case it's the only time.' Jim Fraser laughed as he spoke, but Alex could hear pride in his voice. They all stepped into the library; Sam waved to his parents as they found chairs against the side wall.

The kids greeted Ayla with warmth. Ms Warner stayed by her side, he heard Sam Fraser explaining to Ayla that the vegetable garden was sprouting, and he'd love to show it to her.

Once Ayla began, Ms Warner moved over to where he stood, watching with interest. He hadn't been sure what Ayla was going to cover, but it seemed she was summarising all their bee studies so far. It was very interactive, and the children were fully engaged. She had questions for the younger students that she asked the older ones not to answer. He watched, proud of Ayla's way with the kids, but also proud of the students and how they'd made the bee program their own. He tried to see Ms Warner's response out of the corner of his eye. She smiled and nodded a few times and seemed pleased overall.

Ayla finished and he asked the students to thank her by clapping. It was so loud and so long that he had to ask them to stop clapping after a few minutes. Then he asked Ruby and Sam if they'd like to share their presentation and report. As they got ready, he explained that Ruby and Sam were in Grade Six and had chosen to compile a report on their own. Ms Warner nodded.

Ruby had set her laptop up, and it was only when she turned it on that he realised she had it linked to the big screen on the wall behind her. Ruby began. 'This is what we encountered on our first day of term.' They all looked at the screen, a video of the bee swarm hanging from a branch on the gum tree in school grounds. It was footage Alex had taken himself on his phone. Then Ayla appeared, placing the chairs under the swarm, Skye standing only a metre away.

He glanced at Ms Warner. Her hand was on her mouth, her eyes surprised. Jim and Julie looked amazed, too.

Ruby went on to explain what Ayla was doing, as she warmed her hands and let the large body of bees nestle into them. Seeing it again, himself, he was still astounded at her skill. The bees captured, Ruby paused the video and Sam stepped forward, speaking confidently about the next stage, the vegetable garden, even thanking his dad for helping. He talked through the concept of companion planting and pollination and ended by saying Ayla was going to bring the rescued colony back when the blossoms came out. It would be the school's first beehive.

Ruby stepped up then, talking about the *what ifs*. What if the bees died? What would happen to food production and life on earth? She was passionate and convincing and backed her talk up with researched facts. She also spoke about the recent Varroa Mite outbreak and what it meant for horticulture and agriculture.

They finished with a bit more of the video, the bees in the bee box with Skye sitting right beside it. Skye clapped and called out, 'That's me Ruby!' and everyone laughed.

Alex thanked Sam and Ruby for their presentation and then their guests, including the Frasers, Ayla and Skye and Ms Warner for joining them. Jenny rang the bell and the library erupted into movement and chatter as the students ran back to their own classes to get their school bags, calling goodbye to their friends as they began to depart. Ayla and Skye, with the Frasers and Ms Warner had walked to the vegetable garden. He was about to join them but saw a group of parents gathering at the school gate. He glanced back, Ayla and Ms Warner were speaking together, slightly apart from the others.

He walked to the gate. Joyce Wilson was there with her daughter and son-in-law and a few other parents. Standing near them was Nadia, with Mel and Ben Evans, Drum Murray, Max Masters, Debbie and Jamie Tait, Nik, Robbie and Harry. Avery and Julia were with them too. He had no idea what was going on, and became nervous, the others strolled across from the vegetable garden until Ms Warner was right beside him. His hands were suddenly clammy.

Joyce Wilson stepped forward. She looked at Ms Warner. 'I'm Joyce. We spoke on the phone.'

Oh crap, this was not going to end well. Alex opened his mouth to speak but Ms Warner was quicker.

'I want to thank you Joyce, Mrs Wilson, for bringing the bee program here at Barrington School to my attention. It's been my absolute pleasure to hear from Ayla, The Bee Whisperer.' She raised her eyebrows slightly and Alex let his breath out. 'And some of the students this afternoon. I want to congratulate Mr Macintosh, for turning the unexpected arrival of the bee swarm at the school into a high calibre learning module.' She turned to Ayla. 'I highly commend your engagement with the whole student body, all age groups. It's not easy to do.' She turned then to the parents. 'And to the School Community for your support of the program.'

She faced Alex again, held out her hand to shake his. He wordlessly shook her hand. 'I'm going to ask Mr Macintosh if I can return when the beehive arrives, I'd really like to watch this program develop.' She looked at Ayla then. 'And I've already asked Ayla if she would consider replicating the program at other primary schools in our district.' She chuckled. 'They won't all kick off with a bee swarm, of course.'

Everyone began speaking at once, and Alex stood quietly watching Jessica Warner move through the group of parents, speaking to them individually. He saw her congratulate the Frasers on Sam's presentation and Jim looked especially proud. He wondered if she'd speak again to Joyce, but Drum Murray caught his attention.

He noted that Ms Warner spoke with Joyce and her followers, but he couldn't hear the conversation. He saw Joyce nod her head, but her expression was mutinous, then she ambled away in her signature rolling gait.

Finally, it was just Ayla and himself. Ruby was pushing Skye on the swing.

'Thank you Ayla. You're not just the Bee Whisperer, you're the School Board and Parent Whisperer too.' She laughed but shook her head.

'It wasn't me, Teacher. It was you. The love and respect this community have for you. They were prepared to defend your honour, here at the school gate!' Her eyes twinkled and he chuckled.

'You had a conversation with Jessica Warner, by the vegetable garden. What did she say?' He was curious.

'She had already decided to come and make her own judgement, when Joyce had said I'd be here this afternoon. She asked me only one question.'

'What was that?'

'Was I involved with you before you contracted me for the bee program. I said no, we met the day of the swarm, but we are involved now. Then she smiled and congratulated me and asked if I can run the program in other schools.'

He felt lighter, knew he was grinning. 'And Joyce? Do you think she'll let it go now?'

Ayla shook her head sadly. 'I don't Alex. She was already against me, and now she has you firmly on Team Ayla. I'm not sure what more she can do, but I don't believe this is the last we'll hear from her. I'm sorry.' He felt his grin fade. Ayla was right. There'd be more opposition. For Ayla, and maybe for him.

He missed her next words. 'Sorry, I was thinking. What did you say?'

She turned away from him, looked across at Ruby and Skye, then turned back. 'I think there will always be opposition of some sort toward me Alex. It's a small town, a place of conservative views. I don't conform. Never will. Skye will be labelled too, as she gets older.' She gazed steadily into his eyes, her tone quietly serious. 'You've had a taste of it now. Unreasonable opposition. I understand if it's not a path you want to travel, with me.' She squared her shoulders, he read sadness in her eyes, but not defeat.

'Too late, Bee Whisperer.' He reached for her, wrapped his arms around her, his mouth against her ear. 'I'm on this path with you now. I don't think I can change direction so easily. You know, because I'm conservative.' He kissed her ear lightly, laughing quietly. 'I was going to say I have your back, but you know what, I'd rather be beside you.' He rubbed her back with one hand, tilted her chin up with the other and lowered his lips to hers. Gently. He felt her nod, then a shudder ran through her body. Was she crying? He leaned back and discovered she was laughing quietly, her shoulders shaking. 'What? Why?' He laughed too, although he wasn't sure why.

She looked at him, eyes wide, feigning innocence. Her

words were anything but. '*Beside* me is a lovely sentiment, but it's not going to seal the deal. Teacher, there are a lot of places I'm gonna want you...'

'Stop. I'm kissing you now. Our daughters are watching.'

'Let them.' She kissed him back.

THE END

ACKNOWLEDGMENTS

My thanks, first and foremost, to my daughter Emily for allowing me to use her story as groundwork for this book. Watching this young woman follow her dreams, without compromise, and develop a business from her passion has inspired me. She is saving the world one bee at a time. Now I'm saving the bees too. *@embodybee*

Thank you also to Simon Mulvany from Save the Bees Australia, a great friend to Emily, and even better one to the environment. *@savethebeesaustralia*

The support provided by Trudy Schultz from *@accommodation_gloucester* has been amazing. Trudy is also a talented photographer and I've access many of her great shots of the Barrington and Gloucester region in my promo materials. Thank you also to Wendy Hughes and Lorna Tomkinson for invaluable local intel.

My co-authors (Love in a Sunburnt Land 1 & 2) have provided valuable advice, tips and support. Adore our regular zoom catch ups - you gals rock - Rhonda Forrest, Emma Powell, Louise Forster & Leanne Lovegrove.

If ever I need a pick me up, a little cheer from the sidelines, I speak to daughter Jasmine. She's always on Team Susan. And now I have little Edmund to make me smile too. Blessed. Keep sending those vids.

My biggest supporter is undoubtedly Bloke - thank you for all you do, but especially the accidental meme material. I was bummed when you got social media last year, it has been so much harder to use you in social posts and get away with it. I know you don't mean to provide meme material - yet here we are!

Thank you Fiona @*fionahayesart* for continuing to provide beautiful original art for my covers. This one has been hanging on my wall since late 2022, shaking it's fist, telling me to get on with it!

I need to mention my new *work wife* Allison, 'cos she begged to be included, lol! You're funny and kind and make the days fly by, thank you.

And to you, my readers. Thank you for reading and rating/reviewing. I love reading your comments and adore when a comment on social media turns into a conversation that turns into a friendship. You know who you are! Keep reading, there are so many wonderful writers and stories out there. I'm blessed to be part of such a strong and supportive writing community in Australia, thank you.

ABOUT THE AUTHOR

Susan Mackie is first and foremost a farmer's daughter. Her career as a journalist, small business owner, tourist resort developer, real estate agent and government employee created a wealth of experience from which to develop characters and storylines. Susan has two daughters and two grandchildren and lives in the Southern Downs region of Queensland, with Bloke.

The Bee Whisperer is the third novel in the Barrington Series. There are also two Barrington novellas, soon to be three.

https://www.susanmackie.com/